KU-443-313

BLEED A
RIVER DEEP

BRIAN McGILLOWAY

CONSTABLE

CONSTABLE

First published in Great Britain in 2009 by Macmillan

This edition published in 2021 by Constable

1 3 5 7 9 10 8 6 4 2

Copyright © Brian McGilloway, 2009

The moral right of the author has been asserted.

*All characters and events in this publication, other than
those clearly in the public domain, are fictitious
and any resemblance to real persons,
living or dead, is purely coincidental.*

All rights reserved.
No part of this publication may be reproduced, stored in a retrieval
system, or transmitted, in any form, or by any means, without
the prior permission in writing of the publisher, nor be otherwise
circulated in any form of binding or cover other than that in
which it is published and without a similar condition including
this condition being imposed on the subsequent purchaser.

A CIP catalogue record for this book
is available from the British Library.

ISBN: 978-1-47213-338-0

Typeset by Hewer Text UK Ltd, Edinburgh
Printed and bound in Great Britain by Clays Ltd, Elcograf S.p.A.

Papers used by Constable are from well-managed
forests and other responsible sources.

MIX
Paper from
responsible sources
FSC® C104740

Constable
An imprint of
Little, Brown Book Group
Carmelite House
50 Victoria Embankment
London EC4Y 0DZ

An Hachette UK Company
www.hachette.co.uk

www.littlebrown.co.uk

For Will Atkins

Prologue

The last time I saw Leon Bradley with a gun in his hand, he was standing in our garden at home. Only five years old and a little under three feet tall, he had a cowboy hat tipped back on his head, his hair, strands of fine spun gold, hanging in his eyes. My younger brother, Tom, who was playing the Indian, had taken refuge in our shed, sharpening his plastic knife in preparation for a scalping.

Leon had pointed the gun at me, one eye shut, the tip of his tongue poking out through his lips in concentration while he lined me up in his sights. He kept shaking his fringe from his open eye. 'Hands up, Tonto,' he said.

I raised my hands in surrender as I edged my way down the driveway and out on to the street. My friend – Leon's older brother Fearghal – waited for me in his Ford Fiesta, revving the engine.

'Bang, bang,' I heard Leon shout just as I slammed the car door. As we sped off, I saw Leon in the rear-view mirror, mimicking a gun's recoil with the plastic Smith & Wesson clenched in his tiny fist.

This was different though. Leon must have been in his late twenties now. His hair had darkened or was dyed brown, and hung in unwashed straggles down his neck. Yet his face was again contorted in pantomime concentration as he held the gun steady. Again he had one eye open, his mouth a thin pale line. I followed his gaze, followed the aim of his weapon to where US Senator Cathal Hagan stood, his face frozen in terror.

I pushed through the crowd towards him, my hand raised, a shout of warning caught in my throat. Then I heard the shot and glimpsed the muzzle flash, even as two American Secret Service agents, too late to compensate for the inadequacy of An Garda, grappled Leon to the ground. The gun, knocked loose from Leon's grip, fell on to the floor, where it lay glinting in the autumn sunlight that streamed through the windows.

Chapter One

'They've uncovered a body out at the new mine.'

It took me a few seconds to realize the speaker was addressing me. I looked up from my desk to where Superintendent Harry Patterson loomed over me.

'Excuse me?'

'They've dug up a body out at the mine,' he said irritably. 'We're going out there. It's a dead body,' he explained, turning to leave as he did so.

'They generally are, if they've had to dig them up,' I muttered to his retreating back.

'And keep the smart-arse comments to yourself,' he snapped. 'Get a move on.'

The leaves had just begun to turn, and some green still showed from the massive oaks behind our home when I left that morning; the cherry trees though were predominately golden, the leaves beginning to twist and sag. The air was still ripe and warm, the tannic scent of autumn starting to sharpen.

The fact that Patterson himself was attending the site was indication enough of the priority this find was being given.

It wasn't so much what was found, but more *where* it was found: Orcas, a new goldmine opened two years previous near Barnes Gap, between Ballybofey and Donegal town, built on the promise of untold wealth to be shared with the whole community at some undefined point in the future. The body, Patterson explained in the car, had been found by some of the workers as they dug a new section of the mine. Patterson had been summoned by the owner himself, John Weston.

Weston was a second-generation Irish-American, whose family had moved back to 'the old country' following his father's death. Bill Weston, John's father, had been a senator in the US, as well as being extremely wealthy. John had inherited every cent and had developed a number of business projects in Ireland, supported by friends of his father. The Orcas goldmine was the biggest and, it appeared, the most successful.

Twenty minutes later Patterson turned the car up a narrow side road, and Orcas dove into view: sixteen acres of Donegal bogland which now housed Ireland's largest goldmine. Preliminary tests conducted in the 1990s had shown the presence of several high-quality veins running through the rock under this land. One vein apparently stretched right across the sixteen acres and along the bed of the River Finn.

'I wonder where ...' Patterson began, then stopped. There was no need to ask for directions. A convoy of Garda cars was already parked further up the road, alongside several 4x4s marked with Orcas livery. Half the force in Donegal must have been called out here, I thought. A good day to commit a crime anywhere else in the county.

The car made it almost to the site before getting stuck in a mud-filled puddle. We walked the rest of the way, our feet slipping on the wet path. Ahead of us a group of Guards had gathered, most still in their shirtsleeves. Some of them must have clocked Patterson, for they began to make themselves look busy. Some of the others just moved to the side of the road to let him past.

'This is a right balls-up,' he spat. 'Weston's just turned a record profit. Word was he was going to make a bigger investment. This could be enough to scare the fucker off.'

As we drew level with the pit, the two men standing in it dropped their spades and scrabbled up the bank of clay they had shifted. The soil was almost black and scented the morning air with the smell of mould. It took me a second or two to pick out the body from the surrounding earth, for the only parts visible at this stage were the head and part of the upper arm.

But Patterson had no need to worry about Weston getting scared off. If there was a murder involved here, it had happened a few thousand years earlier, by the look of it.

The corpse was curled in on itself. The underlying muscle was outlined by skin the texture of old leather. The face had been flattened, presumably by the weight of earth pressing on top of it. The eyes were open, though the sockets long emptied. The mouth likewise was fixed ajar, the teeth, slightly gapped and blunted, were still lodged in the jawbone. There was certainly no sense of serenity in death: the face was twisted as if in agony. One arm protruded slightly from the dirt, the fingernails still attached to the talon-like hand.

'Jesus, what is it?' Patterson asked. 'Should we call the State Pathologist or the archaeologist?'

A few of the men standing around grunted good-humouredly.

'Still, at least he didn't die on our watch, eh, boys?' he continued.

'Do we need an ME to declare it dead?' someone called. More laughter.

'Best get Forensics up anyway,' Patterson concluded. 'Just to keep it all official and that.' Then he nodded to me: 'We're to see Weston.'

As we travelled towards the main building, I looked out across the mine. When it first opened, it had been the subject of some controversy from environmental lobby groups, and I had had my own reservations about it, based on the little I had read in the papers. In reality, the mine itself was not at all what I had expected and much smaller than I'd imagined, though the scarring it had already inflicted on the landscape was still significant.

Two large warehouses squatted side by side, their low corrugated roofs painted blood-red. Despite the size, only a few workmen were visible, and I counted a half-dozen cars parked in the staff area. One, a black Lexus with personalized number plates spattered with mud, revealed that Weston was already here.

We were directed to the only brick building in the compound, a white stucco three-storey block. A workman was at the front door, fastening a bronze plaque to the wall with an electric screwdriver. It caught the sun as he

6

shifted it into position. He nodded as we passed, then snuffled into the back of his wrist and continued with his work.

Weston's receptionist was waiting for us when we entered the building. The floor was covered with thick carpet on which the image of a gold torc was repeated in a series of diagonal patterns. To one side of the reception desk stood a mahogany display cabinet, its contents lit by tiny halogen spotlights. The shelves of the cabinet glittered with gold jewellery. I wandered over and scanned the contents and tbeir price tags while Patterson ingratiated himself with the twenty-year-old receptionist behind the desk. The smallest item in the cabinet – a pair of stud earrings – was priced at €350.

John Weston strode down the stairs towards us, his hand already outstretched, his smile fixed, businesslike, friendly, predatory. He smelt of expensive aftershave. His shirt cuffs sat just far enough past his jacket sleeve to reveal both the quality of the cloth and the gold cufflinks, fashioned again in the torc shape of his company's emblem. His skin was tanned, his hair neatly trimmed: he looked younger than his fifty years, despite the slight peppering of grey at his sideburns.

'Gentlemen,' he began, his accent discernible in the way he slurred the word, the 't' almost silent. 'Thanks for coming. Let's grab a coffee.'

Clasping Patterson's hand in both of his, he shook it, tben repeated the gesture with me.

'John Weston,' he said, smiling expansively.

'Ben Devlin,' I replied.

'Ben,' he repeated, with a nod of his head, as if to demonstrate that he was committing my name to memory. Then he placed his hand on my elbow and guided me towards the stairs, physically directing me. I resisted the movement and he stopped.

'Just admiring your collection here,' I said. 'My wife would kill for something like that.'

'Beautiful, aren't they?' he agreed, still smiling. His teeth were perfect and straight, and unnaturally white. I was vaguely aware that I was trying hard to find reasons not to like the man, despite the fact he had been nothing but gracious since our arrival.

'Jackie,' he said to the girl who had welcomed us. 'Have you those packs?'

With a timid smile, Jackie produced two thick folders from beneath the desk where she sat. Both were bound in a leather cover emblazoned with the Orcas emblem. No expense spared.

'And choose something pretty for Ben's wife, would you?' he added, winking at me conspiratorially, then directing me towards the stairs again before I had a chance to decline the offer.

Weston's office itself was the size of the entire ground floor of the Garda station in Lifford where I was based. He occupied a corner room on the top floor of the building so that, from his desk, he could survey his empire both to left and to right As we entered his office he flicked a switch and the blinds on the windows automatically pulled back, revealing both the expanse of his goldmine and, to the other side, the majesty of the Donegal landscape in which he had quite literally carved his niche.

'Beautiful country,' he observed. 'Absolutely stunning.'

I began to suspect that Weston spoke only in superlatives. I also noticed he was being careful to compliment the landscape, and not the additions he had made to it.

I looked down over the forest to our left, through which I could catch a glimpse of the Carrowcreel, a tributary snaking its way towards the River Finn. The light glittered on its surface as if on shards of broken mirror.

'Almost a pity to industrialize it,' I said, earning a warning glance from Patterson, who had continued his ingratiation since our arrival, echoing Weston's observations on the weather as we had climbed the two flights of stairs to his office.

'Almost,' Weston agreed with a smile. 'This is my country too, Inspector. I'm not going to damage it. Part of our licence is our guarantee that we will leave this area as we found it. Every clod that has been dug up will be replaced. It will be as if we were never here.'

'And when will that be?' I asked.

'When it's no longer profitable to remain, I suppose,' he said, his palms held open in front of him in a gesture of honesty. 'I am a businessman, after all.' He waited a beat, then continued, 'Though of course this was all bogland before we arrived. And to bogland it must return, despite the fact that the bogs themselves were artificially created by some Iron Age entrepreneur.'

I nodded slightly, having taken his point.

'Which leads me nicely on to our friend out there. I'm no

9

forensics specialist, but I'm guessing he or she didn't die in this century. Is that right?'

'It would appear so,' Patterson said, eager to assert his role in the conversation. 'It shouldn't cause too much disruption to your works, Mr Weston.'

Weston nodded his head. 'An amazing country,' he stated, then pointed a finger at us. 'I forgot that coffee, didn't I?' he said, still good-humoured. He pressed the intercom button on his phone and instructed Jackie to bring us coffee and some biscuits, which she did with startling speed.

Once we had settled into our drinks, Weston explained why he had summoned us.

'The packs you've been given detail the history of the Orcas mine – including our financial reports for the past tax year. You'll notice that last year we enjoyed record profits. As a result of this, we have a special visitor coming both to formally open the site and, I suppose, to officially acknowledge the Irish-American finances that have made this all possible.'

'Who's the visitor?' Patterson asked.

'An old friend of my father's,' Weston said. 'Senator Cathal Hagan.'

We both nodded. Hagan was well known, even in Ireland. He'd been an outspoken Irish-American senator, who had established links with Heal Ireland, ostensibly an Irish aid charity but in fact a front that funded Republican causes in the North.

'Obviously, anything we can do to help, sir,' Patterson offered.

Weston nodded soberly. 'Thank you, Harry. We'll have to work together on this. The Senator will bring some security with him, and I know a number of the other divisions will be involved in his trip, but we'll be dependent on yourself and Ben to ensure there's no trouble while he's here. Obviously this information is between the three of us for now, gentlemen.'

I didn't need to ask why there would be trouble. Hagan had called on those senators who expressed reservations over the invasion of Iraq a few years back to be strung up for failing America in its hour of need. Post-9/11 he was an outspoken critic of terrorism in all its forms, apparently forgetting that the charity he had spearheaded in the 1980s had paid for most of the Republican movement's weaponry in Ireland. His arrival could attract the growing anti-war lobby, which had already organized more than one demonstration in Ireland over the past few years.

'Do you expect trouble?' Patterson asked, then seemed to gauge the stupidity of the question by our expressions, for he immediately added, 'Beyond the usual, I mean.'

'Senator Hagan has his detractors, both at home and abroad, as I'm sure you're aware, Harry. In addition, the environmental lobby seem determined to vilify us at every turn, despite the fact that, before a sod was cut here, we invested millions in an environmental impact study, to whose recommendations we have adhered in every point.'

'How much security will he be bringing with him?' I asked.

'One or two personal security men, I suspect,' Weston answered. 'He's retired now, Ben, so he isn't afforded quite the level of protection he once was.'

'So we'll be responsible for the bulk of it,' Patterson said. It was a statement rather than a question, but Weston nodded.

'When's the visit?'

Weston grimaced, then, leaning forward in his seat, consulted a document on the desk before him, although he clearly knew the date by heart: 'Monday, ninth of October.'

Following coffee and preliminary security discussions, Patterson and I were escorted back downstairs. Weston gestured to the welcome packs we had been given.

'Everything you could ever want to know about our company is in those packs, gentlemen.'

As we shook hands to leave, the receptionist approached nervously, holding a blue box. She passed it to Weston, who opened it and inspected the contents.

'Beautiful choice, Jackie,' he said, nodding with admiration. Clearly relieved to have completed this latest task to Weston's satisfaction, Jackie smiled and hurried off again. I was a little taken aback when Weston handed me the box. 'I hope your wife likes it, Ben,' he said.

I opened the box, a little confused and feeling my face flush with embarrassment. Inside it sat a thick gold necklace, which I was sure I had seen in the display cabinet earlier with a price tag in excess of €3,000.

I held the box out towards Weston again. 'Thank you, sir, but I can't accept this. It's . . . it's far too much.'

He stood his ground, however, his hands clasped in military fashion behind his back, his smile fixed. 'No, I insist, Ben.'

I could think of nothing to say, and so in the end simply thanked him for his generosity, though as we left the building to return to Patterson's car I could not help feeling that, in some way, I had accepted more than just a gift for my wife.

'Bloody hell, Devlin,' Patterson said as we pulled out on to the main road. 'That thing costs a fucking fortune.'

'I didn't ask him for it,' I said defensively.

'You may as well have done,' he retorted, and I suspected that part of his reaction was jealousy that he had not been similarly gifted. 'You can't fuck up this visit now,' he added, without looking at me.

'Me?'

'You. I'm putting you in charge of it,' he said. Then, nodding towards the box I held in my hand, he added, 'You've already been paid for it, after all.'

We had only travelled a mile or so when a security van accompanied by a convoy of Garda and Army vehicles approached us on the other side of the road, travelling towards Lifford to stock the banks in preparation for wages day. As it passed, a camper van with number plates so muddied they were impossible to read overtook it, then cut across the lane in front of us and trundled up a dirt track just off the main road. Patterson slammed on the brakes, though there was no real prospect of our colliding with it.

13

'Fucking hippies!' he shouted, flicking one finger in the general direction of the van, whose rear bumper we could see disappearing up the laneway.

While we were sitting there a second camper, which had remained behind the security cortège, indicated and pulled across the road in front of us, also heading up the lane.

'Where the fuck is everyone going?' Patterson asked incredulously.

'Maybe we should find out,' I suggested, if only so we wouldn't have to sit in the middle of the road any longer.

He grunted, then turned the car on to the laneway and followed the trail of dust raised by the van in front, up the path and into the pine forest I had seen from Weston's office. The car shuddered along the dirt track, the air cooling as we drove beneath the canopy of the trees. The lower trunks and boughs were completely bare, the forest floor thick with browned pine needles and lumps of cones, the air sharp with the scent of sap when I wound down the window. Above the drone of the car, I could hear the rushing of the Carrowcreel.

Around the next bend, we pulled to a stop behind the two camper vans, which had parked alongside several other cars and trucks. The occupants of each were unloading tents and camping equipment from their respective vehicles. My initial thought was that it was perhaps a group of travellers or crusties, setting up camp illegally. However, as I looked closer, it became apparent that the people around us were of no single age or social group. The second car from the front was being emptied by a middle-aged couple. The camper van did indeed contain crusties, clad in woolly jumpers, with dreadlocked hair, tight jeans and loose boots. There were also single men and women and families, even a local barman I recognized, Patsy McCann, removing camping gear from the boot of his car.

We got out of the squad car. Patterson immediately made a beeline for the camper van, already fitting his cap on his cannonball head. I wandered over to Patsy McCann, taking the opportunity to light up as I did.

'What's up, Patsy?' I said, holding out the box to offer him a cigarette too.

'Here ahead of the rush, Ben,' he said over his shoulder to me, not stopping his unpacking. 'No thanks,' he added, nodding at the proffered cigarettes.

'What rush?'

'The bleedin' gold rush, man,' he said, cocking an eyebrow at my ignorance.

I laughed, assuming it was in some way connected with the record profits Orcas had just announced. I was wrong.

Patsy turned long enough to hand me the local newspaper, then turned again and, having emptied the boot, strained to pull, from the back seat of his car, a rucksack, tied to which was an old kitchen sieve. I opened the paper. The story could not have been more obvious. Under the headline PREPARE FOR THE RUSH was a picture of a middle-aged man holding up a nugget of gold the size of a penny.

His name was Ted Coyle. He had been camped out in this woodland for three weeks now, without anyone knowing. He had come here, he said, because of the goldmine, believing he was fated to strike it rich. Coyle sounded like a

15

lunatic. Whether he was or not, according to the news report, he would soon be a rich lunatic. The nugget in his hand might just make his fortune, the report claimed. He had found it while panning the Carrowcreel.

Chapter Two

Friday, 29 September

On the final Friday of each month, in preparation for wages day, each bank in the East Donegal region is replenished with cash. A security van, containing on some days over ten million euros, travels slowly from bank to bank throughout the county. As it makes its way along deserted country roads and through mountain passes, its safety is guaranteed not simply by the armour plating and time locks on the van but by the fact that it is sandwiched between two Garda cars, and, in front of and behind those again, two Irish Army jeeps, with armed soldiers. At each bank, as the cash is hurried into the branch, soldiers toting M-16s line the road outside. The message is unmistakable. Only an idiot would try to rob a bank on such a day. Or someone too desperate to care.

It is doubtful that the man who decided to hold up the local Ulster Bank branch in Lifford that morning knew this. Just after eleven, when one of the two cashiers had gone upstairs for his tea break, the man had entered the bank. He was unshaven, his skin sallow, his hair unkempt. He wore denim jeans a size too big and a multicoloured sweater unravelling around the hem. He wore no coat. He glanced around the branch, then shuffled over to the stand of pre-printed dockets, as if to complete one for a transaction. The girl behind the desk, Catherine Doherty, began to suspect that something wasn't right. She reached under the desk and placed her finger lightly against the alarm button hidden there, ready to press it if the need arose.

The man stood for a moment flicking through the blank dockets. Then he approached the counter, seemingly unaware that the glass partition in front of him was two inches thick and bulletproof. Behind the counter, Catherine Doherty brushed her hair from her face and smiled, then said, 'Good morning.' The man shouted something she could not understand, and produced a gun from the waistband of his trousers, which he brandished at the window. By this stage, of course, Catherine Doherty had already pressed the alarm button. Then she ducked beneath the counter and waited.

The security van preparing to unload two cashboxes in Lifford pulled up outside the Ulster Bank at 11.03. The guard inside logged the time on his record sheet then waited for the soldiers in front of him to get out of their vehicle. Next the Gardai accompanying him got out. Finally he opened his door and waited for the time lock to click. He was two minutes early. Time for a smoke, perhaps.

They all heard the alarm go off at the same time. Instinctively, he clambered back into the van and shut the door. Likewise instinctively, four Army officers simultaneously shouldered their weapons.

*　　*　　*

Instinctively, the man turned and ran from the counter, his replica weapon still in his hand, blundering through the doorway and out into the car park. Perhaps he wondered how the Guards had arrived so quickly. Perhaps he believed that if he raised his hands they wouldn't shoot. He was wrong.

Patterson had got the call on our way back from the Carrowcreel. The man's body still lay on the pavement when we arrived. The force of the automatic weapons had spun him several feet back towards the door. His legs were splayed, his arms bent unnaturally and twisted behind him. He lay facing the sky, his skin taut against his cheekbones, his mouth hanging open, his jaw slack. He had several bullet wounds to his chest, and one to his forehead. Presumably he had held his hands in front of his face in some final futile survival instinct, for his right palm was marked with a hole reminiscent of the wound of Christ into which Thomas had been able to place his finger.

His head rested on the gravel path, his face turned slightly sideways, bits of grit stuck to his cheek. Behind his head a halo of blood widened slowly, its surface already beginning to congeal. The replica gun which he had been waving as he ran out of the bank lay several feet away from him, its casing shattered.

John Mulrooney, our local doctor, had already pronounced the man dead. He stood now with his back to the body, smoking the cigarette I had offered him while the Scene of Crime team checked the body.

19

'Multiple gunshot wounds. I'm guessing the one to the forehead actually killed him, but even if it hadn't, one of the wounds to his trunk probably would have anyway. Any ideas who he is?'

'*Was*,' Patterson said. 'Looks like a foreigner.'

This pearl of wisdom was soon tested. One of the SOCOs brought over the man's wallet that contained a photograph of a woman and spare change just short of a euro. In the notes section of the wallet was a driving licence featuring a photograph of the dead man in front of us. His name was Joseph Patrick Mackey, and his address was in Coolatee. Folded behind the licence was a small prayer card, written in a language I did not recognize.

'Russian?' Mulrooney suggested.

'God knows,' I said. ' "Joe Mackey" hardly sounds particularly Russian, though, does it?'

'Find out,' Patterson said, handing me the keys to the car he had been driving. 'Take a woman with you to break the news.'

Even before I had knocked at the door, something felt wrong. The house in Coolatee listed as Mackey's address was huge, set up from the road with a winding driveway leading up to the front porch. A drystone wall five feet high surrounded the plot and a new-registration Avensis was parked in front of the garage. Somehow it didn't seem to suit an unshaven robber in torn clothes with less than a euro in his wallet.

'Nice spot,' Helen Gorman said. I had picked her up at the station. Helen was a uniformed Garda officer with whom I had worked on previous cases. Certainly this wasn't the first time she had accompanied me to break such news.

A woman we took to be Mrs Mackey answered the door, though she looked nothing like the young woman in the photograph we had taken from the dead man's wallet. Mackey was in her fifties, with tanned skin and platinum-blonde hair.

'Mrs Mackey?' I asked, somewhat incredulously.

'Yes,' she said, smiling confusedly. 'Is something wrong?'

'We'd best go inside, ma'am,' Gorman said, the implication of her words already filling Mrs Mackey's expression with dread.

The woman stood her ground, refusing to move along the hallway towards where we could see the kitchen. 'It's Joe, isn't it?'

I scanned the walls behind her head, taking in each photograph: a child playing in snow, squinting a smile towards the camera; Mrs Mackey, a little younger, her husband standing beside her, holding her hand, relaxed, smiling; her husband, bald, pale and a little podgy. Not thin, not black-haired, not the man lying dead outside Lifford bank.

'I'm afraid we have some bad news, ma'am,' I heard Gorman say.

'What?' Mrs Mackey stuttered, stretching one hand to steady herself against the wall, her other teaching for her chest. 'Not Joe. He can't be.'

I glanced at Gorman, wishing I'd spoken a second earlier. 'He's not, Mrs Mackey. Look, can we come in and sit down? We need to talk.'

*   *   *

21

I finally assured Mrs Mackey that her husband – her bald, pale, podgy husband – was, to the best of my knowledge, still alive and well and playing golf. Then we fairly quickly established that Mrs Mackey – Diane Mackey – had no relatives matching the description of the man we'd left lying in Lifford Main Street. Finally, for confirmation, I showed her the licence we had taken from her 'husband's' corpse.

'That's his information all right – even his date of birth,' she said. 'But I don't know the man in the picture. He's not my husband.'

'Why would he have your husband's licence?' I asked.

'I have no idea,' Mackey replied. 'But that man's not my husband.' Then something seemed to strike her. 'Shouldn't you people check these things out more carefully? Telling someone their husband's dead when it's not true.'

'It doesn't usually happen, ma'am,' I said. 'It was a genuine mistake.'

'Genuine or not, I'm quite angry about it.'

'I understand, Mrs Mackey,' I said. 'Has your husband ever had his licence stolen?'

'Don't you check *anything?* The whole bloody house was emptied in February. We spent days filling out forms and lists of what was taken. Of course, we never heard another word from you lot. A waste of time.'

She folded her arms and turned her face towards the window to emphasize her disgust at our inefficiency.

Patterson wasted no time in letting the entire station know about his anger at our mistake – *my* mistake, apparently – by loudly repeating each part of the story as I relayed it to him.

I had told Gorman to find something to do until he'd had a chance to react and I was glad that I had. She'd have been even more upset than she already was. For my part, I took what Patterson threw with gritted teeth.

'Have you nothing to say, Devlin?' he spluttered, finally spent.

'It was a genuine mistake, sir. But a mistake, none the less, for which I take full responsibility.'

He looked at me suspiciously, and I could see he was trying to figure out the angle. I suspected he was gathering himself for another tirade, but realized there was little point, for I had mounted no defence.

'Just find out who the hell he actually was then. And no more fuck-ups,' he spat, stabbing the air with his finger.

'I'll try my best, sir,' I said, standing up.

'Try better than that,' he growled.

I sat in a patrol car for a few minutes, risking a cigarette in spite of the smoking ban and trying to decide what to do next. Finally I went back to the site of the shooting, where the dead man's body had been covered with a sheet in preparation for the pathologist's arrival. I retrieved the prayer card I had seen in the man's wallet. Then, with the card safely wrapped in an evidence bag, I drove to our local technical college. The Tech, as it's known, offers a fairly diverse range of subjects, including European languages, so I was hopeful someone would be able to help me identify the language on the card the man had been carrying. It would at least be a first step towards identifying him.

*   *   *

After I had signed in at the reception desk, one of the secretaries took me to the office of the Head of Languages, Marie Collins, a small, middle-aged woman.

She came around from behind her desk and gestured towards one of the two easy chairs in her office, indicating that I should sit.

'I'm hoping I'm not in trouble, Inspector,' she said, smiling mildly.

'Not at all. I was wondering if you could tell me what language this is, please,' I said, holding the card out to her.

'It's the Cyrillic alphabet,' she said, having read the first few lines. 'I'd say Caucasian, possibly Chechen,' she continued. 'Where did you get it?'

'It's part of an ongoing investigation,' I said.

She widened her eyes slightly, as if I had shared privileged information with her. 'It's a prayer to St Jude,' she explained. 'Patron saint of lost causes.'

'I see,' I said.

'The reason I mention it is that Chechens are predominantly Muslim. Quite rare to find a Chechen Catholic.'

I nodded my head, unsure of the significance of this piece of information, but unwilling to disappoint the woman, who was clearly pleased at knowing it.

'So, anything else I can help you with?' she asked.

'Can you tell me the name of the man who was carrying it?' I joked. 'Or where to find his family?'

'Try the Migrant Workers' Information Centre,' she answered, seriously. 'Of course, the only difficulty with that will be, if he is Chechen, he's here illegally.'

*   *   *

The man I spoke to in the Migrant's Centre, Pol, was Polish. He wore dark blue drainpipe jeans and a loose Ireland football shirt. His black hair had been shaved tight, revealing a ragged red scar across the right side of his skull, running from his temple to just below his ear.

He read the prayer card quickly, shrugging non-committally when I said I thought it was Chechen.

'I don't speak it,' he explained. Neither could he suggest where I might start looking for the man's family.

'If he's using a stolen identity card and he's Chechen, he's an illegal immigrant. To be honest, illegals wouldn't really come in here; the migrants who use us are here legally and looking for legal employment.'

'Any ideas where I might start to look for information about him?'

'A lot of migrants do their shopping at the local car-boot sales and markets. There's a new Polish food store opened on Main Street; they might be able to help you. The *Weekly News* is running a Polish column each week now – maybe put something out through there. There's a migrant Mass in the cathedral once a month. And, of course, we can put up a notice.'

I thanked him and turned to leave, then thought better of it.

'You must know something about illegal immigrants – off the record. Where they live, how they get into the country in the first place?'

Pol held my stare. 'They're brought in by Irish gangsters who charge them several thousand euros each. They bring them in the back of freight lorries. Provide them with stolen identities, charge them massive rent, then force them into cheap labour. They can't go to the police or they'll be deported. Can't complain to the people who bring them in or they'll be killed.'

'Then why come here at all?'

'Because it's better than what they're leaving behind. The Celtic Tiger is known all over Europe. Everyone wants a share of the wealth. Some of us can come in legally – other countries are not so fortunate yet. In this case, I suspect he's escaping the killing. The Chechen war may be over, Inspector, but as with Northern Ireland, the killing can continue.'

'What brought *you* here?'

'Work. The chance to earn some money to send back to my wife.'

'You left your wife in Poland?'

'And our two children. I work here for two years, earn enough to cover ten years' work in Poland.'

'But you must miss your family. Your children must miss their father.'

'It will keep them off the poverty line – it's a small sacrifice for me to make for them, to provide for them like a father should. A man needs to have some pride for his children.'

I gestured to the scarring at the side of his head. 'Did that happen here or there?'

'Here. Just after I came over. I was working in a food-packaging factory for minimum wage. One night I was jumped. Told to stay away the next day. My type weren't welcome. They told me they'd kill me if I came back.'

'What did you do?'

'What would you do, Inspector?' he asked me defiantly.

I nodded my head. 'Thanks for your help,' I said.

By the time I got home that evening, the children were already in bed. Debbie had kept my dinner for me and while I waited for it to heat in the microwave I presented her with the box from Orcas.

'A gift,' I explained when she raised her eyebrows at the box. 'From John Weston.'

She opened the case, already half smiling, then, made a silent O with her mouth when she saw the necklace. 'Jesus, Ben,' she whispered. 'It's beautiful.'

Unable to fully share her enthusiasm, I simply nodded my head.

'What's it for?' she asked.

'Putting round your neck,' I answered, earning a slap on the arm.

'You know what I meant,' she said gaily, unhooking the clasp and lifting the piece from the box, cupping the weight of it in her hand.

'I'm wondering that myself,' I said. 'Should we keep it?'

Debbie looked at me, her eyebrows arched, as if daring me to try to take it back.

'Why shouldn't we? How many perks do you get?' she said, holding it around her throat. 'Now hook me up.'

I fixed the clasp at the back of her neck. She'd had her hair cut up short, exposing the slender line of her nape. My fingers trailed along the curve of her skin after I'd fixed the clasp. She reached up and patted my hand with her own, then moved in front of the mirror in our hallway to better see the necklace.

'Beautiful,' she whispered reverently.

'And the necklace isn't bad either,' I added.

She turned, smiling, and looked at me in a manner that required no further conversation.

Chapter Three

Saturday, 30 September – Monday, 2 October

I spent Saturday morning in a meeting with Patterson to discuss the security arrangements for Cathal Hagan's visit. Patterson emphasized several times the importance of the visit and the need for the force to do itself proud. He would coordinate with the other divisions involved if I would take control of all local arrangements.

Following the meeting, I passed an hour wording an appeal for information about the dead Chechen. I eventually traced Marie Collins on Saturday, having contacted the Principal of the Tech to get her phone number. She translated the brief message into Polish, Russian and Chechen, spelling each version out for me letter by letter over the phone. The message made clear that no one was being investigated for illegal entry to the country but that we were attempting to find any relatives of the man in question. It did not mention the fact that he was dead.

I contacted all the local hospitals and PSNI and Garda stations. I guessed that, had the man any living relatives in the area, they would contact some external agency eventually in an attempt to find him. I left a message that anyone doing so be given my number.

On Saturday afternoon I headed back out to Orcas to see how things were progressing with the bog body. The numbers of Guards from the previous day had dropped to one, who sat in his car at the entrance to the mine, his feet on the dashboard and his cap over his face, an unfinished crossword lying beside him. I parped the car horn long enough to wake him up, then waved and drove on up to the site, where a blue tarpaulin had been erected above the scene to protect the body from the elements.

An archaeological pathologist, who had been drafted in from the National Museum in Dublin, was busy at work when I arrived. She wore a white paper forensics suit, though I suspected it was as much to keep herself clean as to reduce contamination. She leant over the remains in the pit, brushing gently at the leg muscles with a thick paint-brush, clearing away the loose soil.

The body itself had been completely exposed now. The form was recognizably female, though her breasts were no more than flaps pressed tight against her chest. Her hair was cropped short, her shoulders hunched up so they touched her lower jaw. Her arms lay at her sides, the musculature depleted.

The pathologist stood up when I arrived and came towards me, hand outstretched. Removing her surgical mask, she introduced herself as Linda Campbell. She brushed the fringe of her brown hair back from her face and squinted against the sunlight as we spoke.

'How are you getting on?' I asked.

She smiled warmly. 'Fantastic,' she said. 'The body's so well preserved.' Though she had come up from Dublin, I could discern a light Northern lilt to her accent.

'A woman, I see,' I said, gesturing towards the body.

'Yes,' she said, looking back at the corpse with something akin to admiration. 'Isn't she beautiful?'

'She's not really my type.'

'She's quite a find,' Linda Campbell continued, with a forbearing smile. 'The bogland here fully preserved her.'

'How?' I asked, knowing she would be eager to tell me.

'The water in bogland contains a lot of organic acids and aldehydes, which act almost like embalming fluid. More importantly, it stops bacteria growing. The body ages without ever decomposing; the skin toughens so much it becomes like tanned leather. It's really rather incredible. And very rare for a woman to be found. Most bog bodies are male.'

'I didn't know that,' I said. 'Any ideas on how she died? Or when?'

'The when, I can't really say yet. I suspect Iron Age probably, but I'll need to take her into the lab. The how is easy; I'll show you.'

I followed her under the tarpaulin again and she lowered herself gently into the pit where the body was lying. I knelt at the side and looked down.

Linda used a small, metal rod to tug lightly at something around the corpse's neck. Peering closely I could see some type of twine tied around her throat and looped at the back around a piece of wood.

'Is that a garrotte?' I asked.

'Absolutely,' she said, smiling and blowing at a stray lock of hair which hung in front of her eyes.

'So she was murdered?'

'Executed,' she corrected. 'Or sacrificed.'

'What makes you say that?'

'If she is Iron Age, she should have been cremated. As far as we know, they only buried those who were very important, or who had been sacrificed.'

'Why would she be sacrificed?' I asked.

'Every year, someone would be sacrificed to one of the gods. The god of the bog, the god of the harvest, the god of spring. Much like the ancient Greeks and Romans. You have different gods for different things. Some criminals, instead of being executed, would be sacrificed instead, and would be buried rather than burnt. It would be quite an honour for her, you'd imagine.'

'I'd imagine she might be a little pissed off, actually.'

'The well-being of her whole community depended on her sacrifice, Inspector,' Linda said with a serious edge to her tone. 'It would absolve her and her family from her crimes, whatever they were.'

'I understand,' I said, sorry that I seemed to have offended her. 'I don't need to start a murder file, though.'

'Unless you spot a four-thousand-year-old man wandering around, I think you're fairly free of this one, Inspector.'

On Sunday, I returned my attention to the more recently deceased. I went to the car-boot sales in Lifford and Letterkenny with a number of uniformed officers to canvass for information about the Chechen's death. We distributed the flyers I'd had translated to anyone interested and asked them to spread the information. Jim Hendry, my counterpart north of the border, had promised to do like-wise around Strabane. Our efforts, however, garnered no further information.

In the afternoon I went to the large market held on the outskirts of Derry. I stopped at various stalls selling eastern European foodstuffs, but no one was able to help me. As I was making my way along the final stretch of the market, I recognized someone working out of the back of one of the white vans parked against the perimeter fence.

Pol from the Migrant Workers' Information Centre was handing bags of toilet rolls to a heavy-set woman. Beside him stood another man, leaning against the side of the van, rolling a cigarette. He was wiry and sharp-featured, with a thin moustache.

'You really are a migrant worker,' I said to Pol when he was finished serving the woman. He looked at me sharply, as if searching for the insult in what I had said.

'I mean, two jobs,' I explained. 'You'll be putting the rest of us lazy buggers to shame.'

'Work is work,' he explained. 'What are you doing here?'

'I'm still looking for information on him,' I said, handing Pol a flyer. 'Will you display it on your table?'

'This is my boss, Vinnie,' he said, gesturing towards the other man. 'Best ask him.'

Vincent stepped away from the van and took the leaflet from me.

'What's he done?' he asked.

'He's got himself shot,' I answered. 'We need to find his family, if he has one.'

'Any leads?' Vinnie asked.

'Not a one,' I replied, suddenly eager to end the conversation.

Vinnie bit the end of his rolled cigarette and spat on to the ground. 'We'll put up the poster and keep an eye out,' he said.

The breakthrough, when it came, did so from an unexpected source. I had begun having panic attacks a while back and my GP, John Mulrooney, had prescribed beta-blockers. On Monday morning I had a check-up with him to get a new prescription. As I waited for him to sign the script he asked about the dead man.

'Any luck with an identity?'

'None. It seems he's an illegal immigrant – Chechen, apparently. But we can't find anyone who'll come forward to identify him.'

'No family?'

'Nothing,' I said. 'I've tried the car-boot sales and markets, and the Migrant Workers' Information Centre. The problem is, if he's an illegal, he's not going to register on any systems.'

'Are you sure he's illegal?' he asked.

'Fairly certain,' I said. 'Why?'

Mulrooney seemed to consider something, then stood up and handed me the script. 'I didn't tell you this, Ben. There's a locum doctor does the evening emergency surgery in Strabane sometimes – a Polish fella. Apparently he sees illegals requiring medical help during the night surgeries on the sly – doesn't charge them. He'd be fired if it were officially known, but no one on the ground cares. End of the day, the Health Service is meant to be helping people. If anyone knows your man, it'll be him.'

'Does it not piss the Irish doctors off – a Pole taking their work? Would someone not report him?'

'He's happy to work the graveyard shift no one else wants to do, and for a third of the cost. No one really cares who he treats at three in the morning, if he's happy enough to get out of his bed to do it.'

I don't know which I found more offensive: that the Polish doctor was being paid a fraction of the going wage, or that it was clearly preferable to whatever the man had been earning in his home country.

It took a phone call to Jim Hendry to get the man's name: Karol Walshyk. As he lived in the North, Hendry told me he'd accompany me to the man's house in Sion Mills.

It was the neatest in a row of five terraced houses. Lace curtains covered the windows and the woodwork had been freshly painted. When Walshyk answered the door, a waft of warm air escaped, heavy with the smell of spices. The man himself, in his forties with a neat grey beard, stood in the doorway wearing an apron over his clothes.

His initial response upon seeing us was to ask if something had happened to his parents in Poland. Reassured on this point, he invited us in with an offer of lunch. Finally he asked us what exactly was wrong.

When we explained why we were there, he was, understandably, wary of helping us. He denied knowing anything about illegal workers in the area, and claimed not to recognize the man whose picture I showed him. It was clear that he was holding back on us, and I began to suspect that the presence of Jim Hendry was the reason. No immigrant, legitimate or otherwise, is going to admit to illegal activity, even of the most justifiable kind, in front of a police officer. I, on the other hand, being out of my jurisdiction, represented no threat to him. I thanked him for his help and left him my card, in case he should think of anything useful.

Sure enough, an hour later he called and told me to come alone to meet him and he would take me to the family of the dead man.

I was surprised to learn that the dead man's residence was in a new housing development along the Urney Road. On our way there, Karol, as he told me to call him, explained the family's background to me. The man had come to the surgery with his wife one evening several months back. She had been in the early months of pregnancy and had suffered a miscarriage. Karol had wanted her to go to the hospital, but she refused. Instead, he had visited her at home each day for a few weeks, until she had recovered. At the time, her husband, one Ruslan Almurzayev, had been working in a local chip van. Karol had not seen either him or his wife, Natalia, since.

I remembered when these houses had been on the market. Despite their size and the paucity of ground around them, they'd had a hefty price tag.

'How the hell can they afford to live here?' I asked.

'You'll see. Wait.'

*　　*　　*

36

When we arrived at the house, Karol offered to prepare the occupants before bringing me in. I sat in the car, smoking and waiting for his signal.

I had just stubbed out my cigarette when Karol appeared at the doorway and beckoned me in.

Once inside, I began to understand. The interior was almost empty of furnishing; seating in the kitchen took the form of an old patio set. The living area was furnished with beanbags and an old coffee table. In the corner was a battered black-and-white TV, in front of which sprawled several children of varying ages. A pot of something steamed on the cooker in the kitchen. Upstairs I could hear the wailing of a woman and the shouts of others.

Karol led us up the uncarpeted steps. A crowd of women blocked the entrance to one of the three bedrooms. Peering between them I could discern a woman sitting on the edge of a camp bed, sobbing, while another woman comforted her.

Karol spoke to the group, presumably in Chechen, for they began to part as we pushed through. He led us into the room and spoke again, and within a minute only we two and the girl were left.

'Are they your friends?' My question was for the woman, though I directed it to Karol.

'They live here,' he replied without speaking to the girl.

'All of them?' I asked incredulously, for there were at least a dozen I had seen, not counting the children downstairs.

'Twenty-four in total,' Karol explained. 'Four families. One per bedroom and one for the living room.'

The girl looked from one to the other of us, her eyes wide and red, her face drawn in an expression that was as much fear as grief.

'Please don't be afraid,' I said, crouching before her. I produced one of the flyers I'd had made, and folded it so that the picture of her husband was visible. 'Is this your husband?'

She pointed to the picture and said something to Karol, then turned to me and nodded her head slowly, before breaking into fresh sobs.

'Ask her when she last saw her husband.'

The two spoke briefly. 'Last Friday,' Karol explained to me eventually. 'He went out looking for work.'

'I thought he worked in a chip van,' I said.

Another conversation ensued. While they spoke, I examined the woman's face. Her hair was blonde and shoulder-length, though pulled back into a pony-tail that seemed to accentuate the sharpness of her features. One of her teeth, slightly crooked, bit her pale lower lip.

Karol turned to me. 'He was fired. He asked for more money, so his boss fired him. He'd been looking for work for a few weeks now.'

'Did she know he was going to rob a bank?' I asked.

The word 'bank' must have registered for she shook her head violently and said something which sounded like 'Naa ha'. She looked from Karol to me. 'Naa . . . no, no,' she said, blinking back her tears. I was unsure whether she was answering my question or vainly protesting her husband's innocence.

'Tell her I'm sorry, but we need her to identify her husband for us,' I said. Any further questioning could be carried out in the station, after she'd had time to grieve a little for her husband. Though I couldn't really see where the questions would lead us – the man had been living in desperate circumstances without a job and was unlucky enough to rob a bank the day half the Irish Army were standing outside.

'I'm sorry, Mrs Almurzayev,' I said, looking her in the eyes. 'I'm very sorry.'

I laid my hand on hers momentarily. Her hands were cold and light, the skin calloused. She looked at me, then withdrew her hand from mine.

As we drove to Letterkenny General to identify the body, Karol and I discussed the likely fates of the immigrants I had seen in the house. Mrs Almurzayev sat in the back of my car, looking out of the window.

'I'm glad you got back to me,' I said. 'I'd never have found anyone else who could speak Chechen.'

'A lot of refugees came into Poland in 2005. I volunteered in the Médecins sans Frontières camp in Warsaw for six months,' he explained. 'You have to learn fast there.'

'I'd believe that,' I said.

We stood beside Natalia Almurzayev while she viewed the dead man. She held his hand in her own and stopped the morgue attendant from pulling the green sheet over his face again until she had kissed him on the forehead. She cradled the side of his head in her hand and rubbed the greying hair at his sideburns with her thumb as she murmured to him words that required no translation.

Afterwards, Karol and Natalia sat in the cafeteria while I went to get three cups of coffee. When I came back, they were deep in conversation. They were an incongruous couple – he in a suit, she dressed in jeans and a hooded top.

'She had no idea that her husband was going to rob a bank, Inspector,' he said when I sat down. 'She thought he was going looking for work.'

'How long have they been here?' I asked.

'Five months,' he answered without asking her, which suggested that he had already established some of the background details while I was buying the coffee.

'Where did her husband get the false driving licence?' I asked. Karol translated the question. Though she shrugged her shoulders in bewilderment, it was clear that she knew what I was talking about.

'She doesn't know about a driving licence,' Karol said.

I took the licence from my pocket, still in an evidence bag, and placed it on the table. 'Tell her she won't get into trouble, if she'll tell me now. If she doesn't, I'll have to report her to Immigration Services.'

Karol started to speak then stopped and looked at me quizzically.

'Just say it, please,' I said.

Reluctantly the girl told us the full story of how she and her husband had ended up in Ireland.

They had both worked in a steelworks in Chechnya for under €200 per month between them. Then Ruslan received word from his cousin who had moved to Ireland: the economy here was booming; it was a land of opportunity. They could earn in a week more than they had been earning in a month at home. They had no children, no dependents, nothing to stop them coming across. They did, however, have to pay €10,000 each for their transport and for a safe house and identity when they got here.

The man who would bring them over would let them pay in instalments when they arrived: half their wages each week, until the debt was cleared. Ruslan's cousin organized the whole thing.

In March they met a group of thirty other people near the border with Ingushetia. They were bundled into the back of an articulated lorry. A thin wooden partition in the cargo area created a false wall behind which they crammed. They each had to pay €1,000 to the driver as a deposit. Then, packed together, they sat and waited to be delivered to Ireland.

They travelled, for some time huddled in the dark. She wasn't sure whether they went east to the Caspian or west to the Black Sea but, within a day of travelling, they reached the coast. They smelt the change in the lorry, the briny quality of the sea air. They heard, when they stopped, the crying of gulls.

Natalia could tell when the lorry had boarded a ship; so deep in the bowels of the vessel, crammed together, the pitch and roll effect exaggerated, many of those in the compartment, particularly the children, vomited for most of the journey. Five bottles of water and a loaf of bread had been left with the occupants. By the second day, the water tasted bitter with the taste of vomit. Natalia managed to refuse subsequent offers of a drink until the fourth morning or so she estimated (there were no windows or lights in the compartment, so day and night became interchangeable). By that stage the lorry was back on solid ground.

They travelled by water once more, a journey of only an hour or two. Within a few more hours they finally arrived at their destination, more than five days after leaving their home.

She felt the truck stop. She heard the thud of the cab door as the driver got out, heard voices outside, heard the grating of the large back doors being opened. She and the others listened in darkness, whilst the cargo was shifted to one side. What if they had been caught? What if it was immigration officers?

When they first saw the man who appeared in the doorway, they were certain they *had* been caught, for he carried a gun in his hand. Some of the children screamed, until he raised it above his head and shouted to them in Russian that they had arrived in Ireland.

It was turning dark when they got out of the lorry and were led, one family at a time, to an old farmhouse. Natalia fell when she tried to walk, her muscles cramped and unaccustomed to use after sitting so long in one position. A man pointed to the gable wall of the house. Several small holes punctured the rendering, which was stained with a rust-coloured residue.

In the cottage a man spoke to her and her husband in Russian. He took their photographs with a digital camera, then directed them to wait in the kitchen area with the others. Chocolate bars were lying on a plate and they gorged themselves. When he returned, a few hours later, the man handed them each a forged driving licence and passport. Her husband's new name was Joseph Mackey; hers was Anna McIlwee.

Fifteen minutes later they and three other families were collected in a convoy of cars. As they drove they were given instructions. They would be taken to their new home; they would remain there until they had paid their debt, collected each month with the rent for the house, which would be an additional £50 per week. They would be provided with jobs until their debt was paid, then they would have to find their own. If they complained, argued back or broke any of their conditions, they'd be dealt with severely. If they contacted the police, hospitals or government agencies while they were still paying their debts, they would be brought back to the cottage, where they would be stood against the gable wall they had all been shown earlier.

An hour later they were dropped at the house in Strabane. A middle-aged man with a pony-tail was waiting for them there. He had milk, bread, butter and eggs. The house had no furniture, no bedding. One of the men complained to him, said he had expected better. The man with the pony-tail and one of the drivers took him upstairs. The others cowered below as they listened to the thuds. They did not see the man again until the next day. He had never complained since.

The pony-tailed man said he'd call each month; he'd collect £400 from the Almurzayevs – £100 each towards the debt and £50 per week for the rent. Larger families were paying almost double that. Anyone who couldn't earn enough, they'd find work for them. Even the children. So far, they'd all made sure they had their rent when he called, after 8 p.m. the first Friday of each month.

We listened in silence until she had finished her story. She asked me for a cigarette and went outside to smoke.

'I can't let this happen,' I said to Karol. 'I need to contact the PSNI.'

'No,' he said. 'They'll be deported.'

'It would be better than what they're doing at the moment.'

'They'd kill anyone not caught by the police, Inspector. They'd assume someone had informed on them.'

'I know someone with the PSNI – someone good. He'll deal with it properly.'

'You told her you wouldn't report her, Inspector. You gave her your word.'

'Better to let them be exploited by a bunch of thugs? Is that what you're suggesting? The state will take care of them.'

'You think they'd be any better off being looked after by the state? There are no-safe houses for illegal immigrants. They won't even get healthcare unless people like me treat them illegally. I'd be struck off, sent back to Poland, if they knew what I did. Your reporting them will change nothing. The people who brought them in will vanish into the woodwork and the only people to suffer will be Natalia and others like her. If you want to help her, actually help her.'

'And how do you suggest I do that?'

'Find out who brought them here. Because they're going to want their money soon, and she has no way of earning it.'

We both looked out through the plate glass to where Natalia stood, hugging herself for warmth, dragging on the end of the butt of her smoke as if it were her final cigarette.

I sat that evening with Debbie, having put our two children to bed. She sat cross-legged on the sofa, a cushion clutched in front of her as she tried to watch a soap opera.

'Either way, I feel culpable,' I said. 'If I do nothing, I'm letting whoever is fleecing these people get away with it. If I report it, I'll be handing them over to be sent home. What would you do?'

'Is there no way you can follow it up without actually reporting them? Trace who brought them in?' she suggested, without averting her eyes from the screen.

'I wouldn't know where to start,' I said. 'And I'm on my own with this.' My partner, Caroline Williams, had left the force following a case we had worked on in which she had almost died. I had not since been given a new partner, partly, I suspected, because our new Super, Patterson, was happy to isolate me a little.

'They must have contact with someone. How do they pay back their debt?'

'Some guy comes to collect it on the first Friday of each month.'

'That's this Friday coming,' Debbie concluded. 'Why not call Jim Hendry and see what he can do?'

I had already considered it, but to do so would be to place Jim in an awkward position. And I wasn't sure how far I could test our friendship.

I explained this to Debbie. 'I'm stuck. I want to do what's right for the woman, you know? I don't want to help her out of one mess into another. Especially with what's happened with her husband. I need to know I've done the right thing.'

Finally, sensing that I wouldn't leave her in peace until she had given me a satisfactory response, she put the cushion she'd been hugging to one side, muted the TV and faced me.

'In that case, speak to Patterson about it. You're working the dead man's case anyway — at least this way you'll have shown you've worked out who he was,' she said, raising her eyebrows, the remote control already pointed again at the TV.

Chapter Four

Tuesday, 3 October

I was first in to the station the following morning and brewed coffee in the kitchen while I collected my mail. I took my mug and the post out the back for a smoke. In the middle of the pile was a card from Caroline Williams, sent from Sligo. She wrote that she was fine, though her son, Peter, was going through a bad patch. She hoped everyone was well. She missed us all, she said. Obviously not enough to come back, I thought.

When Patterson arrived, I went into his office and explained all that I had done in tracing Ruslan Almurzayev, and about his widow's predicament.

'So we know who he was,' Patterson said.

I nodded.

'Good work, Devlin,' he said. 'The rest of this has nothing to do with us.'

'But these people are—' I began to protest, but he held up his hand to silence me.

'These people have chosen to live in the North. Now, while I sympathize with their situation, it is not our responsibility. We've done our bit. Call your friend in the North, Hendrix or whatever he's called, and tell him.'

'They'll deport them,' I said, trying to keep my voice as calm as possible.

'Listen,' Patterson hissed. 'Costello might have indulged your habits, but I won't. We have Cathal Hagan coming here in a week's time and you're in charge. Now do the job you're being fucking paid for and stop chasing cases out of your jurisdiction.'

'He died over here,' I said.

'Past tense: died,' Patterson repeated. 'Dead and buried. Case closed. Drop it.'

I knew there was no point in discussing it further with him as he glared at me across his desk.

'They're moving that body from the mine today. Now why don't you get out to Orcas and kiss Weston's golden arse until it shines.'

I sat in the car near the border for ten minutes, staring across the river towards Strabane as if somehow it would reveal an answer. Finally, I phoned Hendry on my mobile. His line rang out. I had another smoke and redialled. Again, no answer. I got the impression someone was trying to tell me something.

I headed back to Orcas as directed. The traffic was heavier than I had expected and I realized that quite a bit of it was headed out to the camp that had been set up along the stream where Ted Coyle had found his nugget. Riled by Patterson's concluding comments, and always happy to spend half an hour outdoors in weather like this, I pulled in to the camp rather than going directly to Orcas.

The number of cars parked in the area had significantly increased. The scent of fir trees had been thickened with the smells of burning wood and cooking food. The atmosphere under the canopy was carnivalesque. A few kids who should have been in school were playing soccer in a clearing, using the nearest trees as goalposts. A young girl was picking flowers from the woodland floor, in spots where the sun had managed to pierce the canopy.

Rock music played from one of the camper vans and a number of its occupants were sitting in the sunlight outside the open back doors, rolling cigarettes or drinking from beer cans. I noticed a few of those rolling smokes hastily hide them when they saw me getting out of my car. A man who was playing with a mongrel looked up, peered at me for a second as if in recognition, then turned his back and continued to fight with the dog for possession of the stick it had clamped in its mouth. None of them, as far as I could see, were panning for gold.

I nodded over to them, then walked on down to the river, where the atmosphere was very different. I counted twenty-three straining rumps down by the water, each owner sifting through the grit they had gathered in the sieves and colanders they were using.

I recognized Patsy McCann, standing close to the far bank. The spell of dry weather had exposed part of this section of the riverbed, though a good night's rain would soon change things. I was able to cross to him with some care and minimal soaking, stepping from stone to stone.

Patsy threw his sieve down in disgust on the near bank and flopped down beside it. Reclining on the grass, he shielded his eyes with his hand and looked up at me.

'Any luck?' I asked.

'Bugger-all,' he spat. 'I'd be better off back pulling pints.'

'Anyone found anything?' I asked, a little surprised that McCann had given up his job to sift through river dirt.

'Nobody, apart from yer man Coyle.' He nodded upriver to where a stocky middle-aged man stood, trouser legs rolled up to his knees, pan in hand.

I noticed that a number of the other people spotted around the river were likewise watching him and, as he moved around, they followed him, at a distance, as if he possessed some unshared knowledge of the riverbed and its secrets. If he was aware of their gazes, he didn't show it.

Suddenly, a child's shout echoed along the river. A number of prospectors looked up quickly towards the source of the cry, their faces lit with expectation and envy in equal measure when they saw something glistening in his wet hands. Equally quickly they turned away, with palpable relief, when they realized that it was not gold he carried in his hands but a dead fish. He held its curled body on his upturned palms, as if in offering. Coyle alone went over to inspect it, like some tribal elder, prodding it with his finger then turning and wading upstream. One or two of the others, watching him, gathered their things and began to move too, until he turned and glared at them as if warning them to keep away.

'That fish is probably the most valuable thing anyone's found since we got here,' McCann said, drawing my attention back to him. 'I'll give it another week, I think. Then I'm packing it in.'

Wishing him good fortune, I headed on to Orcas, and a meeting with seemingly the only man to really profit from Ireland's gold rush.

Weston suggested we walk to the site where a group from the museum were lifting the bog body from the ground and transporting it to Dublin. He walked with his suit jacket slung over his arm, his sleeves rolled up to his elbows. I faced twin reflections of myself in his sunglasses as we discussed the discovery of the body, which, to Weston's mind, could only be good for business.

'We're perfectly happy to stall production for a few days, helping the museum services to process this discovery. Far from trampling on tradition, we're helping to preserve it,' he said in a manner that made me believe the spiel had been scripted.

I couldn't help but suspect that Weston worked hard to get me to like him – though I didn't flatter myself to believe it was particular to me. He seemed to need people's approbation; or perhaps he was so used to being criticized that he was now automatically politic in his conversation, arguing his defence before an attack had even been made.

'Of course,' he added, 'I might ask them to sell the body back to us; put it on display in the reception area.'

I looked at him and he laughed, though, with his sunglasses shielding his eyes, I couldn't assess the sincerity of the emotion.

'Maybe just a loan then, eh, Ben?'

We reached the site slightly out of breath. Linda Campbell was there, though no longer in charge. I noticed that her paper suit from the previous day had hidden a slight frame.

'Back again, Inspector?'

'Can't keep away,' I said. 'Even if I wanted to.'

'Ben Devlin!' a voice boomed, and I turned to see a man my age and size struggle his way out of the pit. 'Jesus Christ, Ben Devlin in the Guards!'

He stood before me. His face was jowly, his eyes narrowed by the pudginess of his cheeks. His hair was receding, though still naturally black. He held out his arms, as if to give me a hug, and I instinctively stepped back.

'Jesus,' he said, turning to Linda Campbell and lowering his arms. 'Four years together at college and the blackguard pretends not to know me.'

And then it struck me. 'Fearghal Bradley,' I said, shaking my head. 'Good to see you.'

'Benny,' he said, smiling broadly, clasping me to him in a bear hug. I patted his upper arms lightly in return and extricated myself from his embrace.

'Fearghal, what brings you to Donegal?'

'Kate, of course.'

I smiled a little uncertainly and looked at Linda. 'Kate?'

'Kate Moss,' he explained, laughing at his own joke. I vaguely remembered that a body found several years ago in a bog had been named Peat Moss by some wag in the press. It hadn't taken a massive leap to christen this new find.

'Except she'd need to lose a few pounds to look like the real thing,' I added.

Fearghal guffawed loudly. 'Ben Devlin,' he repeated, as if

for the benefit of those standing around, who looked as bemused as I felt.

'Are you in the museum now?' I asked.

'Professor Bradley *is* the museum,' Linda Campbell said.

'Listen to her,' Fearghal laughed. I wondered for a second if there was something going on between them.

'So, what happens with her next?' I asked, nodding towards 'Kate'.

'Full forensics, Benny,' Fearghal said. 'Same as you'd do yourself. We'll find out when she lived, how she died, maybe even why she died. It's the discovery of a lifetime.'

'I see,' I said.

'Ben Devlin in the Guards!' Fearghal repeated, as much, I suspected, for something to say. 'Who'd have thought it?'

We struggled to make small-talk for a few moments, having not seen one another in over a decade. Finally we parted with the half-hearted promise to meet for a drink sometime. As we shook hands to part he said again, 'You a Guard!' Then he added darkly, 'Did they know about your criminal record?'

Linda Campbell looked quizzically at me. I laughed as good-humouredly as I could manage.

After returning to his office, Weston and I discussed the arrangements for the following week. He ran through Hagan's itinerary with me, and details of the security he would be bringing with him. I in turn outlined the arrangements Patterson and I had discussed. Satisfied with our plans, Weston thanked me for my work and walked me to the door.

'I have to ask,' he said, smiling. 'What's the criminal record your friend mentioned?' Before I could even respond he continued, 'I shouldn't pry, but I'm guessing it's nothing serious or he wouldn't have brought it up.'

'It's nothing,' I said. 'When we were students we broke into the admin building of the university. It was a student prank thing.'

'You've a bit of the Irish rebel in you, Ben,' Weston said, slapping me lightly on the back and laughing as if we were old friends. I was reminded again of how I felt on the day he had given me a gold necklace for Debbie. 'Keep me posted,' he said, patting me on the upper back once more, then turned back into his office, allowing the door to swing quietly closed behind him.

Chapter Five

Wednesday, 4 October–Thursday, 5 October

On Wednesday I attended the funeral of Ruslan Almurzayev. Karol Walshyk had helped make the arrangements, finding the priest in Derry who said the Polish Mass in the cathedral and persuading him to lead the service.

The turn-out was tiny. Clearly most of the other immigrants were fearful of Immigration Control attending the event. Natalia Almurzayev stood flanked by two female companions. She wore a simple floral summer dress and a pair of plain shoes. Her face was bleary with tears throughout the service.

She stood alone by the graveside as her husband was laid to rest, and I wondered how this woman, alone in a foreign country, having lost her unborn child and her husband within the space of a few months, had the strength to even stand. I was certain that, as she had huddled in the back of a lorry making its way across Europe, she must have held her breath and dared to hope that the future could only bring good things.

Before leaving, I went over to see her to express my condolences in a language she did not understand. Still, she held my gaze with dignity, her jaw set. But behind her strength I could sense a fear of what was to come. She must have realized that the rent collector would be calling on Friday for money she did not have.

I leant close to her, kissed her lightly on a cheek still damp with tears. 'Don't worry,' I said. 'I'll not let them hurt you. I promise.' I handed her my card, on which was printed my mobile number. 'Call me if you need anything,' I said.

She looked me in the eye and smiled lightly, as though she understood the sentiment, even if the words meant little to her.

'Anything,' I repeated.

The rest of the day passed with meetings to discuss security arrangements for Hagan's impending visit. Patterson had relieved me of all other duties to focus on the event; my preparations required a visit to Dublin on Thursday with Patterson, to meet with a number of other regional commanders. It was the first such meeting since Patterson had taken over as Superintendent and he took advantage of the opportunity to go for drinks with his new colleagues during the afternoon. For my part, I decided to visit an old friend.

The girl at the desk of the museum phoned through to Fearghal Bradley for me and as I waited for him to come up from 'the bowels', as his message relayed through her put it. I examined the nearest display cases.

One in particular stood out: a massive torc – a golden neckband – which had been discovered in Meath in the 1920s was the centrepiece of the biggest display, surrounded by smaller gold pieces discovered in the same dig. The information sheet beside the cabinet related details of the find and the fact that the jewellery had been fashioned from Irish gold during the Bronze Age, when mining had been a common feature of life in Ireland.

A few minutes later Fearghal appeared by my side. I was a little surprised to see him wearing a white medical coat.

'Benny boy, good to see you,' he said, continuing his hail-fellow-well-met routine.

'Fearghal,' I said, shaking his hand. 'I was down for a conference; thought I'd drop in and see how Kate is doing.'

'Great to see you,' he said, pumping my hand in his but noticeably toning down his voice. 'Come and see her.'

As I followed him to the door, I asked about his family. His parents had both been architects, and I remembered them as kind, good-living people. They were both well, he assured me, as was his younger brother, Leon, who had been friendly with my younger brother, Tom, when Fearghal and I had known each other. Leon had been a computing expert, then had thrown it up and had gone off to some commune, apparently. Tom, meanwhile, had become a mechanical engineer.

'That's how people change,' Fearghal concluded as he led me down several flights of steps to a basement laboratory not unlike a surgical theatre.

Kate's body lay curled on top of a stainless-steel table, her features much clearer now that all the dirt had been cleaned from her. Her hair was red, her teeth almost golden in colour.

'She's a beauty, isn't she?' Fearghal said.

'Considering her age,' I said.

'Two and a half thousand years,' he said. 'Carbon dating will give us a more accurate date, but we suspect early Iron Age.'

'Have you been able to verify cause of death?' I asked.

He smiled. 'Typical cop,' he said. 'The how's not really important, Benny. It's the why that's interesting.'

'Why then?' I asked, and then, perhaps through pure contrariness, he answered the 'how' anyway.

'She was strangled,' he said. 'Garrotted.'

'Miss Campbell thought that,' I nodded. 'And why?'

'We think she was a sacrifice. She was probably a criminal who was to be executed anyway so they offered her as a sacrifice instead.'

'A sacrifice to whom?'

'Probably Aine,' he said. 'Goddess of love and fertility.'

'What makes you think that?'

'Detective work, Benny,' Bradley said. 'And a lot of guessing.'

'That's mostly the same thing,' I said.

'There's a whole load of things we've picked up on,' he said. 'Firstly, the fact that she was buried at all. Early Iron Age man cremated his dead. If they buried someone, it was probably as a gift to the bog or to the gods.'

'Why do you think she was a gift to the gods then and not the bog?'

'Two reasons,' he said, clearly enjoying discussing his work. 'Linda examined Kate's stomach contents, her last meal. She ate, or was forced to eat, a gruel or soup of flow-ers: barley, lin-seed, knotgrass, gold-of-pleasure. The fact

58

that she ate a mixture of flowers and cereals suggests either the harvest or the spring.'

'Forced?'

He beamed broadly. 'C'mere.' He beckoned me over to a shelf where a tupperware container sat, half filled with a thick yellow substance. Bradley lifted a spoon from the desk, wiped it on the tail of his white coat and spooned out some of the yellow mix.

'Taste that,' he said, offering me the spoon as I backed away.

'No thanks,' I said, raising my hand.

'Go on,' he persisted, raising the spoon to my mouth. 'It won't kill you.'

'Is this her actual stomach contents?' I asked, trying hard not to gag.

'Jesus, Ben, we're not mad, you know. One of the botanists here made it up from modern ingredients. It's as close as she can get it to the original. Try it.'

I took a small mouthful of the gruel. The initial taste was malty, though very quickly a bitter aftertaste developed. Suppressing the urge to spit, I grimaced and swallowed.

Bradley laughed loudly, tapping the remains of the gruel off the spoon back into the container. 'Exactly,' he said. 'Would you eat that voluntarily?'

'Fair enough,' I said.

'So that's that. Plus, of course, the fact that she's a woman . suggests something to do with fertility – which is why I think she was sacrificed to Aine. Which, in turn, would suggest that she was killed on her feast day, Midsummer's Eve.'

'What age was she?'

'In her early twenties. She's measuring in at 154 centimetres, though she'll have shrunk in the bog. Plus it dyed her skin and her hair; she may not have been a redhead in real life.'

'Linda told me it would have been a great honour for someone to have been sacrificed.'

'She was right,' Fearghal said. 'Her family would have been very proud. Her death would have been one of great dignity.'

'Any damage to her hands?' I asked, angling my head slightly to examine them.

'Nothing much,' he said, interested now.

'If she were strangled, you'd imagine her fingers would be damaged from fighting against the noose. You'd expect her fingernails to have broken at least. She didn't fight it.'

'She may well have been drugged beforehand.'

'Maybe,' I agreed. 'Might be worth doing toxicology.'

He laughed. 'This isn't a murder case, Ben.'

'You'd just like to know, though. Wouldn't you?'

He nodded. 'I guess you would, Ben,' he said.

We stood by her body for a moment in silence, then I announced I'd better get back to Patterson.

'What did you say had you down here?' Fearghal asked as we mounted the stairs back up to the street.

'Security conference,' I said.

'Must be big,' he said.

'Cathal Hagan, the US senator, is coming to Orcas next week to officially open the place.'

'Hagan,' Bradley said. 'Isn't he the one that—'

'Yep,' I said, glad to see the final flight of steps ahead. 'He's that one.'

'Good luck to you,' he said. 'You'll need it with that bastard,' he laughed, standing on the top step, hand held aloft in a farewell salute.

Chapter Six

Friday, 6 October

Friday morning dawned to blue skies, with a thick bank of white cloud low to the east. The forecast promised rain by evening, but until then a fine day stretched ahead.

Natalia Almurzayev had told us that the rent collector, whom I had christened Pony Tail, would be calling to collect his payment after 8 p.m. on the first Friday of the month. I had mulled over the problem all week; to tell Hendry would almost certainly result in the immigrants being shipped back to Chechnya. To say nothing would leave them at the mercy of whoever was exploiting them. I figured if I could trace whoever the rent collector delivered to, I might be able to direct Hendry towards him without necessarily landing Mrs Almurzayev in trouble with the Police Service of Northern Ireland.

Not for the first time, I missed my old partner, Caroline Williams, who had left both An Garda and Donegal following our last case together. I needed help – in particular a woman's help. My plan was to have Natalia Almurzayev removed from the house before the collector arrived. I would then watch the house and follow him when he left.

In the end, I contacted Helen Gorman. She had proved herself hard-working and sensible enough; plus she was involved to some extent in the case already, having mistakenly broken the news of 'Mackey's' death to his wife. I didn't know how discreet she would be, but I had little other choice.

I caught up with her in Letterkenny over coffee. She agreed to help in any way she could, but in fact all I needed her to do for now was baby-sit Natalia for an hour or two.

I met Helen at 6 p.m. in Lifford and we drove in two separate unmarked Garda cars to the house in Strabane where Karol Walshyk had brought me the previous week. The man who opened the door to us immediately tried to slam it shut again, perhaps thinking we were Northern police. With luck and speed, I managed to wedge my foot in the doorjamb, then used my considerable weight to force the door back. Realizing he was on to a loser, the man let go of the door and scuttled into the house shouting a warning. I, in turn, fell through the door-way and found myself sprawled on the floor.

I was aware of a number of people running to the kitchen to escape through the back door. A hand helped me to my feet and I turned, assuming it was Helen Gorman. Instead, Natalia Almurzayev stood before me.

'Thank you,' I said.

She nodded as if she understood, not just what I had said, but why I was there. I pointed to Helen. 'Go with her,' I said. Natalia looked at Helen who, in turn, smiled sheepishly and waved from the doorstep.

Natalia looked from Helen to me and spoke in Chechen, then rubbed her fingers together in a gesture of money, before pointing at her watch. She was referring to the money collector.

I pointed to my chest. 'I'll take care of it,' I said. 'Go with Helen.'

She looked doubtful still, but finally called to some of the others in the house and a few faces peered out from the kitchen. One woman called something back and, whatever Natalia's response was, it seemed to placate them, for they began to move back into the body of the house again.

Natalia placed her hand on my arm as she walked past. She nodded and said something approximating 'Thank you'. She smiled sadly, then lowered her head and allowed Helen Gorman to guide her out to the car.

I followed them and watched as they drove away. In my turn I went over to my own car, broke open a new packet of cigarettes, and sat and waited.

At just after 8.15, a silver Ford Fiesta pulled up outside the house. From where I was sitting, I could make out two men in the car. The passenger door opened and Pony Tail climbed out and shuffled up towards the house. His accomplice, who wore a baseball cap, remained in the car. Exhaust fumes continued to escape from the back of the car – the engine was still running. The visibility of the fumes also suggested the engine was cold; the men had not driven far. Unfortunately, the driver was facing me, which made it difficult for me to watch him openly, not to mention follow them unnoticed. I could, however, jot down the registration number.

I slid down a little in the seat and stubbed out my smoke. I felt certain the driver was watching me watching him. Soon, though, he got bored and leant back to retrieve something from the back seat.

A few minutes later Pony Tail came out of the house and I got a proper look at him. He was wiry-framed with greying hair. His face was thin and lean and he chewed gum as he walked, blowing and popping a bubble as he reached the car.

The driver said something to him and he looked back at the house he had just left. Then, as he turned to get into the car, he glanced directly at me for a second.

As he closed the door I phoned Gorman, who had taken Natalia for a drive, patching the call through the hands-free set so that the two men in the car opposite would not see me using my phone. I explained the situation.

As the Fiesta drove off, I was aware that both men were looking across at me as they passed and I had to resist the compulsion to look back. I'd know Pony Tail if I saw him again but I'd no idea what the other man looked like, beyond the feeling that he had black hair beneath his cap.

When they turned the corner I started the car and drove after them in the same direction. They knew they were being followed, so it made no difference if they saw me behind them. I only needed to know which direction they were going when they got to the bypass which would take them either north towards Lifford, south to Omagh, or else straight ahead into the centre of Strabane. Helen Gorman had dropped Natalia at a local fast-food place on the edge of town and was making her way up the bypass. If they headed towards Omagh or into Strabane, she'd catch them; if they headed towards Lifford, I'd have to follow them.

At the lights they indicated right, in the direction of Omagh. Gorman had just reached the junction opposite and slowed sufficiently to miss the traffic lights, thereby ensuring she'd be behind them when she got a chance to pull out. The lights changed and they drove out onto the junction and up the bypass. Following them at a distance, I stopped at the lights, although they were green, so that they would think they had lost me. When the lights changed, Gorman pulled out and drove up the bypass after them.

We followed them like that for over an hour as they visited three other houses in the surrounding area. Gorman was able to stay fairly close to them without being spotted, she assured me.

The last house they visited was an old bungalow about two miles outside Artigarvan. To reach it, they had had to turn off the main road and drive up a country lane. Gorman had been following at a distance, but when the men reached their destination, they stopped so abruptly that she had no choice but to drive past the house and continue on up the laneway. Whilst she wanted to drive back down and follow them back out onto the main road when they left again, it was too dangerous. She would be exposed on a country road and, more importantly, isolated and alone. I told her to sit at the top of the lane in case they continued on up the road. If they came back down the way they had gone, I'd wait for them at the bottom and try my best to pick up the trail from there.

I picked the most inconspicuous spot I could find along the main road with a view of the junction they would have to pass through if they came this way. Sure enough, a few moments later I was able to make out the car coming back down the laneway. I started the engine and drove past the junction, fairly sure that their final destination would be Strabane. All I could do was drive ahead and keep track of them in the rear-view mirror.

As expected, they pulled out onto the road behind me. The road ahead was straight and clear and I hoped I was far enough ahead of them that they wouldn't recognize my car as the one they had seen outside Natalia's house.

However, I was aware they were approaching the rear of my car very quickly. Just when I thought they were going to ram me, the car indicated and began to overtake. I decided to risk a look at the men.

I turned, glancing to my right, just as Pony Tail lowered his window and stuck a sawn-off shotgun out. I slammed on my brakes as he fired off a shot which peppered the side of my car, spider-webbing the reinforced windscreen. I twisted the steering wheel and my car jerked out of control and hit the grass banking to my left. The impact happened as if in slow motion and I watched my glasses hit the steering wheel, just before the airbag inflated and enveloped my head.

Gorman decided it was more important to check on me than chase the shooter's car. It was the right decision; having already opened fire on me, I had no doubt they would have done the same to her.

I sat for a few moments at the side of the road and smoked a cigarette. Beyond being a little shaken, I wasn't hurt, though I was acutely aware that I would have to explain to Patterson why a Garda car was shot at north of the border. In turn I would have to explain about the immigrants and the fact that I had ignored his instructions; there seemed no other way out.

After managing to get the car started, I drove slowly behind Gorman to the fast-food restaurant where she had dropped Natalia. We learnt that she had left an hour earlier, walking in the direction of the Urney Road, according to the boy serving at the counter.

We returned to the house where the immigrants lived, but there was no response to our banging on the door. No lights shone from any of the windows, despite the encroaching dark.

I sat outside the house until 2 a.m. waiting for someone to return. When it became apparent that this was not going to happen, I reluctantly made my way home, wondering what further suffering my actions had caused Natalia.

Chapter Seven

Saturday, 7 October

The following morning I finally did what I should have done all along and contacted Jim Hendry, my counterpart in the North, asking him to meet me at the house. I was not wholly surprised when I drove over in my own car that morning to find the remains of Almurzayev's house charred and smouldering, the heat still palpable from the ruins. A fire tender was still there, finishing what had been several hours' work for the local fire service. Panic rising, I asked one of the firemen at the scene about fatalities and was relieved to learn that there had been no one in the house. It did not, however, remove the dread from my conscience that something would happen to Natalia. In attempting to save her from deportation, I had left her to a much worse fate.

Hendry arrived a few minutes after me. We sat in my car, watching the last firemen picking up pieces of debris and throwing them out into the garden. I explained what had happened the night before and all that had brought me to that point. He was, unsurprisingly, pissed off, both at our incursion into the North and at my failure to tell him about the house or its occupants.

'We got reports of gunfire last night, outside Artigarvan. One of our men spotted the accident site where your car must have hit. We figured it couldn't be that bad if the car had been able to drive off again,' he said, bitterly.

'I'm sorry, Jim. I didn't know what else to do,' I explained.

'Ignorance is no excuse. You should have told us you were coming across here, Devlin. Following suspects; withholding information relating to a crime; losing a houseful of illegal immigrants,' he said, counting each incident off on his fingers. 'You've royally fucked this one up.'

I wanted to argue, to defend myself on the grounds of good intentions, but I knew he was right. 'I got the registration plate,' I said, as if this in some way compensated for the mess I had caused.

'Not a silver Ford Fiesta by any chance, was it?' he asked. I nodded.

'Burnt out at the head of the town. No doubt it was stolen,' he said. 'You've got fuck-all, Devlin.'

'Have you traced it?' I asked.

'Are you telling me my job?' Hendry exploded. 'Fuck you. Piss off back to Lifford.'

With that he got out of the car, slammed the door and went over to talk with the firemen. I started the engine and drove off.

It was scant consolation that he was less annoyed with me than Patterson was. The Super almost had a stroke when I explained to him what had happened. He told me he would have suspended me on the spot if plans for the Hagan

70

visit on Monday hadn't been so far advanced, and had Weston not seemed so keen to have me involved. I would pay for it in the long run, he warned me, before we left for another meeting at Orcas. I didn't doubt it.

Weston was less solicitous during our meeting this time. He said little as we ran through arrangements for Hagan's visit. We would meet the Senator at the border after he had conducted a few engagements in Derry. Two unmarked cars would accompany him to Orcas through Lifford and Ballybofey; Hagan would travel with his own two security men, ex-Secret Service. I would be in one of the cars with a second escort behind, whilst Patterson would take care of dealings with Weston personally. Local Gardai would be on the ground at Orcas, ensuring crowd control, though the only crowd would be a small group of local primary-school children. Presumably anyone older might have reservations about waving flags at a warmonger such as Hagan.

Finally Weston got around to the subject that seemed to be bothering him. 'Have you gentlemen read the newspapers today?' Without waiting for a reply, he produced one of the Dublin broadsheets: CONTROVERSIAL SENATOR IN DONEGAL the headline read. He produced a second paper, this one from the North: WARNING TO US SENATOR AHEAD OF VISIT.

I glanced up at Weston as he showed us the stories, aware that he was reading our reactions to see if either of us was responsible for the leak.

'What was the warning?' I asked, gesturing towards the headline of the second story.

'Death threats,' he said. 'Phoned in to the Samaritans in Downpatrick, apparently. Probably nothing, but that's not the point.'

'Absolutely,' Patterson said, having finished reading. 'We'll have to take it seriously.'

'Of course you will,' Weston snapped. 'My biggest concern is how the fuck they heard about his visit.'

Harry had so far done all he could to appease him. This time, though, it seemed Weston had overstepped the mark.

'Well, it didn't come from our office, Mr Weston, and I'm not sure I like your tone. Every Garda force in the country knows he's coming, plus all the people involved in his trip to the North. Hell, the local primary-school teachers must know.'

'The school was only informed this morning,' Weston said, though his tone had changed somewhat. 'I apologize, Superintendent. I'm a little worried about all this.'

'No need to worry, sir,' Patterson said curtly. 'We have everything under control. I'll investigate these claims myself,' he added. 'Though I can assure you that neither I nor Inspector Devlin here would have mentioned this to *anyone*.'

'Janet Moore,' Patterson said when we were back in the car after our meeting. 'She wrote the first story. She's a freelancer, lives in Strabane. I play indoor football with her husband sometimes. Find out where she got her information.'

'Would it not be better you asking her, if you know the family?'

'I said I know her *husband*,' Patterson said irritably. 'Better a stranger asking her. You can lean on her more than I could.'

I silently wondered how he expected me to get her to reveal her sources. After a moment I said, 'Thanks for your support back there, Harry.'

'It was the force I was supporting,' he snapped. 'If I find out you did leak it, I'll rip you a new arsehole.'

I shook my head and looked away. I wondered if Fearghal Bradley had had anything to do with the leak. And I wondered just how many more mistakes I could get away with.

I reached Moore's house just after two o' clock. She and her husband, Karl, lived in a detached house at the far end of Strabane, just off the Derry Road.

Karl Moore was crouching over a motorcycle, which lay on its side on the front lawn. He had removed a section of the engine and was spraying the parts with oil when I arrived.

He offered his hand, then looked at it, rubbed it on his jeans leg and shook.

'I'm looking for your wife, Mr Moore,' I explained.

He squinted at me.

'Aye,' he said. 'What's she done?'

'Nothing, sir. I'd like to discuss a story she wrote about in the paper.'

'Is it that bloody environment thing?' he asked.

I shook my head. I had no idea what he meant. 'She wrote a story about a US senator coming to Donegal. I need to check some information with her.'

'What information?'

'Where she heard about it, for starters,' I said genially, hoping he might tell me.

'Fuck knows,' he said. 'Probably that Bradley fella.'

My surprise at the ease with which I had gleaned that piece of information did nothing to outweigh the anger I felt at myself for having told Fearghal in the first place.

'Is your wife about?' I asked.

'She's out at that gold place,' he said, wiping his forehead with the shoulder of his T-shirt.

'The mine?' I said.

'No,' he said. Then, making speech marks with his fingers, he guffawed, 'The "gold rush".'

'Thanks, Mr Moore,' I said, surprised by how forthcoming he'd been. 'You've been a great help.'

'Oh, it's my pleasure,' he said.

I caught up with Janet Moore in the clearing where the prospectors had parked their cars and vans. On the back seat of her electric-blue Tigra I noticed a number of documents and envelopes.

Patsy McCann pointed her out to me, though I could have identified her myself: for a start, she was better dressed than the other people on site, in jeans and a grey sweater under a Barbour coat. She was sporting green wellingtons, wet with river water.

She was talking to Ted Coyle and one of the crusties I had seen before. He slunk away when he saw me approaching, rubbing out the spliff he carried as he did so and slipping it into his pocket.

Ted Coyle straightened himself up and placed his hands on his hips. Janet Moore simply drew deeply on a cigarette and blew the stream of smoke upwards as she glanced in my direction.

'Mrs Moore,' I said, extending my hand. 'I'm Inspector Benedict Devlin. I was wondering if I could have a word.'

'Certainly, Inspector,' she said, pointedly. Then she turned to Coyle. 'Thanks, Ted. Keep in touch.'

We walked over to her car together.

'How did you find me?' she asked, then pursed her lips and nodded her head when I told her that her husband had directed me, as if it made sense of some sort. 'So, what can I do for you?'

'We were wondering about the story you wrote about Cathal Hagan,' I said.

'So, that's official confirmation,' she said, smiling. 'Hagan's coming here.'

I tried to keep my expression as neutral as possible. 'I don't suppose you'd tell me who told you about it, would you?'

Unsurprisingly, she laughed. 'You're right,' she said.

'Your husband tells me it was Fearghal Bradley,' I said.

She looked perplexed. 'My husband is talking out his arse, Inspector. I don't know any Fearghal Bradley. Who is he?'

'Never mind,' I said. 'Do you know anything about these death threats?'

'No,' she said, a little haughtily.

'If I find you've been withholding information that may have prevented a crime, you'll be—' I began.

'Give it a rest,' she said, dropping her cigarette butt on to the ground and treading on it. 'You were doing better when you were playing the good cop. What's it worth?'

'That depends. What do you want?'

'Two tickets to see Hagan. Good seats,' she said, crossing her arms in front of her chest.

'Why do you need to bribe me for tickets? Surely you'll get invited, as a member of the press.'

'I'm a freelancer,' she said. 'We're the last to get anything. I want two good seats – at the front, mind you.'

'And in return?'

'Do we have a deal?' she persisted, refusing to show her hand yet.

I didn't see that we had anything to lose, and I said so. If her information were of no use to us, she knew she'd end up sitting in the car park for the duration of Hagan's visit.

She smiled. 'I don't know Fearghal Bradley,' she said. 'Whoever he is. As for the death threats, they're not serious. It's a prank, a publicity stunt dreamt up by an environmental group called the Green Alliance.'

'What have they against Hagan?' I asked.

'Where should I start?' she said. 'Anyway, I think that's worth two tickets.'

'You're sure of this?'

'Absolutely. From the horse's mouth, so to speak.'

I considered what she had said, watching her face to see if I could tease out the angle she was playing, but I couldn't read her.

'Why are you telling me this?' I asked.

'Public conscience,' she said, almost managing not to smile. 'And I don't want anyone getting shot now, do I?'

'You and I both, Mrs Moore,' I said, though in the event we were thinking of two different people.

Chapter Eight

Sunday, 8 October

Debbie, the kids and I went to early Mass. The days were turning now, the sky darkening earlier each evening. After Mass we spoke with Father Brennan, our local priest, and I gave him a Mass offering for Natalia Almurzayev's safety.

We drove to Derry that afternoon and had lunch in town. Penny's birthday was a few weeks away, and we had promised we'd take her to the toyshops to pick what she'd like. Shane was walking unaided now, his squat body shifting from side to side as he moved. Every so often, when he came to a high kerb that required extra balance to step off, he raised his small fist in the air in the expectation that Debbie or I would take hold and support him till he had stepped down. Then the fist would be withdrawn and he'd continue on his way.

Penny was trying on an outfit when my mobile rang.

'They're bringing that bog body back to Orcas this evening, ahead of the Hagan visit,' Harry Patterson said, without introduction. 'Get over there and show your face.'

'I'm on my day off, Harry,' I said, raising a hand to placate Debbie.

'You tell me that like I'd give a fuck. Get out there, Devlin.'

'Why?' I asked, refusing to be drawn into a swearing match while Penny and Shane were standing in front of me.

'Because I'm telling you to,' he replied, then hung up.

When I reached the main building, a museum truck was parked at the front doors, the hum of its air-conditioning unit audible. Fearghal Bradley and Linda Campbell were in the foyer of the main reception area when I arrived. John Weston was speaking on his phone near by.

Fearghal was not as effusive in his greeting this time, merely nodding and winking once as he worked the electric controls on a glass presentation case that sat in the centre of the area. The box was perhaps five feet long, sitting atop a mahogany plinth.

The workman I had seen on my first day out at the mine was standing nearby, fixing up the frame on a noticeboard, inside of which was a hastily produced poster about the bog body and its discovery. The rest of the building was in darkness.

Weston snapped his phone shut and came over to me, smiling expansively as always, hand outstretched. 'Good to see you, Ben. Out on a Sunday – that's above and beyond the call of duty.' He paused for a beat. 'Tell me, did your wife like the gift?'

'She did, sir,' I said, earning a glance from Linda and Fearghal, who then went back to their work. I gestured towards the truck outside with a nod. 'So you managed to get a loan after all,' I said.

'More than that, Ben,' he said, smiling, then placed his manicured finger against his lips and motioned towards

Fearghal's back, intimating that I shouldn't say anything more. I suspected it was a sore point with Fearghal.

When Fearghal was finally happy that a constant temperature and humidity level could be maintained inside the case, he asked for our help carrying Kate in.

She lay on a plastic board, clay and browned leaves cushioning her body. She was much lighter than I had expected and smaller than I remembered. Her skin shone now, as if polished, and her hair's redness was more vivid than before. We carried her as one might a coffin, each taking one corner of the plastic board on which she lay, shuffling sideways through the main doors and into the reception area.

We positioned her on the plinth and Bradley lowered the glass cover and pressed a small button to the side. Air hissed as the body was sealed in a vacuum and several small spotlights within the unit flickered on. Then all the lights in the reception area went out and I became aware that Weston was standing at the switch by the wall, gazing in wonder at his newest acquisition.

The spotlights threw shadows upwards on our faces and I wondered if it were that or something else, that made Fearghal's mood seem so dark. The thought registered only for a second, though, and then was gone. He laid his hand on top of the case for a moment, then wiped away his handprint with a cloth.

After they had completed the necessary paperwork, Fearghal announced that he was hungry. I suggested getting something to eat. Though none of us had extended an invitation, Weston excused himself on the grounds that he had too much to do to prepare for the following day's visit but insisted that dinner would be on him, handing Linda Campbell a hundred-euro note.

'*Bon appétit*, folks,' he said. 'See you all tomorrow.'

We drove back to Lifford to the Old Courthouse, beneath which is an Italian restaurant, built in the converted cells where criminals and lunatics were detained side by side centuries ago.

Fearghal ordered two bottles of wine for the group along with our meal. I added a soft drink to the order, on the grounds that I had to be up early the following day in preparation for Hagan's visit.

'Speaking of which,' I said, 'you didn't happen to mention the visit to anyone, did you?'

Fearghal was stuffing a chunk of ciabatta in his mouth and attempting to down a glass of red wine simultaneously. 'You didn't tell me not to,' he said defensively, when he had swallowed his food.

'I know I didn't, Fearghal. Just the same, did you tell anyone?' I persisted, smiling as best I could.

He shook his head sulkily.

We sat in silence for a few minutes.

'So, how did you two know each other?' Linda asked finally.

'We lived near one another. Then we were at college together,' I said. 'University. We were both doing Politics modules in our first year. We became drinking buddies.'

Bradley seemed to warm to the recollection. 'Our kid brothers were friends once too. Then at uni, Benny was

81

doing English or something; I was doing History. We were arrested together,' he stated. 'Benny Devlin in handcuffs.'

Linda laughed lightly. 'What for?' she asked, directing the question to me.

'We broke into one of the admin offices for a sit-in protest,' Fearghal said. 'In protest at – what was it, Benny?'

'The university refused to recycle paper,' I explained, aware of how ridiculous it sounded. 'They said it was too expensive to separate all its rubbish. We were part of an Environmental Club. Five of us got drunk one night and thought it would be very clever to break into the admin building. We thought the press would cover it and highlight the travesty.'

'Instead,' Bradley continued, 'they called the cops and had us all lifted. We had to pay a fine and they wouldn't let us graduate.'

'Seriously?' Linda said, her face bright with smiling, looking from one of us to the other.

I looked at Fearghal and smiled at the memory, though for long enough it had not been a particularly happy one.

'You wouldn't think it to look at him now,' Fearghal said, 'but he used to be a bit of a rebel. He used to give it to "the man". Now he's paid by him.'

The comment hurt more than I would have thought, but I tried to brush it aside with a laugh.

'Not you, though, Fearghal, eh? Always the rebel!'

'Do you think?' he said, a little sadly. 'Not these days. Do you know how that fucker Weston got Kate back? He sponsored an entire wing of the museum for five years.'

I figured this wasn't the first time Fearghal had mentioned it, for as he spoke Linda Campbell placed her hand on top of his in reassurance.

'What can you do, Ben, eh? Refuse the man and a whole wing of exhibits closes.'

'It's a tough one, Fearghal,' I agreed.

'It shouldn't be,' he said, spitting bits of bread on to the tablecloth. 'We wouldn't have taken it when we were youngsters.'

'The price of growing older, Fearghal,' I said, smiling a little uncertainly. He seemed to be getting drunk very quickly. His face was flushed and red, and beads of sweat were visible at his hairline.

Linda squeezed his hand in hers and, with her free hand, rubbed his shoulder.

'Fearghal argued against Kate being brought up here. He was overruled. Threatened with the sack if he didn't get behind the management.'

'I know how he feels,' I said, as if he wasn't sitting in front of me.

Fearghal looked at me pathetically, his head hanging slightly, flecks of bread drying on his lips.

Chapter Nine

Monday, 9 October

I was sitting in a squad car at the border at 10.30 the following morning. Hagan was due to cross the border near 11. I had asked Helen Gorman to accompany me and we spoke briefly about the events of Friday night. I could tell she was uncomfortable with the situation. Perhaps she resented me for involving her in something that had gone so badly wrong. I assured her that I had made no mention of her involvement when I reported back to Patterson.

I got out of the car and smoked a cigarette as I leant on the parapet of the bridge over the confluence of the Foyle, Finn and Mourne rivers. Several men were fishing further upriver, one wading in the depths. I recalled Janet Moore's attire on Saturday and the damp on her boots. She must have been wading in the Carrowcreel, I guessed. She didn't strike me as someone likely to go prospecting, and it made me wonder what she and Coyle had been discussing.

Below me a heron was stepping cautiously across the stones on the riverbed, his neck craned, his beak poised several centimetres above the water's surface. Two seagulls circled around him, attempting to chase him away. He held his stance, his eyes fixed on the water, then in a fluid movement his beak dipped just beneath the surface and he lifted off with a single beat of his massive wings. A fish curled in his bill, its skin glittering.

I made to flick my cigarette butt into the water, then thought better of it, crushing it out on the metal railing and returning it to the packet.

Hagan's jeep turned the bend at the metal sculptures on the border just shy of eleven o'clock, sandwiched between two PSNI cars, which drove as far as the restaurant before the border then pulled in.

I drove out in front of the jeep and turned on my hazard lights. I was aware of our other unmarked car pulling out behind it. Then we set off for Orcas.

A small crowd had gathered by the time we arrived. A group of thirty or so primary-school children lined the driveway, waving small plastic American flags as if the President himself were passing. Their teacher stood at the top of the line, smiling at her children and encouraging them to cheer at the darkened windows of the jeep.

I became aware that the distance between my car and the jeep behind me was widening, and realized that Hagan had asked his driver to stop and was out on the roadway, speaking to the children. Ahead of us, a similar-sized group of adults stood, some on tiptoes, some with cameras, clearly hoping that Hagan would extend the same courtesy to them when the time came.

After a few minutes he made his way up to the teacher. He placed his hand on her elbow and leant in to kiss her cheek. She turned her head and he ended up kissing her hair. She apologized and attempted to move her head the other way. They both laughed good-humouredly. Hagan waved to the children once more, then stepped back into his jeep.

Around a hundred people now stood outside the main building. Considering the mine only employed a dozen or so, I guessed most were invited guests, any one of whom could have revealed details of the visit to the press. Near the front was our local councillor, Miriam Powell. She smiled coldly at me as I drew up alongside her and parked the car. Harry Patterson and John Weston came forward to the kerb to welcome Hagan officially.

Cameras clicked and flashed as they shook hands. I spotted Janet Moore out of the corner of my eye and she smiled and nodded at me. Several plain-clothes officers mingled with the crowd and a number of uniformed men stood on the roof, with binoculars.

Hagan made his way through the crowd, slapping backs or clasping hands with each person to whom he was introduced. He came to Miriam Powell and called her Miriam without being introduced. They kissed like old friends, and stood conferring while the next in line rubbed the sweat from the palms of his hands on his trouser legs.

Hagan himself was not what I had expected. He was smaller in stature, standing just over five and a half feet tall. His hair was thin and grey, brushed back sternly on to his scalp. His eyes were magnified by thick glasses that sat on a long, hooked nose. He wore a grey suit and starched white shirt, with an emerald-green tie. His manner was easy; his handshakes firm; and his jokes deeply funny – or at least that was the impression given by the raucous laughter of those around him.

Just behind him, to left and right, walked the two Secret Service agents, who had travelled in his jeep with him, though 'secret' seemed a misnomer. Both were the size and shape of gorillas and were crammed into black suits. Both wore sunglasses and earpieces, but since there were only two of them there, and they were walking side by side, I couldn't see the need for earpieces.

Hagan's first official engagement was to draw back a small blue velvet curtain from the case in which 'Kate' had been placed. In so doing, he said, it gave him great pleasure to officially open Orcas Mine. Applause and the whirr of cameras accompanied the action.

Then he was taken to a lectern, placed at the bottom of the staircase that led up to Weston's office. A bench had been set behind, on which sat Miriam Powell and Harry Patterson. There was a space between them, presumably for John Weston.

Weston approached the lectern first, inviting guests to take their seats. I had arranged for Janet Moore to get two seats near the front, but the seat beside her, which I had assumed was for her husband, was empty. Further back I could see Linda, and beside her Fearghal, who looked decidedly uncomfortable.

When people had settled, Weston began. He thanked all who had come, then spoke at some length about the various difficulties he had overcome in setting up his mine. He spoke of Cathal Hagan and his relationship with his father.

He spoke of his fondness for his 'old country' and his hopes that he could put something back into the local economy. Then he welcomed Cathal Hagan to the lectern.

Hagan likewise went through the formalities and required thanks. Then, leaning one arm on the lectern and loosening his tie, he adopted a more conversational tone.

'Despite the talk of recession, the Celtic Tiger's roar has been heard across the globe,' he began. 'You folks gathered here today represent the best of it, the strength behind the tiger. You know,' he leant further forward, 'it's strange to think that, a hundred-odd years ago, the people of this great island – this whole island – came to my country looking for shelter, looking for work. They came in their thousands, braving the most adverse conditions to start a new life in the US. And what a great contribution they made, in all areas of life.'

Several people applauded lightly at this point, allowing Hagan to pause, take a sip of water from the glass on the lectern and lean his weight on his other arm.

'It seems to me that Ireland is now affording that opportunity to other countries. During my visit to Dublin I met many immigrant workers, grateful for the succour Mother Ireland has given them. It seems you have become a mini-America – a land of the free, a land of opportunity. Heck, you folks even have your own gold rush, I believe.'

There was more applause and laughter, the loudest coming from behind the lectern, where Weston was clearly relishing his moment in the spotlight.

'That's an awesome responsibility, folks,' he continued. 'But places like this, built on Irish-American finances, represent all that's good about the dream of wealth and prosperity; the pursuit of happiness. We will help you rise to the challenges that that responsibility brings. Hand in hand, we face a golden future. God bless you all.'

At this, as if by some signal, all those in attendance rose to their feet in applause, though I noticed Fearghal was the slowest out of his seat and the least enthusiastic. The standing crowd blocked the view of the two security men for a few seconds, but it was all that was needed.

At first I thought the man was returning to his seat, but he kept moving forwards. He was a crusty, one of those from the camp by the stream, and I recognized him as the one with whom Moore had been speaking the day I met her there. He glanced to the side, caught someone's eye, smiled. I followed his gaze to Fearghal Bradley, who stood quite still, his expression frozen. I read his lips as he mouthed his brother's name: 'Leon.'

Then Leon Bradley raised the gun.

His face was contorted in pantomime concentration as his hand held the gun steady. I followed his gaze, followed the aim of his weapon to where Hagan stood, his face drawn in terror.

I pushed through the crowd towards him, my hand raised, my shout of warning caught in my throat. Then I heard the shot, glimpsed the muzzle flash, even as Leon was grappled to the ground by the two Secret Service agents, attempting too late to compensate for the inadequacy of the protection offered by An Garda. The gun, knocked loose from Leon's grip, fell on to the floor, where it lay glinting in the autumn sunlight that streamed through the windows.

*　　*　　*

In the panic that ensued, Patterson and Weston bundled Hagan away, while several other Guards assisted Hagan's security agents in subduing Leon Bradley. I went over and lifted the gun Leon had dropped, carefully holding it by the muzzle. I realized quickly that it was no more than a starter pistol. Hagan might be shaken up, but he wouldn't be hurt. Checking that Leon was cuffed, I made my way over to where Hagan was standing surrounded by well-wishers.

I didn't make it that far, for Patterson blocked my way, his face red with anger.

I held up the gun. 'It's a starter pistol—' I began, but Patterson grabbed me by the collar and shunted me against the wall.

'You useless prick,' he hissed through clenched teeth, then he shoved me once and stalked back through the crowd.

Several onlookers glanced in my direction, then turned away and spoke among themselves as the gunman was bundled away.

Chapter Ten

Monday, 9 October

By six o clock that evening Hagan had left for his next engagement and Patterson had spent the best part of three hours apologizing to both him and Weston. Leon Bradley had resolutely refused to reveal how he had gained access to the main reception area. CCTV footage from the main gate showed him entering through the front and presenting a ticket. My initial thought had been that his brother had given him it, but on checking, it appeared that Fearghal had only been given two tickets, one for Linda and one for himself. Then I followed a hunch. The first time I had seen Janet Moore, she had been talking with Ted Coyle and one of the crusties, whom I now suspected to be Leon Bradley. A quick check confirmed that, despite her husband's absence, both of Janet Moore's tickets had been presented at the gate.

Leon was sitting in the holding cell in Lifford. Someone had left him with a black eye and a purple bruise on his jaw. It had yet to be established if it had been one of our men or one of Hagan's who had caused the injuries. No one was in a rush to find out.

He sat hunched on the lower bunk. His height meant that he had to stoop to prevent banging his head on the upper one. His skin was pale but darkened with stubble. On his left cheek, just below his eye, he sported a small home-made tattoo of a Chinese symbol, almost obscured by the bruise. His hair was dull with grease and rat-tailed in dread-locks. He wore stone-washed drainpipe jeans, tattered at the hems. The laces of his workmen's boots had been removed.

The Army jacket he had worn when he shot at Hagan lay on the floor. He was rolling a cigarette when I came in, though he would not be allowed to smoke it inside.

He glanced up at me, then ran his tongue along the pasted edge of a Rizla paper, rolling it into a cigarette and twisting the end. Then he started on another to add to a small pile on the bed beside him.

I sat down on the plastic chair opposite him.

'Hi, Leon,' I said. 'I don't know if you remember me—' I began.

He glanced up again. 'I remember you. Fearghal told me you were based here now. How's Tom?'

'He's fine, Leon,' I said.

'Tell him I said hi,' he said, then went back to rolling his cigarettes.

'So, what was the point of today, then?' I asked.

'To scare the shit out of that prick,' Leon replied, measuring out a pinch of tobacco and teasing it out the length of the paper.

'And us,' I added.

Leon shrugged, then twisted his head sharply to flick his dreadlocks over his shoulder.

'Why, Leon?' I asked again.

'He's a dickhead,' he stated, as if this explained, everything.

'I understand why you might not like Hagan,' I said. 'I have my own issues with him, but I wouldn't shoot at the man.'

'That's your choice,' he said.

'Did Janet Moore give you a ticket?' I asked.

Leon didn't look up, but for a brief second he paused in his cigarette production. He did not, however, answer the question.

'She had two tickets, Leon. One for her, one for her husband. Her husband obviously wasn't there. What's the connection between you and her?'

He looked at me from under his brow, then licked the edge of the paper slowly, still holding my gaze as he did so.

I went into Patterson's office. We had not spoken since the incident earlier. If either of us expected the other to apologize, we were both to be disappointed.

'I believe he got his ticket from Janet Moore,' I said.

'Which she got from you,' he stated, the accusation clear.

'I want to bring her in, to establish the connection between her and Bradley.'

Patterson shook his head, but didn't look at me. Instead he fidgeted with a number of paper clips that he had twisted together on his desk. 'Not a chance,' he said, dropping the clips on to the desk and steepling his fingers. 'You're being stood down for a week or two.

'Excuse me?' I said.

'You're suspended, for two weeks,' he explained. 'It's just been one balls-up after another recently, Devlin. You shouldn't be doing this job, and you're going to get someone killed. You're to have a few weeks to assess your position.'

'Assess my position?' I asked incredulously.

He nodded his head gravely.

'You're fucking kidding,' I said.

He smiled coldly. 'Not at all,' he said. 'Though I'd be lying if I said I didn't derive some pleasure from this.'

'You're a prick,' I said, angrily.

'Whatever you think,' he said, picking up the clips again. 'Now get out. And do us all a favour and don't come back.'

I stared at him for a few seconds, wondering if it was worth continuing the discussion, but he had already dismissed me. I got up and walked out, leaving the door lying open.

Chapter Eleven

Tuesday, 10 October

I slept late the following morning. Debbie had left, to take Penny to school and Shane shopping for Hallowe'en costumes. I ate breakfast in my dressing gown, padding around the kitchen aimlessly, not entirely sure how to spend the first day of my suspension. The fence at the front of the house needed painting, but a thick head of cloud was gathering towards Letterkenny and the first fat drops of rain were already exploding in puffs of dust along the roadway outside.

At around ten-thirty I heard a knock at the door. Expecting it to be the postman, I opened the door only an inch or two so as not to reveal the fact that I was still wearing my robe. I was a little surprised, and even more gratified, to see Jim Hendry standing there, a greasy brown-paper bag held aloft.

'I brought the gravy rings, if you make the coffee,' he said.

'Is this a peace offering?' I asked.

'Thought I'd help you celebrate the first day of your suspension.' He glanced down. 'But get dressed, for God's sake.'

I directed him into the kitchen and went upstairs to change while Jim filled the kettle. By the time I came down he had two mugs of coffee set on the table and a plate of gravy rings, the sugar coating sparkling.

'Tough luck with the Hagan thing,' he said, raising his mug in salute. 'Nothing you could have done about it, from what I've heard. Bit shitty of them to blame you for it.'

'One in a long list of recent fuck-ups, Jim. As you know yourself.'

Hendry nodded. 'Understandable, I suppose. Still a bit harsh.'

'So, what brings you over to the enemy territory?' I asked.

Jim produced a folded piece of paper from his pocket. 'I got you a name on your car from the other night. Thought you might be interested. Then when I called the station to tell you, they told me you were off indefinitely.'

'So you came to commiserate. Thanks, Jim,' I said. 'I appreciate it a lot.'

He waved away the sentiment, a chunk of gravy ring in his hand. 'I'd miss you, Devlin, if you stopped illegally coming into the North and causing chaos. Where would the craic be in having somebody over here who does things the old-fashioned, legal way?'

'True enough,' I said. 'So who's the car owner?'

'Some guy from Ballykelly, Michael Hines,' Jim said, handing me the paper. 'I did a quick background check on him, but nothing showing; not so much as a speeding ticket.'

I didn't recognize the name. 'What age is he?' I asked, scanning the sheet for his date of birth.

'Mid-fifties, from what I can remember; why?'

'One of the guys had a pony-tail, seemed a bit older than the other. I didn't get a great look at the second; he wore a cap, though I think he had black hair.'

'Do you want to call Hines or will I?' he asked.

I shook my head. 'I'd need to see him face to face, in case he is one of our guys.'

'*Our* guys?' he said, smiling lightly. 'OK; let's take a run to Ballykelly. You might be suspended, but I'm not.'

'You're coming?' I asked, a little surprised.

'Of course,' he spluttered. 'Sure the bloody crime was committed over on my side. Besides, I'm the only one with any authority in the North.'

Michael Hines, when we found him, was indeed in his mid-fifties, but any remnants of greying hair he had left certainly wouldn't have been enough to scrape into a pony-tail.

He explained that he'd sold his car several months earlier, through a local classifieds page.

'I filled in the form and everything,' he said. 'I'm not responsible.'

'Do you remember who you sold it to?' I asked. 'You didn't get his name, by any chance?'

Hines shook his head. 'I can't remember,' he said. 'Paul something. He was a foreigner. I have it written down somewhere, though I don't have his address now, before you ask.'

'What kind of foreigner? Black, Asian, American?'

'If he'd been black, do you not think I'd have mentioned it right off?' he said. 'He was European; Polish or Russian, or one of those new countries.'

97

'What colour hair did he have, do you know, Mr Hines?'

'Black,' he stated. 'With a scar running along here, now that I think about it,' he added, pointing out the approximate area of the scar on his own skull. 'I'll just get the name for you,' he said, turning back down the hallway.

'So, where do we go from here?' Hendry asked as we headed back to his car.

'The Migrant Workers' Information Centre,' I replied. 'I think I know who "Paul" is.'

At the migrants' centre we were told that Pol Strandmann had taken a few days off work. With some persuasion Hendry managed to get an address for him, in Ballymagorry, just outside of Strabane.

'Would you recognize him as the other guy in the car?' Hendry asked, as we drove up the road.

'I don't think so,' I said. 'The driver was wearing a cap.'

'Best we can do then is to rattle his cage a bit, see what happens,' Jim concluded, tapping out some internal rhythm on the steering wheel as he spoke.

'We can at least find out how he can account for the car ending up burnt out,' I said.

The house was at the end of a row. Greying lace curtains blocked out the windows; the grass in the yard was overgrown, the dandelions a good foot high. I thought of the contrast between this and Karol Walshyk's home.

Pol answered the door almost as soon as Hendry had hammered on it. He wore skin-tight jeans and a pair of baseball boots, laced but untied. His T-shirt sported an image of a smiley face. Pol held a rollie cigarette in his hand. He leant against the doorjamb, his legs crossed at the ankles, put the cigarette in his mouth, his eyes squinting against the smoke.

'I know your face,' he said, nodding at me. 'What do you want?'

Jim answered. 'I'm PSNI Inspector Hendry. You've met Garda Inspector Devlin before, I believe. Can we have a word?'

Pol held his position for a second longer, as if considering Hendry's request, then shrugged and stood aside so we could enter the house.

The living room was furnished in a basic manner. A small settee was against one wall, in front of which was a badly scored coffee table on which sat a box of tobacco and a packet of Rizlas.

In the far corner was a new-looking television, a DVD player and a satellite receiver. A few prints hung on the walls; on the mantelpiece was a photograph of a young woman and two children.

'Is this your family?' I asked, picking up the picture.

Pol glanced at the picture and nodded curtly. 'So, is this about the car? Have you found it?'

'We have indeed,' Hendry said, sitting on the edge of the settee.

'It was stolen from outside my work on Friday. I called the police station in Derry and reported it.' He glanced from Hendry to myself.

'We found it burnt out in Strabane, after it had been used in a shooting,' Hendry said.

'That's terrible,' Pol said, though his voice was devoid of emotion. 'Was anyone hurt?'

I could have sworn he glanced at me when he asked this, though if he did it was too brief to be obviously significant.

'Thankfully not,' Hendry said. 'So, what time was your car lifted?'

'I'm not sure. I noticed it gone that night. I was out with some friends after work. Came back to the car park after ten and noticed it was gone. I called the police then.'

'Can your friends verify that you were out with them until after ten?'

'I'm sure they could,' he said. 'Though they've gone back to Poland, I'm afraid. Not much use to you.'

Hendry shifted in his seat. 'Excuse me,' he said, taking his mobile from his pocket. 'I've a call to take.'

He went outside and I guessed he was phoning the Derry station to see if and when Pol had called the car in.

'I remember you now,' Pol said, as we stood in the silence following Hendry's departure. 'You were looking for a Chechen.'

'That's right.'

'Did you find him?'

'We'd never lost him,' I said. 'He was dead.'

'That's terrible,' he repeated.

I examined the scar on his skull as we spoke. The tissue was puckered, the line uneven. It seemed more livid this evening, the skin shiny red.

'That's a sore-looking cut,' I said.

He instinctively touched at it, and grunted in agreement.

Hendry came back into the room again and nodded at me. 'I think that's us, Mr Strandmann. Maybe you'll arrange to pick up your car. We've brought it to the station in Strabane. You can send your insurance people to see it there if they want.'

'Piece of crap anyway,' Pol said. 'I picked it up cheap when I came here.'

Hendry filled me in on what he had learnt as we drove bade to my house. Pol Strandmann had reported the car stolen at ten-thirty on Friday, which was an hour after I'd been shot at. That didn't mean that he was involved though.

'What do you think?' Hendry asked me. 'Did you recognize him as the driver?'

I shook my head. 'Much as I wanted to. There's something not right about him, though.'

'Cheap, crap car and a top-of-the-range TV and Sky? He's getting money from somewhere, and it's unlikely to be the Migrant Workers' Centre.'

'We can't lift him on that. Maybe he's just not sending as much to his family as he should be. Enjoying the good life here.'

'Maybe,' Hendry said, unconvinced. 'Though we've nothing on him unless you or the wee lassie you had running around with you recognize him. Or if we find that houseload of Chechens you lost.'

Chapter Twelve

Friday, 13 October

The rest of the week passed fairly uneventfully, though daytime television eventually drove me to fence-painting. I was just finishing the last stretch, on Friday morning, when a car with a Dublin registration parked at the bottom of our driveway.

I was pleased to see Fearghal Bradley. He came up the drive a little sheepishly, and extended his hand.

'Benny,' he said.

'Fearghal,' I replied. 'What brings you out here?'

'I . . . I thought I'd call and see how you were doing. I'd heard you'd been sidelined. I'm sorry. For Leon.' He wrung his hands as he spoke, his face twisted in a frown.

'How is he?' I asked.

'He's . . . he's OK. He got charged with misuse of firearms or something. Bailed at ten thousand to appear in Letterkenny at the end of the month.'

I nodded my head, having guessed as much. He'd never do time for the prank, but a high bail would be a sufficient smack on the wrist. And if he stayed over the border and missed his court appearance, they'd still made ten grand out of him.

'An expensive prank.'

Fearghal nodded, but did not speak, and I got the impression that something else was preoccupying him.

'And how's Kate?' I asked.

I thought I heard Fearghal groan involuntarily. 'Weston's giving her to Hagan as a gift, after what happened. She's going to be sent to America.'

'I'm sorry—' I began, but Fearghal finally said what was really on his mind.

'I feel shitty doing this, but I need your help. Leon needs your help.'

'Why?' I asked.

'Have you heard about the Eligius break-in?'

I felt my face muscles tighten, even as I tried to keep smiling. 'Probably best if we go inside,' I said.

Eligius was a US defence company which had opened several years ago outside Omagh. At the time it had attracted a lot of bad press, not least due to the US involvement in Iraq and the perception that the newly employed people of the town would be able to watch the fruits of their labours explode over Baghdad on *Sky News*. As it turned out, the factory was producing a microchip for inclusion in armoured personnel carriers, though the offices were also the European headquarters of the firm.

I had heard about the break-in on the news that morning. The previous evening, four people had broken into the Eligius offices and had unrolled an anti-war banner from the windows at the front of the offices. One, a well-known local figure called Seamus Curran, had shouted anti-American slogans through a loud-hailer to the gathering press and police.

At one point, several computers were thrown from a first-floor window and, later, a number of burning sheets of paper. Television images had shown, from a distance, the other three people involved in the break-in, but none of them clearly enough to be identifiable. Fearghal, however, assured me that there was little room for doubt over Leon's involvement.

'The fucking idiot called me from the offices last night. They brought him out just after three this morning.'

'Why did he do it?' I asked.

'Another one of these bloody publicity stunts.'

'Why come to me? What can I do?'

'We were hoping you could put in a good word for him. With the cops up North.'

I said nothing, but Fearghal obviously read my feelings clearly.

'Look, I know he's fucked things up here for you,' he said. 'If you don't want to help him, I'd understand, but help *me*. Please.'

I called Hendry, who was able to give me the name of the arresting officer in Omagh, though by the time I phoned, Leon and his three co-accused were already on their way to appear in court.

I changed out of my paint-splattered clothes as quickly as I could, but by the time we reached Omagh the Eligius Four, as they had been dubbed, had already appeared before the magistrate. The barrister representing them spoke briefly with Fearghal, explaining what had happened during their appearance. He named the four men, though the only name I knew other than Leon's was Seamus Curran; he had been in the papers some years back over a miscarriage of justice. In the 1970s, Curran had been one of a number of men arrested on terrorism charges in England, who had been denied legal representation and had confessions beaten from them. Curran's conviction had finally been overturned several years ago with an unspecified settlement and an apology from the Home Office. Whether or not he had been political before his arrest thirty years ago, his time inside had certainly politicized him, and he was frequently pictured in the local papers leading demonstrations against one thing or another, though without affiliation to any particular party. The other two men's names meant nothing to me.

The hearing had been quick and uneventful, apparently. A PSNI officer who introduced himself to the court as Inspector Sweeney outlined the facts of the case and stated that he could connect the four accused with the break-in.

Leon Bradley spoke only long enough to confirm his name and age. The magistrate set bail at £2,000 for each of the accused, to reappear again on the 28th. Sweeney in turn suggested that Bradley might pose a flight risk following an incident in Donegal and requested that he be refused bail. However, instead the magistrate ruled that his bail be set at £5,000 and that he report to Omagh PSNI station once a day until the trial.

*　　*　　*

Fearghal organized the bail as quickly as he could, and later that morning we collected Leon from the Gortin Road station where he was being held. Fearghal asked to speak to Leon alone before he was released, and I guessed he was preparing him for my presence.

While I waited in the station foyer, I read through the local newspaper, the *Tyrone Herald*, and was surprised to see a story about Ted Coyle, the Carrowcreel prospector. He claimed to have been attacked, at his campsite by the river, and had been admitted to hospital with fractured ribs and a broken ankle. Gardai believed that the attack was a mugging; someone perhaps looking for his gold nugget. Supt Harry Patterson appealed to people to stay away from the camp-site, stating that, in the time that prospectors had been working the river, only Coyle had found anything worth mentioning. The level of human activity on the river was also having an adverse effect on local wildlife, he said, as well as permitting the type of lawlessness that had resulted in the attack on Mr Coyle.

Leon smiled at me sheepishly as he was led out from the holding cells. His hair was even more dishevelled than the last time I had seen him and his clothes smelt of the smoke of both cigarettes and wood fires. I noticed he wore faint eyeliner around his eyes and this, coupled with his thin build, the paleness of his skin and his prominent cheek-bones, gave him a vaguely feminine appearance – in marked contrast with the bear-like physique and sanguine colour-ing of his elder brother.

'Ben,' he said, raising his head.

'Leon,' I replied, folding the newspaper and replacing it on the seat where I'd found it.

'Right,' Fearghal said, rubbing his hands together. 'Let's get some food, men, shall we?'

We went to a café on the outskirts of Omagh. While Fearghal and I ate cooked breakfasts, Leon contented himself with coffee and a rolled cigarette, despite having not eaten in almost a day. He said little as Fearghal admonished him for his actions and, every so often, read and replied to text messages he received on his mobile.

'What the fuck were you thinking?' Fearghal asked. 'Bad enough the stunt you played in Donegal, never mind breaking into a bloody missile factory,'

'It was a protest,' Leon shrugged.

'Against what?' his brother replied with exasperation.

'Against *whom*,' Leon corrected him. 'Hagan.'

'What about him?' I asked.

'He's a major shareholder in Eligius,' Leon replied. 'Another finger in another pie.'

'What have you got against him?' I asked.

'He's an arsehole. He funded terrorism over here for years, and now he's trying to stifle debate in the US over Iraq.'

Neither Fearghal nor I spoke.

'Of course, what nobody says is that Hagan is part-owner of a company that sells parts to the US Army. He has a vested interest in keeping the war on terror going for as long as he can.'

'People responsible for wars generally do,' I said. 'Breaking into their offices or shooting starter pistols at them won't make a difference.'

'We'll see,' Leon replied darkly.

'You used to think it did,' Fearghal protested, turning to face me. 'When we were young. You used to think stunts like that could make a difference. You did it yourself, for Christ's sake!'

I was taken aback by the shift in the tone of the conversation, and realized I had ignored the cardinal rule that blood is thicker than water. Fearghal could take digs at his brother, but when an outsider did so they closed ranks.

I felt I had to defend my position. 'The only people it affects are those doing it. The university didn't change its recycling policy because of us, Fearghal, and America won't change its foreign policy because Hagan had the shit scared out of him with a starter pistol.'

'You used to have a bit of spirit about you, Benny.'

'Did you protest against Weston being given Kate? Or Weston giving it to Hagan? Would it have made a difference?' I knew it to be a sore point with Fearghal. He did not respond. 'I make what difference I can in my own way,' I concluded.

The Bradley brothers looked at each other.

'You hardly expected a cop to understand, did you, Ferg?' Leon said, looking at his brother. 'Sure, he's one of them.'

Fearghal dropped me back home after lunch. We exchanged pleasantries and agreed to keep in touch, though I suspected, and even hoped, that I wouldn't see him again after our conversation.

Chapter Thirteen

Saturday, 14 October

Debbie and I spent Saturday morning with the kids, shopping in Derry. On the way to town, Penny complained of being thirsty, so we stopped at the shop on the border and I took her inside to buy drinks for the family.

As we waited in the queue to pay, I recognized the man at the front. Dressed in a suit and bow-tie, his hand covering his mouth as he attempted to stifle a yawn, stood Karol Walshyk. He apologized to the girl at the till, lifted his milk and bread and turned towards us. His eyes were slits in his face from lack of sleep and I guessed he had just completed another night shift. As he passed us, he smiled in semi-recognition, then seemed to realize how he knew me and stopped.

'Inspector Divine?' he said, pointing at me.

'Devlin,' I nodded. 'Good morning, Doctor. Late night?'

'Busy night,' he replied. Then he looked down at Penny, who was peering up at him, one hand gripping my waist.

'And who's this young lady?' he asked.

'This is my daughter, Penelope,' I said, ruffling her hair as I spoke. She squinted up at me, then glanced back at Walshyk.

'How do you do?' Walshyk said, extending his hand. Penny looked at me once more, smiled uncertainly, then shook his hand quickly before wrapping both her arms around my waist again.

'I called to see out mutual friend,' he said, straightening up. 'Her house was burnt down.'

'That's right,' I said.

'Do you know where she is now?'

I shook my head, uneasy about the direction our conversation was taking, both because I was reluctant to discuss the case with him professionally, and also because I was aware of the fact that it had been my fault that Natalia had vanished.

'Did you not help her?'

'I did,' I protested. 'I tried to. She – we lost her,' I said, as quietly as I could.

'You told her you would help her,' he stated, his gaze steely. I was aware of Penny looking up at me with concern, seemingly following the direction of our conversation. 'You promised her you'd help,' he continued, the accusation clear.

'I tried my best.'

'Is that so? I was wrong to trust you.'

I felt Penny's hold on me loosen slightly.

'I'm sorry you feel that way,' I said, my face flushed. 'I have to get my daughter a drink. Excuse me.'

In the car afterwards, Penny asked me about the conversation. Debbie looked at me quizzically and I attempted to shrug off her concern as I started the engine.

110

'Why was that man cross, Daddy?' she asked, twisting the lid off her drink.

'He . . . I told him I would do something and I wasn't able to.'

'Why?'

'It's complicated. He asked me to look after someone and I wasn't able to do it.'

'He said you promised. Did you break a promise?' she asked.

'It's complicated,' Debbie said, though the response did nothing to reduce the judgemental look I saw reflected in the rear-view mirror.

'You have to keep your promises, Daddy.'

'I know, sweetie. I know.'

I attempted to forget the events of the day before, though the comments of Fearghal and his brother had stung me more than I cared to admit. I had convinced myself that joining the Guards was the only way I could make a difference and apply my own beliefs and principles in a manner that would have a real and lasting impact. But increasingly I was beginning to suspect that that was not the case. Caroline Williams, my former partner, had taken a leave of absence because she no longer felt that the rewards of the job justified the risks. Increasingly I was aware that, no matter what we did or how we acted, it didn't stop crime, and it certainly didn't stop people like Cathal Hagan delivering hawkish speeches about the need for military intervention while lining his pockets with the profits of such action.

I tried to explain this to Debbie as we drove back home that afternoon, the two children asleep in the back.

'You can't change the world,' she said, fiddling with the radio. 'You can only make your little corner of it a nicer place to live.'

'Is that good enough?' I asked.

'It has to be,' she stated with a simplicity of reason I found difficult to dispute.

She found a station to her liking, turned the volume up slightly, and settled down in the passenger seat, pulling her knees up against her chest and resting her feet on the dash in front of her.

I was considering what she had said when the news headlines were read on the radio. The first headline concerned the discovery of a dead body near Orcas goldmine. A man's body had been pulled from the Carrowcreel.

Five minutes later, Fearghal Bradley phoned my mobile to tell me that he believed the body was Leon's.

He called at our house and collected me before driving on towards the Carrowcreel.

'Leon has been missing since last night,' he explained. 'I called the Guards and that arsehole Patterson told me he couldn't help me, but that a body had been found out by the river. It was too early to tell anything, he said.'

'He said that?' I asked, a little surprised. It seemed a fairly callous way to deal with a concerned relative, even by Harry Patterson's standards.

'He didn't say it was Leon as such. He said Leon wasn't gone long enough to be considered a missing person. He might just have gone to a friend's, or something.'

'Might he not have done?' I asked.

Fearghal shook his head, then, as we drove, explained his concerns.

After we had parted company yesterday, he had taken Leon back to his hotel and booked a room for him. He said he had wanted to keep him away from the crusties at the campsite for a while, in the hope that Leon might keep his nose clean long enough for the events of the past week to settle.

He and Leon had argued; Leon felt his brother was treating him like a child. Fearghal told him he had fallen in with a bad crowd. He reasoned with Leon, telling him that he would get in trouble if he breached bail and went back over the border. And he explained to Leon that, having stood his bail, it would be Fearghal who would bear the financial burden if he broke his bail conditions.

Finally, Leon had agreed to book in to the hotel but explained that he had someone to meet out at the Carrowcreel. He would come straight back after the meeting. He gave Fearghal his word.

'You might be worrying over nothing, Fearghal,' I reasoned. 'Maybe he lied when he said he would come back.'

Fearghal shook his head curtly. 'Leon always keeps his word. Especially after yesterday. He was so pleased at me sticking up for him he wouldn't let me down. Something's happened to him, I know it.'

'Have you tried his mobile?'

'Dead,' he replied.

'Did you contact any other Garda stations? Or the PSNI? Maybe he's been lifted doing something else?'

'Patterson said he'd have heard if they'd picked him up. But he was being awkward about it, probably because of what Leon did to Hagan at Orcas. I was hoping you might come with me to the site. Maybe you might find out if it is Leon. They'll tell you things they won't tell me.'

I believed Patterson would be no more forthcoming with me, but I said nothing; I wanted to help Fearghal, despite all that had happened. And if I was honest, I missed my work and was eager to be at the scene.

When we pulled into the campsite beneath the giant pines, a Garda cordon had already been set up. I could see several officers I knew questioning the occupants of the various camper vans and mobile homes. Patterson was nowhere to be seen, but I suspected that we were still some distance from the site of the body and he would probably be there.

I spotted Helen Gorman standing guard at the far end of the cordon. She was standing laughing with a young male officer I didn't recognize. As I approached, she parted from him and waved to me.

'How's the time off?' she asked, careful not to use the word 'suspension', as if I were on voluntary leave.

'Fine,' I said. 'I couldn't keep away from you all, though,' I added, tentatively raising the scene tape to step to beneath it.

Helen smiled uncertainly, then looked around her before lifting the tape and gesturing with a flick of her head that I should come in.

'Thanks, Helen,' I said. 'Bradley's brother's being kept in the dark. He's afraid it's Leon in there.'

She lowered her gaze slightly and pursed her lips, and I guessed that they had already identified the corpse as belonging to Leon Bradley.

I approached the scene from the west, in the hope that I might get as far as Leon's body before encountering Patterson. Within a few hundred yards I spotted a huddle of Guards and, on the ground, a clothed body over which knelt a woman I took to be the medical examiner, whose job would be to officially pronounce death.

As I came closer, one or two of the Guards looked across. A few nodded and smiled in recognition, but others glared. I turned my attention from them to the body lying on the forest floor and my breath caught in my chest a little, even though I had been prepared for the sight of Leon's corpse.

His hair lay in wet tangles across his pale and slightly bloated face. His eyes were open but clouded, and leaves from the river were lodged in his gaping mouth. Seeing small black marks along his neck and jawline, I moved a little closer. The ME looked up at me from her work, her gloved hands holding Leon's arm.

'Who are you?' she asked.

'Inspector Devlin,' I replied. 'What happened to him?'

'Gunshot,' she stated bluntly, continuing with her work.

'Shotgun?' I guessed, gesturing towards the black spots on his neck.

She nodded. 'The main wound's on his back. That's just pellet spray.'

'How long ago?'

She twisted her mouth. 'Hard to tell. That's the pathologist's job.'

115

'Rough guess?'

She looked up at me with annoyance. 'I don't do rough guesses.'

I didn't get a chance to continue our conversation, for someone gripped my arm from behind. I turned to face Harry Patterson.

'What the fuck are you doing here?' he asked.

'He told me he was an inspector,' the ME added helpfully from behind me.

'I am,' I said. 'I'm also a friend of the victim's family.'

'You're on suspension,' Patterson said. 'That's all that matters to me. When I want you at a scene I'll send you to one. Otherwise, piss off – unless you want another week off.'

'You'd better tell his brother he's dead. He's up at the cordon, waiting to hear.'

'He'll be told in due course,' Patterson said, letting go of my arm.

'Have a fucking heart, Harry,' I said. 'He's lost his brother.'

'His brother got what he deserved. He's caused nothing but trouble since he got here. I suppose I shouldn't be surprised that he's a friend of yours.'

With that, he stalked off, though I noticed that when he had gone some distance, he changed his direction and headed up towards the cordon and Fearghal Bradley.

I made my way back along the path I had come, to where Gorman was standing.

'It was him, then?' she said.

I nodded grimly. 'What happened?'

She shrugged lightly. 'I haven't heard it all. He was shot in the back somewhere upriver. One of the prospectors was on the riverbank when the body floated past. It got snagged on some branches over the other side and a couple of them managed to pull him out.'

'Any leads on who shot him?' I asked. 'Or where it happened?'

'Not so's I've heard,' she said.

'Thanks, Helen,' I said.

She nodded and pulled her cap down a little over her forehead, then turned away.

I stood by Fearghal's car and had a smoke while I waited for him. I guessed Patterson had taken him somewhere to break the news of Leon's death. Over to my left the group of crusties with whom I had occasionally spotted Leon were sitting in a circle outside their vans, each with a can of beer. In the middle someone had lit a fire and they watched in silence as the smoke curled upwards. Several of them were crying, leaning against each other for support.

I finished my smoke, glanced around to make sure none of my colleagues was nearby, then approached the group. One or two of them looked up at me when I reached them; the others continued staring at the flames, as if in a trance. Their mongrel barked at me lazily, raising its head an inch off its front paws then lying down again when its owner, an older man with lengthy matted grey hair, whistled through his teeth at it.

'Thanks,' I said, and he nodded in reply. 'I'm sorry about Leon,' I continued. 'I knew him too. When he was a kid. He was a friend of my younger brother.'

The grey-haired man nodded. 'He told us,' he said, raising his can to his mouth and draining off the contents.

'Can I have a second?' I said, unwilling to conduct an interview in front of the silent circle assembled before me.

The man paused a moment, as if to show he wasn't jumping to accommodate me, then struggled to his feet. We walked away from the group and I offered him one of my cigarettes before lighting one for myself. I introduced myself and the man told me his name was Peter.

'Who told you it was him?' I asked, sensing that they were already in mourning.

'A couple of the lads helped pull him out of the water, before the pigs even arrived here.' He glanced at me and added, 'No offence.'

'None taken. Any ideas what might have happened to him?' I asked.

'You'd know that better than us,' he spat. 'You're the cop.'

'Fair enough. Any idea who might want to kill him, then?'

'I don't know, man. Leon was one of the good guys. He didn't make enemies.'

'Apart from Cathal Hagan and Eligius, you mean,' I said.

'I'd start there, then, if I were you,' he replied bitterly. 'The Guards had it in for him over the Hagan thing. He told me your crowd beat him in custody.'

'What was he doing with Janet Moore?' I asked.

Peter stopped and squinted at me with suspicion. 'Why?'

'Were they involved with each other?'

He raised his chin slightly, which I took to be affirmation. Janet would have to be questioned.

'When did you last see him?'

'Yesterday evening. He was going somewhere.'

'Where?' I asked.

'I don't know. He got a message.'

'What about?'

Peter shrugged. 'To meet someone, I guess. And I don't know who, before you ask.' He pinched out his cigarette between his forefinger and thumb. 'I'd better get back to the rest of them,' he said. 'Thanks for the smoke.'

Fearghal was sitting in the car when I went back. His face was puffy and flushed, his eyes red with crying. When I opened the door he hastily rubbed at his face with the heels of his palms, and stretched his jaw muscles.

'I'm sorry, Fearghal,' I said, sitting in the seat beside him and placing my hand on his shoulder.

'Thanks, Benny,' he said. 'Thanks for coming out with me, too. Sorry if it was a wasted journey. That Superintendent came and told me anyway.'

'No bother,' I said.

'Did you see him?' Fearghal asked. 'Leon? How did he look?'

I struggled to think of an appropriate response, but Fearghal had already moved on. 'I haven't seen him yet. I have to go to the hospital to identify him.'

I nodded.

'Might they have got it wrong? Mightn't it be someone else?' he asked urgently, his face brightening.

I shook my head. 'I'm sorry.'

'No,' he said. 'You're right.' He sniffed deeply several times, cleared his throat and turned the key in the ignition.

'I'll drop you home before I go to the hospital. I'll need you to give me directions, if you don't mind.'

'I'll come with you, Fearghal,' I said. 'If you want.'

He looked across the car at me and smiled, then his expression crumpled in sobs again and he lowered his head against the steering wheel. I sat beside him in silence, my hand on his shoulder, until the shuddering stopped.

For the second time in a fortnight, I found myself standing in the morgue of Letterkenny Hospital.

Fearghal Bradley studied his brother's face, as if in so doing he might somehow discover a reason for what had happened. The morgue attendant attempted to adjust the green sheet she'd lowered to expose Leon's face, in order to cover the shot-gun marks, but Fearghal had already spotted them.

'Someone shot him?' he asked, his voice rising in incredulity. 'I thought he drowned.'

The morgue assistant fitted the green sheet back over Leon's head again and made to move the body back to where it would be examined by the State Pathologist.

'Why would someone shoot him?' Fearghal asked me, his hand gripping my lower arm.

'I don't know, Fearghal,' I said. 'But I promise you, I'll find out.'

Outside the morgue, Fearghal was given a plastic bag containing those of Leon's possessions not held by Forensics. As we sat in the car outside, he looked through the assortment: a watch; a Zippo lighter; ear studs; a mobile phone; some washed-out five-euro notes, pulped together.

'Not much to show for thirty years on this fucking planet, is it?'

'They're just things, Fearghal,' I said. 'Your memories of Leon are the important things. The friends he had; the people he knew.'

'Why would someone kill him? I know he could be an arsehole sometimes, but he wasn't a bad guy,' he said with an almost pleading tone, as if he needed to convince me of how unworthy his brother was of death.

He left the bag of items on the floor beside me, then started the car. As we drove, I reflected on what Peter had told me. Leon had gone to meet someone. He had got a message.

'Do you mind if I take a look at Leon's phone?' I asked.

'Why? Do you think it might be important?' Fearghal said.

'I don't know, Fearghal,' I said. 'It might not even work from the water. I just want to check it.'

Initially the phone wouldn't work. I removed the battery and dried it with my shirt-tail, and after a few attempts it came to life. On the Home screen was an image of Leon and Janet Moore, taken at arm's length by Leon. Their faces were pressed together, both of them smiling, and I was a little embarrassed to be looking at something so intimate.

I looked first at the messages received. The final message he had received was dated early on the morning previous from JANET, who I assumed to be Janet Moore. It read simply: 'Meet @ 8. McElroys.' McElroys was the name of a bar in Lifford. It certainly was something that would need to be followed up with Janet Moore.

I flicked into the Sent folder and scrolled through the messages there to see if he had arranged a meeting with anyone, but there was nothing. I scrolled through the list of calls made. Many were to Janet, including, I noted, one at two o'clock on Friday morning, minutes before a call to Fearghal. Leon had obviously called her from Eligius, to tell her of his role in the break-in.

I glanced at the clock on the dash: 10.30. It would be too late to contact Janet Moore now, though I resolved to do so at the earliest opportunity the following day, to find out about the meeting they had had on Friday night. It may well have been the last time Leon had been seen alive. I was also aware that Harry Patterson would be holding a grudge against Leon Bradley, and I was pretty sure he wouldn't be putting too much pressure on those working the case. For my part, I needed to know if Janet Moore had met Leon the night before he died.

Chapter Fourteen

Sunday, 15 October

I went to early Mass alone that morning and headed across into Strabane to see Janet Moore.

The small blue sports car I had seen her in was parked on the driveway. I noticed the motorbike her husband had been working on, lying on its side at the edge of the drive, the helmet on the lawn several feet to its left.

I knocked at the door, but no one answered. I hammered louder, stepping back to view the upper windows, but there was no sign of life. Through the glass door I could see that the lights were on in a room at the back of the house, despite the brightness of the morning.

Stepping across the flowerbeds to my left, I reached the window of a room I took to be the living room. It was then that I saw, half hidden from view by the sofa, what I took to be a body.

Calling the emergency services on my mobile, I ran back to the front door, but it was locked. I skirted the side of the house to see if I could gain entry from the rear, but a six-foot fence enclosed the back yard. Finally I went back to the front of the house and, after several attempts, managed to kick the door in.

My calls were met with silence as I entered the house. Janet Moore's body lay just inside the living room. She had been laid on her side, her arms in front of her, crossed over each other. Her hair covered her face and her lipstick was smeared around her mouth, as if someone had covered her mouth with a hand. Her muscles were still flexible, but her skin was cold to the touch, suggesting she had been dead for at least a day. I could guess at the cause: there were livid red and purpling bruises on her neck and I could make out the distinctive pattern of finger marks around her throat.

There was nothing more I could do for her. While I could justify breaking in on the grounds that Janet Moore might still have been alive, I was acutely aware that I had no grounds to search the house. Having ascertained that she was dead, I would have to wait for the PSNI to arrive.

I was, however, also aware that Karl Moore's bike had been abandoned outside the house, which meant that perhaps he too was injured somewhere in the house.

The other downstairs rooms were empty. Taking the stairs two at a time I checked the first-floor rooms next, starting in the bedroom to the front. The double bed was unmade but cold. The next room was a small study, where Janet must have worked. Newspapers stacked a foot high were piled around the floor. Her desk was strewn with files and Dictaphone tapes. The third room looked like a guest bedroom, everything neat, a small teddy bear perched on one of the pillows.

It was in the bathroom that I finally found Karl Moore, lying in front of an opened medicine cabinet. Various bottles of pills lay spilt on the floor around him, alongside an empty bottle of vodka. In the pool of vomit around his head, I could see the remains of several tablets.

Just as I bent to check him for vital signs, I heard someone enter through the front door below. 'Police!' he shouted.

'I'm up in the bathroom,' I called out in reply.

Just as I turned, Karl Moore sighed so lightly I thought I might have imagined it. I shivered involuntarily.

'There's one alive up here!' I roared, dropping to my knees to check for a pulse. I struggled to find one and in the end grabbed the shaving mirror from the windowsill and held it in front of Moore's face. Sure enough, light condensation misted its surface.

I shouted for the man making his way upstairs to check for the ambulance I'd called, but even as I did so I could hear the urgent wail of the siren in the distance, getting closer.

Karl Moore was on his way to Altnagelvin Hospital in Derry within ten minutes, an oxygen mask strapped to his face. Janet Moore, however, still lay where I had found her while a PSNI Scene of Crime officer edged around her, taking photographs of the body. Jim Hendry had arrived by now. He wore jeans and a loose-fitting shirt. He tugged at his moustache while I explained to him why I had been at Moore's house at 10.30 on a Sunday morning.

'Leon Bradley was contacted by Janet Moore to meet the night before he died. She might have been the last person to see him alive. I wanted to find out if she knew what he had been doing, or where he had gone that night,' I said.

'Are you not still suspended?' Jim asked.

'Leon was the brother of a friend. I'm doing him a favour.'

Jim grunted something unintelligible. 'Anything you particularly want us to look out for?'

'Her phone would be useful. I need to verify that it was definitely her who sent him the message,' I explained.

Hendry nodded and called to one of the SOCOs, asking him to look for a mobile phone. A few minutes later, the man came out to us in the kitchen and handed us a pink phone.

Hendry snapped on a pair of gloves and began working with it as I stood at his shoulder. He searched the Sent Messages folder and asked me when the message to Bradley had been received.

'After eight in the morning on Friday,' I said.

'It wasn't sent from this phone,' he said.

'Let me see,' I said, reaching out for the phone, but Hendry held it slightly away from me.

'I can do it,' he said. 'I'm telling you there's no message here like that.'

'Maybe she deleted it,' I suggested.

'No reason why she would,' Hendry said. 'There are plenty of other messages here she hasn't deleted.'

'Maybe she wiped the ones to Bradley in case her husband saw them,' I said, even as Hendry shook his head.

'No, there are older messages to "Leon" here going back weeks. If she was going to wipe one, she'd wipe them all, surely. Unless it wasn't her who texted him.'

'There is one way to find out,' I said, heading outside for a cigarette and to make a call. I apologized to Fearghal for calling so early in the day, and asked if he could check the

126

number of the phone from which the message was sent to Leon arranging the meeting last Friday. He called me back a few moments later with the number, which I scribbled on the back of my cigarette packet. When I'd finished my smoke, I headed back in and gave Hendry the number to check. He nodded; the message had come from Janet's phone.

'Why then did she delete it? It's innocuous enough in comparison with some of the other messages she'd sent him. Or the ones he'd sent her,' Hendry said. He had clearly been making his way through the messages while I'd been outside.

'It proves nothing, either way,' I said. 'Though worth keeping in mind. What about voice messages? Anything saved there?'

Hendry played with the phone's controls, angling the screen and squinting to read it. Having pressed the necessary buttons, he placed the phone to his ear and listened. For several minutes he said nothing. Then he pursed his lips and raised his eyebrows. He pressed a button and held the phone out for me to hear.

'Only one of interest. Sent at two a.m. on Friday,' he explained, nodding towards the handset.

I heard a tinny voice speak excitedly and realized it was Leon Bradley. I had to listen several times to get the whole message, for in the background I could hear people chanting slogans to do with burning Bush.

'We got in, Jan. I think I got something – something big. I'm not sure what it is, though. I'll need you to look at it. I'll not be able to bring it out, but I've stuck copies in the post. I'll speak to you later, love.'

'What do you think he's talking about?' Hendry asked when I'd finished listening.

'No idea. If he posted something out to her it might be worth searching the house.'

Hendry and the team worked the house for several hours, though they found nothing that looked to have come from Eligius, nor could they find any signs of forced entry, other than my own, nor anything that would suggest that anyone other than Karl and Janet Moore had been in the house at the time of Janet's death. Which meant, Hendry concluded, that Karl had probably killed his wife, then taken an overdose himself.

I used the opportunity to check Janet's study, which was in reality a small bedroom with a desk and several well-stocked bookcases. Her diary lay on the desk beside her laptop.

I read through her appointments for the week previous and noticed that she'd had a meeting arranged with someone called Nuala at 6 on Friday night, two hours before she arranged to meet Leon. She'd written a number in pencil beside the name. Using my own mobile, I tried calling the number, which had a Belfast prefix. An answering machine cut in:

'Hi, this is Nuala. Leave a message and I'll call you back when I get a chance.'

I left my name and number and said I wanted to speak to her about a case. Jim Hendry must have heard me speaking for he appeared at the doorway.

'Anything?' he asked.

'I found her diary. She was to meet someone called Nuala at six on Friday. The contact is a Belfast number, though that doesn't necessarily mean they were going to meet there. I've left a message for her to contact me.'

I realized what I had said just as Hendry's expression changed.

'Contact *you*?' he said, a little angrily. 'You're not even meant to be here, Ben. This is our case.'

'Sorry, Jim. Force of habit.'

'*We'll* contact her, if we need to,' Hendry said, taking the diary from me. Fortunately, her number would be saved on my own phone anyway, if I wanted to contact her again.

Jim continued to stand in front of me, diary in hand, looking at me expectantly.

'What?' I asked, smiling uncertainly.

'You need to leave, Ben. Some of the fellas down there are wondering why a suspended Garda officer is working their crime scene.'

'I . . . I'm sorry, Jim,' I said, finally. 'You're right, of course.'

Jim smiled apologetically and stood back to let me leave the room. He walked down the stairs behind me.

'Anything further on the missing immigrants?' I asked.

'No sign,' Hendry replied. 'That's a dead end, I think.'

A dead end of my creating, I thought.

'So, do you reckon the hubby did Bradley too?' Hendry asked.

'Maybe he followed her, saw them meet, saw them doing whatever. He catches up with Bradley afterwards, kills him, then confronts the wife, kills her, tries to do himself in.'

'Depressingly likely,' Hendry said. He looked back at the house. 'I am sorry about asking you to . . . you know.'

'I know,' I said. Then I held out my hand and we shook.

That evening I phoned my brother, Tom, to organize meeting for Leon's funeral the following morning. We had not seen one another for a month or so and I was looking forward to catching up with him. As children we had fought continually, over toys, over grades in school and, once, over a girl. Tom was three years my junior and, when he turned sixteen, my parents insisted that I take him out with me one Saturday night, 'to keep him out of trouble', they'd suggested. We'd gone clubbing and both hit on the same girl, whose name now I can't even remember. The night ended with the two of us tussling with one another near the dance floor, before the bouncers threw us out. Tom had stomped off in disgust and had not come home till after four in the morning, by which stage my parents had already called the police to look for him. It was several more years before we spent another evening out together.

As we had grown older, though, we had begun to recognize our similarities more clearly, and accept one another a little better because of it. If Tom was stubborn, then he was no more so than I. And in him I saw reflected my own determination to do my best, though Tom carried with that a good-heartedness that made those who knew him well love him well.

Afterwards Debbie and I sat and watched a movie. She lay stretched on the settee, her legs on my lap, wriggling her toes in a vain request for a foot rub.

'What's up?' she asked.

'Nothing,' I said, though privately my thoughts were with Fearghal Bradley, who would be sitting vigil that night by his brother's coffin.

Chapter Fifteen

Monday, 16 October

The church was almost full by the time I arrived that morning. In fact I'd had difficulty getting a parking space, for the street outside was lined with cars and several camper vans.

I recognized a number of the people in the congregation. Fearghal stood at the front, Linda Campbell in the pew behind him. The crusties had gathered to one side and I noticed the older man, Peter, with whom I had spoken on Saturday. He nodded over at me solemnly, his greyed hair tied back from his face. I scanned the pews for An Garda representatives but saw none.

Tom had told me he would meet me in the churchyard, though he had yet to arrive. I did, however, spot someone unexpected. Ted Coyle stood near the back doors, dragging a last pull from a rolled cigarette before the funeral started. His arm was in a cast and he leant on a crutch. I approached him on the pre- text of needing a light for my own cigarette.

'You're that cop,' he said.

'That's right. You're the nutcase that started the gold rush.'

He bowed slightly. 'Guilty as charged.'

'I was sorry to hear about the attack you suffered. You were mugged, is that right?' I asked as he held out a lit match.

He snorted dismissively while I puffed on my smoke to get it lit. 'So they say.'

'Who?'

'Your crowd. It was no mugging. I caught them in my tent. They took my water. Not my gold piece; just my water.'

'What water?' I asked.

At that moment, the choir inside broke into song and the service began just as Tom came running up the church drive-way towards us.

'We'll speak later,' I said to Coyle, nipping the tip off my cigarette, though not quickly enough to prevent Tom saying, 'Still smoking, I see,' as we made our way back inside.

The service was more ceremonial than I had expected. Fearghal had never been particularly observant and I knew Leon had little interest in organized religion, though I suspected he had been spiritual in the manner of one who sees God in the forest, or in rivers.

The priest spoke about Leon affectionately. He commended him on his stance on the environment and the principled stand he had taken against war and aggression.

'Have you arrested anyone for this yet?' Tom whispered, as we sat during the offertory.

I shook my head.

'Any suspects?'

'A few.'

'Did you tell me he was playing around with a married woman?'

I nodded and attempted to look disapproving at his raising the topic at the funeral.

'Is she here?' Tom went on, regardless.

'She's dead too.'

'Jesus Christ. Were they together when they died?'

I shook my head.

'Was it over their affair?' he persisted.

I glanced sideways at my brother. Though he was younger than me, the years had worn us equally. His hair was thinning a little, his midriff widening.

'Possibly,' I said.

Fearghal had helped carry the cruets of water and wine to the altar. The priest was adding a drop of water to the wine, in remembrance of the water that had mixed with the blood of Christ as it ran down his side. But Fearghal didn't see this. His head was turned, one of his hands resting on the lid of his brother's coffin, his tears running freely down his cheeks. I placed my hand momentarily on my brother's, before some impulse drove us both to straighten up and simultaneously fold our arms.

At the end of Mass, the priest led the procession down the aisle and out into the autumn sunlight, swinging the thurible, the smell of incense sweet and heady in the still air of the church. Tom and I waited to join the back of the procession. As Fearghal passed, Leon's coffin heavy on his shoulders, he looked in our direction. He saw Tom and seemed unable to catch his breath. The pallbearer next to him must have sensed this, for his grip on Fearghal's shoulder tightened.

Outside, Tom went over to speak to Fearghal while I hunted out Coyle. I wanted to know what he had meant when he'd said his water had been taken. I also wanted to find out what Janet Moore had been speaking to him about the day I saw her out at the Carrowcreel.

He was standing with a few of the crusties, including Peter, sharing a match to light their cigarettes. Someone must have said something for they turned and looked at me as I approached.

'I'd like to finish that conversation, Mr Coyle,' I said, taking out my own cigarettes.

He squinted against the light, then nodded.

'Tell him nothing,' one of the crusties muttered.

'You were saying you didn't believe the attack on you was a mugging. Is that right?'

He nodded vigorously. 'They took the water from my tent. I've been collecting it for weeks.'

I began to suspect that his reputation as an eccentric was not exaggerated.

'What water?'

'I've seen things since I've been there. Changes. That's how I got friendly with Leon. I told him and he said he knew someone who could help.'

I was lost in the conversation and said as much. 'You need to explain to me what you're talking about,' I said.

135

'The dead fish,' he stated with exasperation.

Since his arrival, weeks ago, Coyle had noticed an increasing number of dead fish floating downstream. At first it had been one every few days. Now he was seeing a couple per day. He figured that there must be something wrong with the water and had begun collecting samples, taken each day from different parts of the river. One day, as he was collecting a sample, he realized he was being watched by Leon Bradley, and he had told him that he believed the river was being polluted. Leon had told him he thought he knew someone who could help him; a few days later, he introduced Coyle to Janet Moore. Leon reckoned the pollution in the river must have been coming from Orcas, which lay a mile or two upstream. Janet had said she would run a story on it, if it were true. She had taken one water sample from Coyle for testing and had promised to get back to him.

'I'm still waiting for her to call,' he said.

'I'm afraid you're going to have a long wait,' I said.

Tom came back to our house for dinner. The kids were delighted to see him, their only uncle, and even happier when he produced presents. For a few hours, I tried to forget about the events of the past weeks. I reminded myself that I was suspended. Yet I watched the clock frequently, wondering when I would get a chance to phone Nuala and find out whether or not she had met Janet on Friday night and, if so, where. Belfast was almost two hours' drive away, so it was unlikely Janet would have met Leon at 8 p.m.

After dinner, Tom and I stood outside the back door so I could have a cigarette. He sat on the doorstep, far enough away from me to avoid the smoke but close enough for me to see his look of disapproval.

'You're going to kill yourself with those, you know,' he said. 'And you with a young family.'

'I got shot at a few weeks ago,' I said.

'Jesus. Were you hurt?'

I shook my head, took a final drag of my cigarette and stepped on the butt.

'Does Debbie not worry about you?'

'I'm sure she does. It doesn't happen that often, to be honest.'

'Still and all, Ben, you have a family. Maybe you should be taking it a bit easier. Look after yourself, you know.'

'What about you?' I asked, keen to change the subject. 'Still with What's-her-name?'

'Emma? Nah.'

'Sorry to hear that. Was it serious?'

He smiled up at me. 'The fact you don't know her name should tell you.'

'Fair enough.' Tom had been in a long-term relationship which had ended just under a year ago. Since then he had drifted restlessly through a string of one-night stands and short-term romances.

'Are you OK? With things, you know?'

He arched an eyebrow, feigned nonchalance. 'I'm fine. It's you I'd be worried about.'

'Nothing's going to happen to me.'

'I'm sure Leon Bradley thought the same thing,' he said,

standing up and opening the kitchen door to go back inside.

Tom left just after nine and we got Penny and Shane ready for bed. Penny had begun asking God for a new brother or sister – not to replace Shane, she stressed, but so the two of them wouldn't get lonely. The last time she had asked for something, it had been a hamster called Harry, who had survived for just over a year. Frank, our basset hound, had been on the receiving end of Penny's affections in the immediate aftermath of Harry's death, but she had now apparently moved on. Shane, strangely, had become more attentive to the dog, frequently pulling on Frank's one remaining ear and earning a lick on the face in return.

'We'll see, sweetie,' I said to her latest request. 'You've got Shane no matter what.'

'Why did God give you Shane and me?' she asked, propping herself up in bed on her elbows.

'Because I must have been really good when I was younger, He gave me you to take care of for Him.'

'That's why you can't break any more promises, like the one to that man in the shop,' she said, earnestly.

'I'm trying my best, sweetie,' I managed, even as my stomach turned at the reminder of Natalia and her fate since her disappearance.

'If you keep being good, He might give you another one of us to take care of,' Penny suggested.

'Only if you're *very* good though, mind,' Debbie said, her eyes twinkling.

Penny looked between us for a few seconds, as if aware that there was a layer to the conversation she couldn't quite grasp. Finally she seemed to give up and simply stated instead, 'I'm glad God gave you Shane and me.'

'So am I, sweetie,' I said.

Chapter Sixteen

Tuesday, 17 October

The following morning I drove Penny to school. As we walked across from the car park to her classroom, she held my hand as she discussed what she wanted for her upcoming ninth birthday. Then, outside her classroom, she met one of her classmates and, chattering excitedly, they walked into the room without so much as a goodbye.

When I got back into the car I noticed a missed call message on my phone. I recognized the number as belonging to Nuala, Janet Moore's friend. I had tried calling her several times the previous night after the kids had gone to bed, but each time had been transferred to her answering machine.

'Is this Nuala . . .?' I asked tentatively, hoping she would provide her surname, which she did.

'McGonagle. Who's this?'

'I'm a Garda inspector. Benedict Devlin,' I said. 'I'd like to ask you a few questions about Janet Moore, if you wouldn't mind.' I wasn't sure if she knew what had happened to Janet.

'She's not got herself arrested, has she?' she laughed.

'I'm afraid not,' I said. 'It's a . . . I thought you'd have been told. There's been an incident. I'm afraid Mrs Moore is dead.'

Nuala laughed once, a snort of derision, as if she suspected me of some prank. Then the line went quiet, though I could hear her breath fuzzing against the receiver. 'Are you serious?'

'I'm afraid so, ma'am. I thought you'd have heard.'

'Jesus Christ!' The exclamation was punctuated with a sob, then the line went silent.

'Ms McGonagle? Are you OK?'

I could hear her sobbing, muffled over the phone. After a moment she spoke again, her voice raw.

'I've been away over the weekend. I had Monday off; I've only just got your . . . what happened to her?'

'We're not entirely sure. Were the two of you very close?'

'Yes,' she said. 'We've known one another for years. Are you sure it's Janet?'

'I'm afraid so, ma'am, yes. I'm sorry.'

'How did she . . . how did it happen?'

'It's being investigated at the moment,' I said, a little ambiguously. I guessed the PSNI would be doing some sort of an investigation, even if it meant waiting for Karl Moore to recover sufficiently to explain what had happened to his wife. 'When did you last see Mrs Moore?'

'Well, was it an accident? Was Karl hurt?'

'I can't really say, ma'am,' I said. 'It's being investigated. I can tell you that it wasn't an accident.'

'Jesus Christ,' she muttered. 'And what about Karl?'

'It's being investigated,' I repeated, more firmly. 'So, when did you last see Mrs Moore?'

141

She paused for a moment before responding. 'At the weekend. She came 'up here on Friday?

'Here being . . .?'

'Belfast. She came up to the labs.'

'This is where you work, is that right?' I said, hazarding a guess.

'Yes. I'm a lecturer in Queen's University. Janet called me last week and asked me to analyse something for her. A story she was working on. She came back up on Friday to get the results. I assumed you knew where I worked; you phoned my office number.'

'We found it in Janet's diary.'

'Yes,' the woman interrupted. 'The number is new. She wouldn't have known it by heart yet,' she explained, though I hadn't asked.

'I see. At what time did you meet her on Friday?'

'After my last class; after six sometime. She stayed up for the night. We had a few drinks and something to eat. To catch up.'

'Was this organized at short notice?' I asked, wondering why she would arrange a meeting with Leon at eight that night, when there was no way she could have made it in time if she was meeting Nuala in Belfast after six.

'No. We'd been planning it for weeks. A girly night.'

'Did she ever mention Leon Bradley?' I asked.

Nuala paused and I guessed she knew about Janet's affair.

'We think she'd arranged to meet him on Friday night here in Donegal at eight.'

'Not a chance.'

'But you know the name Leon Bradley?'

'Yes, Inspector, I know the name,' she said, a little bitterly.

'This sample she'd asked you to examine. It wasn't a water sample, was it?'

Again, Nuala did not speak for a moment. 'Why?' she asked, finally. 'Does it have any bearing on her death?'

'It might, ma'am,' I said. 'At this stage, anything might help.'

'She told me it was a sample taken from a local river. She wanted it tested for pollutants.'

'And were there any?'

'Yes. Significant amounts of acid. Sulphuric acid, mainly.'

Ted Coyle had been right.

'When will Janet be buried, Inspector?' Nuala asked, interrupting my thoughts.

'I'll find out and let you know,' I said. 'Perhaps we could meet for a chat when you're down here. I'd appreciate copies of those test results, if you still have them.'

Coyle, Janet and Leon had all been involved in investigating pollution in the Carrowcreel. Each of them had been attacked or killed within the past week. And it still didn't explain why Janet would organize a meeting with Leon on Friday night, when she knew she'd be almost a hundred miles away at the time.

I called Jim Hendry and told him I had spoken with Nuala McGonagle. I added quickly that *she* had called *me*.

'What's the big issue with you and Janet Moore anyway?' he asked.

'She arranged to meet with Leon Bradley. I promised his brother I would find out what happened to him. Someone shot him. If Janet didn't make the arrangement to meet him, someone else did. Someone who had access to her phone.'

'The husband would seem to be the obvious one for all this, Ben. Finds out about the affair and cracks.'

'Has he been questioned yet?'

'He's still unconscious. They tell us he'll live; they just can't say when we'll be able to speak with him. Don't worry, I'll keep you informed.'

'What about Janet? Was a post-mortem done?'

'Yes, Ben, it was,' he replied with exasperation. 'She was strangled, pure and simple. No mystery there.'

'When will the funeral be? Ms McGonagle wants to know,' I explained.

'Tomorrow at ten in St Mary's,' Hendry said.

'Did anything turn up from Eligius?'

'Nothing.'

'Maybe it was held up in the post,' I suggested.

'Forensics were at the house again yesterday, Ben; there's nothing there. When are you back on the clock, by the way?' he added, a tacit reminder that I was on suspension.

'Monday,' I said.

'Take a rest, Ben. Enjoy a few days' break.'

I contacted Nuala McGonagle again and told her of the funeral arrangements. I also suggested we meet at the cemetery after the funeral, and said I would take her for a coffee.

Despite Hendry's advice, I couldn't let go. And I also realized that, while he had said Janet Moore's post-mortem had not revealed anything, Leon Bradley's may have done.

I phoned Lifford station, hoping that Burgess, the desk

sergeant, wouldn't recognize my voice. I asked to speak to Helen Gorman.

'Thought you'd want to speak to the Super first, Inspector,' Burgess said.

Damn. 'No, thanks. Helen'll be fine.'

'I'll put you through,' he said. Then surprised me by adding, 'You're being missed.'

'Thanks,' I said, sincerely.

'I didn't say *I* missed you,' he retorted, then I heard the line click as I was transferred.

I could tell Helen was reluctant to do what I asked. She didn't want to refuse me, but at the same time she didn't volunteer her help.

'All I need to see is the pathologist's report on Leon,' I said. 'I want to check some details. You'll be gone for ten minutes, nothing more.'

Finally she agreed, and told me she would meet me on Gallows Lane, where we were unlikely to be spotted.

Ten minutes later, Gorman pulled up in a squad car. I was leaning against the bonnet of my own, having a smoke and enjoying the view that the top of Gallows Lane afforded, well into Tyrone.

She carried a thin manila folder in her hand.

'That's everything,' she said. 'I printed you off a copy. It only took a moment.'

The entire file held around twenty pages. The pathologist's report accounted for almost a quarter of them. There were a few witness statements, and some cursory handwritten notes and diagrams illustrating where the body had been found.

'Is this everything?' I asked incredulously.

Gorman nodded, grimly. 'It's not being made a priority. The Super is worried that Orcas will pull out. He wants the Bradley shooting buried. The official version is that Janet Moore's husband killed him.'

'What's the unofficial version?' I asked.

'The same,' she said. 'He killed his wife, you know.'

'I know,' I said. 'I found her.'

Gorman seemed taken aback, and I figured that Patterson hadn't heard about my involvement in that discovery. I scanned the post-mortem results while I finished my smoke. Leon had been shot from behind, fairly close range, by a shotgun. He had died at between eight and midnight on Friday, which didn't narrow things down much. I scanned the report looking for any reference to water in his lungs. I hoped that if the pathologist had tested the water and found pollutants, the damage Orcas was doing to the river would become a matter of public record.

'Did anyone check the water from his lungs?' I asked.

Gorman looked quizzically at me. 'Why?'

'Orcas is pumping pollutants into the river. Leon Bradley and Janet Moore were investigating it.'

'How do you know this?' Gorman asked.

'Good old-fashioned police work,' I said, offering her back the folder she'd given me.

'Keep it,' she said, ignoring the diversion. 'What police work? You're meant to be on suspension.'

'So everyone keeps reminding me,' I said.

*   *   *

146

That evening I went through the murder folder again in more detail. It looked increasingly likely that Karl Moore had killed Leon, though I was reluctant to simply sit on my hands until he woke and confessed. I wondered if the murder weapon had turned up anywhere yet. I also wanted to know what it was that Leon had posted to Janet from Eligius. If they had been working on a story to do with river pollution, what was the connection with a missile-building company, beyond the fact that Hagan funded – and profited from – both? I would need to ask a different source: one of the remaining members of the Eligius four.

I rooted through the recycling bin until I found the weekend papers. The names of the four men and their home towns were listed as part of the story of the break-in. All I had to do now was find them.

Chapter Seventeen

Wednesday, 18 October

As it had been the day before, my first task the next morning was to attend a funeral – Janet Moore's this time. This was the third funeral in as many weeks, and the brightness of the day could do little to lighten the leaden weight that seemed to have settled in my guts.

The funeral was even better attended than Leon's. Janet had known a lot of people and I recognized faces from the various papers and television channels amongst the mourners. I also noticed a number of PSNI officers, including Jim Hendry, who winked when we caught one another's eye.

The only conspicuous absence was Karl Moore, and I noticed that the front pew of the church had been left vacant. It was also clear from the priest's homily that he was struggling to avoid mention of the manner of Janet's death, or its presumed perpetrator. Indeed, he referred throughout to 'this senseless, tragic incident'. It struck me, though, that *all* of the incidents in which I'd been involved were senseless and carried with them their own unique tragic overtones.

I hung back at the cemetery after the burial and, as the mourners dispersed, a woman approached me. She had an athletic physique and blonde hair tied up in a bun.

'Inspector Devlin,' she stated, her hand already extended.

'Ms McGonagle?'

She nodded curtly. 'Nuala,' she said.

'Thanks for meeting me. I'm sorry about your friend.'

'Karl killed her, is that right?'

The PSNI had yet to release details of how she had died, so I wondered if Jim Hendry had told her when he had spoken to her. She sensed my reluctance to answer.

'Karl's not here, and no one's mentioned him. I'm guessing he did it, is that right?'

'It looks that way.'

'What about Leon Bradley? Where is he?'

'I can't . . .'

'He's dead too, isn't he?'

'Ms McGonagle—'

'Nuala,' she corrected. 'He's dead too, isn't he? Karl killed him as well?'

'We're not sure. If he knew about the affair . . .'

'Oh, he knew,' she stated darkly. 'Or he had his suspicions.'

I recalled the first time I had met him; he had mentioned 'Bradley' when I asked how Janet knew about Hagan's visit. I had assumed he meant Fearghal.

'Did Janet say anything to you at the weekend? Anything that made you think she might be at risk?'

'They'd had a row on Thursday,' she said, glancing at her watch. 'Perhaps you could buy me that coffee. I need to be back in Belfast for three,' she said, and began striding down towards the gates of the cemetery.

*   *   *

149

'They'd had a row,' she resumed, once we'd got settled into the café near the Old Courthouse. 'Karl found out that she'd been involved in that stunt at the goldmine.'

'The shooting at Hagan?'

She nodded as she tore a chunk off her panini and bit into it and chewed for a few seconds. 'Uh huh. One of your crowd told him that she gave one of her tickets to Leon, to get into the mine.'

'What do you mean "one of my crowd"?'

'A policeman who'd been working at the mine. He and Karl play football together, apparently. Karl came back from the match swearing blue murder. She denied it, said she was using Leon for research, but she didn't think he bought it.'

I wasn't quite following what she had said. A policeman Karl played football with – and someone stupid or crass enough to reveal details like that to a cheated husband. Patterson had told me himself they played football together. It was unlikely that Patterson had intended to set in motion the chain of events that had subsequently unfolded, but the fact remained that his stupidity had already cost two people their lives – three, perhaps, before this whole thing would be finished.

'So do you think he killed Leon then?' she asked again.

'Honestly, I can't say,' I replied. 'We know that someone had arranged a meeting with Leon on Friday night using Janet's phone. As she was in Belfast with you, it's unlikely that she also arranged to meet Leon at the same time.'

'So Karl did,' she concluded. 'Killed him, then came back and—'

She was extremely matter-of-fact about the events, and it struck me as strange that she seemed so little affected emotionally by the funeral and the death of her friend. I decided to get off the subject of the killings.

'So Janet brought you water to test, you said.'

She placed the cup back on the saucer and lifted her handbag from where she had placed it on the ground at her feet.

'She brought me a bottle of water she said had been taken from a river near this new goldmine. Someone had told her they'd noticed a lot of fish dead in the water. Janet was convinced that this mine was pouring stuff out that was killing them.'

'Was she right?' I asked. Weston had told me they had conducted a full environmental-impact survey before they had started building. A pollution scandal would severely damage the place's credibility, and possibly put a dent in its record profits.

'It seems so. As I told you on the phone, I found significant levels of sulphuric acid in the water. Enough to kill fish life, certainly.'

'And could this have come from the goldmine?' I asked.

She produced a sheaf of papers from her bag and passed them across the table to me.

'The gold in that mine is found in sulphides. It's quite rare to find a vein of pure gold; that's the stuff they make jewellery from. Most gold is found in sulphide compounds. The rock containing these compounds is crushed and put through a number of processes, including being washed with detergents to remove the gold sulphide. Cyanide is then used to extract the gold. Gold mined that way isn't as pure, but it's fine for use in computer circuit boards, needles and cables and that.'

'You didn't find cyanide in the water though,' I pointed out.

She raised her index finger. 'An eighteen-carat gold ring leaves behind over twenty tonnes of polluted waste, Inspector. Cyanide is just one of the problems. In Romania in 2000, heavy rains caused one of the dams holding in the polluted waste from a mine to burst. The cyanide that made it into the local river killed all the fish in the area and made the drinking water for over two million people undrinkable for months. In the US in 1992, gold-mining waste made it into a local river, killing all aquatic life for twenty-five kilometres downstream.'

'But you haven't found cyanide in the Carrowcreel,' I persisted.

'Cyanide is only one of the problems,' she repeated. 'Even without it, the waste products of mining still contain sulphides. Rainwater can combine with this to create sulphuric acid, which then leaches into the water table or, in this case, the local river. Undiluted, it would be as toxic as battery acid.'

'Could anything else be responsible for it, besides the mine?' I asked.

'It could occur naturally in sulphide-rich rock, but not at the levels I found,' she said.

'Is it enough to close the place down?' I asked. I had my own issues with Weston and his mine, but its closure would be a big blow to the local economy.

'That depends on whether there's the political will to do

something about it,' she stated. 'As always, these things come down to who you know, and how well.'

I thought again of our local politician, Miriam Powell, joking with Cathal Hagan at the mine.

'I've included the results of my tests there, inspector. You'd be better contacting the Rivers Agency here in the Republic and letting them do their own tests.'

'I might have a problem arranging that,' I said, then immediately regretted it.

'Why?' Nuala asked sharply.

'I'm not actually on duty at the moment.'

She nodded curdy. 'The Northern policeman told me that,' she said.

'Why did you agree to see me then?'

'Is anybody else really bothered that Janet is dead?' she asked, her head tilted, her expression free from guile. She raised an eyebrow. 'Well?'

As I made my way back to the car, I caught a glimpse of Harry Patterson, watching me from his office window across the street.

The first of the remaining three of the Eligius protesters was a twenty-year-old from Omagh named John Young. I phoned him from a payphone across the border and asked if he would mind speaking with me about the break-in.

'I've nothing to say,' Young stated. 'I made a mistake.'

'In what way?'

'I imagined it was gonna be a bit of craic. It got too serious.'

'What happened inside there? Did you see Leon Bradley lifting anything before you were brought out?'

'He wasn't there like us.'

'What do you mean?'

'I went in to protest about the war. So did the other guys, Curran and Daniels. Bradley was looking for something definite.'

I guessed 'Daniels' was Peter Daniels, a forty-eight-year-old from Navan. I'd tried to track him through the Garda database, but there was no listed address for him. The other man, Seamus Curran, was a name I already knew.

'Why do you say that?' I asked.

'He spent the whole time on the computer, printing off stuff, going through filing cabinets, photocopying sheets. I tell you – I'm sorry I ever set foot in the place.'

'Do you know who might know what Bradley was looking for?' I asked.

'No idea,' Young said. 'The other guy might know; the Provo.'

Whilst Young had referred to him as a Republican, Seamus Curran had in reality become a convinced pacifist. He had been outspoken in the media about the war in Iraq when it had started and I had little doubt as to the reasons behind his involvement in the break-in.

I found him, as expected, in a pub he part-owned in Derry. The bar was small and dark, the roof low, the tables divided between small nooks where, despite the smoking ban, lunch-time drinkers sat in a fug of smoke, poring over the day's racing form in the papers.

The walls were decorated with a mixture of political memorabilia and black-and-white photographs of local celebrities who had graced the bar at one stage or another. A framed copy of the 1916 Declaration of Independence, which had led eventually to the partition of Ireland, hung beside a signed photograph of John F. Kennedy that some-one had gifted to the bar.

Curran was sitting in front of the bar when I came in. The place was mutedly busy, the numbers of drinkers greater than the hush of conversation they collectively produced. Curran was spooning Irish stew on to a heel of bread which he crammed into his mouth before standing up and moving behind the bar when he saw me enter.

He wiped his mouth with his hand, which he then rubbed clean against his trouser leg.

'What can I get you?' he asked, his hand already lifting a pint glass from the counter to fill.

'Just a Coke will be fine,' I said, producing my warrant card. 'I'd like to speak to you for a moment.'

He flipped the glass once and caught it, then placed it on the counter before glancing at my card. He turned his back to me to lift a Coke bottle from the shelf behind him. As he did so he said, 'You're a bit off your patch.'

'I'm just looking for some information,' I explained, taking a seat at the bar.

'Aren't youse always,' Curran said, pouring the Coke into a glass and dropping in a few cubes of ice before placing the drink in front of me.

'About the Eligius break-in . . .' I continued.

He smiled a little sheepishly. 'Seemed a good idea at the time,' he said. 'Depends what you want to know.' He leant on the bar.

'The young fella Bradley who went in with you is dead. I'm investigating the killing. I believe he posted some documents out from Eligius; I'm wondering if you know what they were about? Or if he mentioned to you why he was there?'

'He was protesting against the war. And that arsehole Hagan, poncing about like the saviour of Ireland.'

'Do you know what he was looking for?'

Curran shook his head. 'Did you not see the footage? I spent the evening hanging out a window wi' a megaphone. I know he was looking for something, but to be honest I don't know what and I don't give a fuck.'

'Did you organize the protest?' I asked. 'How did you all meet?'

'We didn't. Leon put an appeal on Bebo and some of those other Internet sites, looking for protesters to join him. Twenty-five signed up – only four of us went in.'

'What about the other twenty-one?'

'They bottled out.'

'That must have been a pisser,' I observed. I was reminded of my own aborted attempt at protest in college. A load of our friends had said they'd come along with us. They never showed.

'You get used to it,' Curran said. 'Everyone cries about the introduction of water charges, then you organize a demo and the same fifty people arrive every time. People like to complain, but that's all they do.'

'What was Leon Bradley's beef with Eligius?' I asked. 'I spoke to John Young and he seemed uncomfortable with the whole thing.'

'I dunno. I thought Bradley was a bit of an amateur.'

'We believe he posted some things out from Eligius – but we haven't been able to find them.'

'Posted? What do you mean?'

'He left someone a message saying he was posting documents out to her.'

'Maybe he brought them out with him? Posting them out seems a bit strange.'

I shook my head. 'No, he was searched when he came out.'

Curran nodded. 'We all were,' he agreed.

'We know he posted something, but we can't work out where. It hasn't turned up.'

Curran grimaced in concentration. 'It wouldn't have, of course,' he said finally, smiling, his hands slapping on the bar counter. 'Sure the place only opened today.'

'What place?' I asked, a little confused.

'Eligius. It's been closed since we broke in. Doing security checks and that. It opened this morning again. If Bradley did post the stuff in Eligius, they're sending the stuff out for him without even realizing it. Christ, that's genius. Maybe he wasn't such an amateur at all.' He laughed, then added, 'This stuff he posted? Does it have anything to do with his death?'

'Possibly not,' I conceded.

'Then why the fuck are you so wrapped up in finding it?' he asked, his smile twisting on his lips.

I couldn't think of a satisfactory response. The Coke in my glass suddenly tasted sickeningly syrupy.

After I left Curran, I called Jim Hendry and told him about the closure of Eligius and the possibility that whatever Leon had posted out of the building would be arriving the following morning. He promised me he would do what he could, but I began to suspect that he was getting fed up with my requests.

That night, Debbie and I got the kids to bed and had just sat down to watch something on the TV when my mobile rang. I didn't recognize the number and it took me a moment to place the voice.

'Inspector Devlin?'

'Yes,' I said, shrugging to Debbie, who was demanding to know who had interrupted our night on the sofa.

'Linda Campbell here, Inspector. We met at—'

'Ms Campbell, I remember. How can I help you?'

She paused for a moment. 'It's not me who needs your help. It's Fearghal. He's been arrested at Orcas.'

The previous day, Weston had contacted the National Museum, requesting that Fearghal and Linda be sent up to Orcas. He wanted their help with the preparations for 'Kate's' transportation to America, where she was to join the personal collection of Cathal Hagan.

Fearghal confided to Linda that he suspected the decision to involve him constituted a public smack on the wrists for his brother's actions. Weston had apparently wasted no opportunity in reminding Fearghal that Ireland was losing this unique cultural artefact because of Leon's recklessness. It was a national embarrassment, he said.

Biting his tongue, Fearghal had gone for dinner with Linda. During the meal, he had become increasingly drunk and agitated. He had spoken about the loss of his brother and the loss of Kate as if they were somehow connected. If they had never found Kate, he said, none of this might have happened. And if he could keep Kate in the country, he might retain some dignity. His brother might be proud of him, wherever he was. Halfway through the meal he lifted his keys and strode out of the restaurant.

Apparently he made his way to the goldmine, where Kate was lying in her transport case, ready for her journey to America the following morning.

Using the wheel brace from the boot of his car, Fearghal had smashed his way into the building. He was caught on security cameras, clambering through the shattered remains of the front door and making a beeline for the crate he had helped pack hours earlier. Using the edge of the brace intended for removing wheel trims, Fearghal had managed to prize open the top of the crate.

He was then filmed smashing in the container in which Kate was sealed. Pushing his hands though the broken glass, he lifted the woman's body out and made his way back to the car park.

Alerted by the burglar alarm, the Guards found him struggling back towards the pit in which Kate had been discovered, her desiccated body cradled in his arms.

*   *   *

I collected Linda from her hotel and we drove together to the station. She was on edge for the duration of the journey and I tried with little luck to engage her in conversation.

'Have you and Fearghal been dating long?' I asked.

She turned her face towards me. 'We're not dating,' she snapped quickly. 'He was my tutor at college.'

'Sorry,' I said. 'I thought . . .'

'Fearghal helped me through a bad patch when I was a student. He's a good man.'

'We were good friends once,' I agreed.

'He told me so,' she replied. 'He used to look up to you, he said.'

It was my turn to look at her. She turned her head away and did not speak again for the rest of the journey.

When we got to the station, Fearghal had already been charged and bailed. He sat on a plastic chair in the foyer, a brown envelope on the floor beside him into which his possessions had been placed following his arrest. He was bent double in the chair, as if winded, his head resting on his hands. When we came in he looked up. His face was puffy and pale, his forehead shining with sweat. His eyes were red-ringed and bleary.

He swallowed drily and attempted to say my name. I put my hand on his shoulder, while Linda sat down next to him and asked him how he had been treated.

'Fine,' he muttered. 'How's Kate?'

Linda looked up at me before answering, which in itself told him all he needed to know.

'She's . . . she's badly damaged,' she said.

'Come on, Fearghal,' I said, helping him up off his seat. 'Time to go.'

He leant his weight on me as we crossed the road to my car.

'I'm sorry, Benny,' he said, patting my back with his hand. 'I've caused nothing but trouble since I got here.'

'Don't worry about it, Fearghal,' I said. 'Still fighting the good fight, eh?'

'I couldn't let Hagan get his fucking hands on her. They'll not be able to sell her now,' Fearghal said.

'Get that drunk out of here,' a voice called from behind us. Still holding on to Fearghal, I turned around.

Harry Patterson and John Weston stood at the door of the station. Weston had obviously given his orders to Patterson, who was shaking hands with him as he left.

I should have turned and kept walking. I shouldn't have spoken.

Fuck it, I thought. Leading Fearghal to the car and handing Linda my keys, I made my way back across to the station.

'I want the Rivers Agency to test the water in the Carrowcreel,' I said, standing in front of the two men. 'I believe they'll find pollutants in the river coming from his goldmine.'

'I want to hump that wee girl that works over in the café there,' Patterson said, nodding towards the building opposite. 'But it's not going to happen, is it?' He laughed forcedly and turned to Weston, encouraging him to share his joke.

Weston, however, was not smiling. 'That's a serious allegation,' he said. 'Have you any proof?'

'Janet Moore knew it. I believe that she and Leon Bradley were gathering the evidence to prove it.'

'It's fucking nonsense,' Patterson interrupted. 'Is this what you had Gorman checking post-mortem results for?' My surprise must have shown.

'Do you think she'd go running behind my back for the likes of you? She came in and told me the minute you asked,' he said.

'I want this done before I return to work on Monday, Harry,' I persisted, regardless.

'You think you'll be back on Monday, do you?' he asked, smiling. 'I think another week or two yet must be needed to really hammer the message home.' With that he stepped closer to me and mouthed the words carefully. 'You're not fucking wanted here.'

I nodded my head. 'You told Karl Moore that his wife was having an affair.'

Patterson stopped moving. His eyelids drooped a little, hooding his expression. 'What are you slabbering about?'

'You told Karl Moore about his wife and Leon. He killed her days later. To my mind, that makes you responsible.'

'You're full of shite,' Patterson spat.

'We'll see,' I said. 'When Moore wakes up, we'll find out. I'm betting he'll tell us what you said to him at football on Thursday night.'

'She couldn't keep her mouth shut – or her legs,' Patterson hissed. 'Not my fault he topped the bitch.'

'Actually, I think it is, Harry,' I said. 'You gave him a motive.'

'Fuck off,' Patterson said, though the comment lacked his earlier conviction.

162

'I want results by Monday, Harry,' I said. 'We'll sort out the rest later.'

I turned and strode across the street, half expecting some final comment to be thrown behind me, but none came.

I got into the car and fired the ignition.

'Is everything all right?' Linda asked, leaning in from the back seat where Fearghal lay slumped against her.

'Not by a mile,' I muttered, glancing once more at where Patterson and Weston stood in the gathering darkness.

Chapter Eighteen

Thursday, 19 October

Next morning I drove to Janet Moore's house. If I could at least see an envelope, or perhaps even catch the postman, I might learn what Leon Bradley had posted to her.

By eleven o'clock the postman had yet to arrive, and one of the Moores' neighbours had evidently grown suspicious, for a PSNI jeep pulled up beside me.

Jim Hendry rolled down the window of the jeep and leant out. 'I thought it might have been you. What the fuck are you planning on doing? You've no key.'

'I was going to mug the postman,' I joked.

'You're too late,' Hendry replied – except from his expression it was clear that he wasn't joking.

'What?' I said.

'You're too late. Someone knocked him down this morning on his way out the Derry Road on his bike. Clipped him with a car.'

'Did he see who did it?'

'Some guy with a pony-tail,' he said. 'Got out to help him up, then grabbed his post-bag and drove off.'

'Pony Tail again?' I said. Things were starting to take shape. But how did Pony Tail fit in with Eligius?

'Now don't start seeing conspiracies,' Hendry said, tossing me a cigarette from the jeep window before lighting one himself. 'It might have been a genuine accident.'

'Except they stole his bloody post-bag,' I argued. Then I realized the full impact of the theft. 'So, we'll never know what Leon Bradley found in Eligius. Someone beat us to it.'

Hendry nodded his head. 'Almost,' he said, his moustache twitching above his smile. He lifted a brown envelope off the dashboard and handed it to me. It was stamped with the Eligius logo and Janet Moore's address was written on it by hand.

'How did you get this?' I asked.

'I went to the Sorting Office last night. Explained that the woman in question was murdered and that.'

The envelope had already been opened. 'What's in here?' I asked.

'I wouldn't be getting my hopes up,' Hendry said. 'A bunch of figures. Shipping orders. Productivity reports. Nothing anyone could make head nor tail of.'

I opened the envelope and took out the sheaf of documents inside. Hendry was right. Several pages listed productivity percentages over several months, with abbreviations at the top of the page above each column: Ag, Au, Cu, Fe. The next sheet listed shipping orders over the previous year. The name on the invoice was V M Haulage.

As I was replacing the documents in the envelope, my mobile rang. The number on the screen had a Northern prefix. When I answered, a man's voice snapped, 'Who's this?'

'You called me,' I said. 'Who's this?'

'Is your name Devlin?' the man demanded.

'Who the hell is this?'

'This is Sergeant Burke. I'm a PSNI officer in Omagh. We've arrested a woman for soliciting. She had your phone number.'

'Who is she?'

'We don't know. She doesn't seem to be able to speak English. She gave us a card with your number to phone.'

'I'm on my way,' I said, turning my key in the ignition.

Hendry agreed to contact Burke for me while I drove to Omagh. I had pulled out of the estate and started up the road when I realized that I had forgotten to return the Eligius envelope to Jim.

The sky was already greying with the threat of rain as I drove up the Omagh Road. It took me some time to find the PSNI station and then I had to wait for a further ten minutes for Burke to appear. I began to realize that I hadn't eaten since breakfast, and the realization brought with it a craving for food.

Burke was a young sergeant, which may have explained his supercilious phone manner. His hair was long, his face darkened with designer stubble. He continually ran his hand through his hair and flicked his head to the side while we spoke. As he led me to the cell where Natalia was being held, he explained how they had come to arrest her.

They had been working on a tip-off. A local clergyman had been told by one of his congregation that foreign girls were working the street corners in one of the rougher areas of town. Cars were stopping and picking them up, then leaving them off again fifteen minutes later. It didn't take Holmesian deduction to work out what was going on.

Burke and three other plain-clothes officers had staked out the street. There had been three girls working. Two of them had made a run for it when they saw the police coming, recognizing them for what they were, even in plain clothes. Only Natalia had been arrested.

'She didn't even *try* to run away,' Burke snorted.

'Maybe she wanted to get caught,' I suggested.

'Huh?' He looked at me sceptically, one eyebrow raised, his lip curled slightly. 'Now why would she want to do that?'

He pushed open the door of the interview room. Natalia looked significantly older than the last time I had seen her. She wore a tight white T-shirt and a frayed denim skirt that barely passed her crotch. Her arms were purple with bruises and her hair hung in straggles over her face. The yellowed remains of a bruise shadowed her left eye. She had wrapped one arm across her breasts.

'Jesus Christ,' I said.

She looked up, her eyes flinty, her jaw set. When she saw me her expression softened for a second and her mouth twitched in recognition, as if she would smile. Then, as if remembering that I was the one who had been responsible for her fate, her expression hardened once more and she looked away.

I went over and knelt in front of her chair, placing my hands on her shoulders, though she shrugged them away. I moved my head in the hope of catching her eye, but she avoided me.

'I'm so sorry,' I said. 'Jesus, I'm so sorry.'

Finally she turned and looked at me. Something inside her seemed to crack. Her nose twitched suddenly and her eyes filled with tears. She spluttered something in Chechen, and hit at me with her fists, the blows glancing off my shoulders and the side of my head. I knelt in front of her and let her strike me, until her tears had subsided. Then I drew her against me and held her tight. Initially she felt rigid in my arms, but then she relaxed and returned the embrace.

'I see now why she had your card,' Burke said.

'Shut the fuck up,' I snapped, without looking at him.

Burke left and his superior came in, an inspector named Charlie Gilmore.

'You were a bit sharp with Peter,' he said.

'Is that so?'

Gilmore nodded. 'He's young. No need to be rude with him. You're off your turf here.'

'This isn't about turf; it's about dealing with people like we're all part of the same species.'

'Oh, we know we're all part of the same species, all right. What we're a bit more confused about though is where exactly she's from. My money's on Russian.' He nodded slightly, as if this piece of information might influence my response.

'She's Chechen. Her name's Natalia Almurzayev,' I said.

'And how do you know her?' he asked, scraping back the chair from the opposite side of the table to us and sitting down.

'Her husband was shot in Lifford three weeks ago.'

He nodded. 'The bank job; the guy with the plastic pistol.'

'That's right.'

'The wife's attempt at crime hasn't been much more successful,' he chuckled. 'So, how do we speak to her?'

An hour later, Karol Walshyk was brought into the interview room. Someone had rustled up a plate of sandwiches and some tea. I had attempted to communicate with Natalia several times, but to little avail. She repeated the word 'good' as she ate, and smiled forcedly. The smile that greeted Karol's arrival, though, was genuine, and for a second I saw a hint of the woman she must have been before setting foot in Ireland.

Karol's reaction was one of both shock and pity. He spoke to her immediately in Chechen, ignoring the rest of us in the room. Finally, seemingly satisfied with her responses, he stood beside her, her hand in his, and faced us.

Gilmore came in with Burke. Instinctively I lifted the chair that had been left for me beside the PSNI officers and moved it to the side of the table, next to Natalia.

Gilmore inserted two fresh tapes into the tape recorder attached to the desk and turned it on. He then stated the date and time, introduced each person in the room, and commenced the interview.

'Can you explain to us what you were doing when you were arrested?' he asked.

On the night I had taken her from the house in Strabane she had gone to a local fast-food restaurant with Helen

Gorman. Gorman had told her she had to leave her for a few moments, after I called her to assist in following Pony Tail's car. An hour later she had not returned and Natalia had started to worry that something bad had happened. Then the waitress had approached her table to warn her that the group of young boys in the corner were looking over at her. One of them, dressed in a tracksuit, his hair dyed blond, had called something over at her, something that caused his friends to snigger. His expression left her in little doubt as to his meaning.

Frightened, she had left the restaurant, fearful that the boys would follow her. She had walked up the bypass, making her way back to the house. By the time she arrived, her friends were in a panic. Angered by her absence, the pony-tailed man had warned he would return the following night. If she didn't have the money by then, the other people in the house would have to pay it for her.

She would think of something, she had promised them. She would ask the policeman to help.

At that point, the front door had been flung open. Pony Tail made straight for her, his mouth an angry slash. He grabbed her by the hair and slammed her face against the wall. He called her names. 'Bitch,' she said. 'Bitch.'

The force of the blows shattered her nose. She screamed, while one of the other women jumped on Pony Tail's back. He punched Natalia in the face, knocking her to the floor, then slammed his back against the wall, badly winding the woman who had helped her. As two of the men in the house rounded on Pony Tail, his accomplice entered with a baseball bat. He barked at the men in Polish, raising the bat.

170

When they had backed off he grabbed Natalia by the hair, dragging her into the kitchen while Pony Tail dealt with the two men.

She understood some of what the man said to her. He wanted to know what she had told the police. She told him she hadn't spoken to the police and he ripped the front of her dress. He lifted a knife from the counter and, grabbing her by the hair, pressed it against her throat. He asked her again, and again she denied involving the police. Finally he pressed the knife against her windpipe, working the tip gently until it just pierced the skin. Then he began to push it deeper. Natalia had screamed and told him she would tell him everything. It was because of her husband, she shouted. He'd died and the police had come.

The man pulled away from her. He seemed to consider something. Then Pony Tail came into the kitchen, a mobile phone in his hand. He spoke to the younger man, seeming to give him an order. The younger man looked at her, his gaze lingering on the swell of her chest, which was spattered with blood. He seemed reluctant to leave, wetting his lips with the tip of his tongue. Pony Tail spoke again, more sharply, and his partner stomped out of the room.

Five minutes later a white transit van pulled into the driveway. The residents were loaded into the back. Natalia stood waiting to join her countrymen, but Pony Tail gripped her upper arm and jostled her down the driveway towards their car. He opened the back door, forced her in, pushing down her head to avoid hitting the car roof.

The younger man was sitting in the driving seat. He winked at her when she got in. He spoke again in Polish.

She was going to earn her rent, he said. He pushed out his cheek with his tongue. The red scar that ran down the side of his skull was livid in the car's interior light.

She had not seen her friends since, nor, it seemed, did she know that their old house had been burnt down. She was driven somewhere in the car. They travelled for about thirty minutes before pulling into the driveway of an old red-brick house, hidden from the roadway by mature trees along the perimeter of the garden. Pony Tail and the scarred man led her inside the house. It was fairly well furnished inside, better than Natalia's previous house. While Pony Tail made a phone call, the scarred man had taken her to an upstairs room where he tore her dress from her. Then he forced her on to the floor.

The story broke there, both because Natalia herself was so upset and because Karol Walshyk asked to be given a break. His face was drawn, his eyes wet with tears. Gilmore, though reluctant to stop the tapes, agreed to a break and sent out for a woman officer.

I stood to stretch my legs, and joined Gilmore at the door of the interview room.

'I know who the scarred man is,' I said.

He squinted at me slightly. 'Who?'

'His name's Pol Strandmann. He sells stuff at the market outside Derry on a Sunday.'

'That's good to know,' he said, turning from me again. Something about his reaction worried me.

'You're not going to lift him, are you?' I asked.

'There are other things going on here, Inspector Devlin. We'll get to him in due course.'

'He raped her. He can be charged with that,' I said, placing my hand on his arm.

He looked down at my hand. 'You're here on a limited welcome; remember that.'

'He raped her,' I repeated forcefully, trying to keep my voice calm.

'Could you step outside?' Gilmore asked through gritted teeth, opening the door and stepping out onto the corridor.

'Why—' I began, but Gilmore stopped me short, stabbing a finger against my shoulder.

'Let's get something straight here. Devlin. You can't come up here, mouthing off to my team, and then tell me what to do—'

'You're not going to arrest him, are you?'

'One thug rapes a prostitute. So what? I'm sorry for her, really I am. You're not the only one with feelings, you know. But there are other women involved here. We believe this guy with the pony-tail is involved in several brothels between here and Strabane, all involving eastern Europeans. If we can get him – and whoever is behind him, more importantly – we'll achieve a hell of a lot more than picking up one rapist.'

It sickened me to the stomach, but I had to concede that Gilmore was making a sound operational judgement. That didn't make it any less unpalatable. I would catch up with Pol down the line, of that there was no doubt.

I nodded. 'I'm sorry,' I said.

Gilmore looked at me a moment. 'Forget about it. We'd best get back in there.'

The atmosphere in the room darkened even further as the interview resumed. Gilmore asked about the man with the pony-tail; had he mentioned any names, given any indication of who he worked for? Natalia listened to Karol's translation of his questions, then shook her head.

'What happened after you were attacked?' he asked.

Again, Natalia watched Karol as he relayed the question to her, her gaze on his mouth, as if lip-reading. Then she began to speak, her words tumbling together.

'She was forced to prostitute,' Karol said, looking between Natalia and Gilmore. 'In order to pay her debt.'

'Did you ever see anyone you thought was in charge?'

She shook her head. 'Only the man with the pony-tail and the one with the scar,' Karol translated.

'Tell her we need her to look at mug shots. To see if she can identify the pony-tailed man for us.'

Karol translated and she nodded.

'What about Strandmann?' I asked. 'We have a lead on him. His car was spotted outside the house where Natalia was originally based. It's enough to bring him in.'

'I've told you already – we'll follow it up,' Gilmore said.

I sat in the station until past midnight, while Natalia sat flicking through several lever-arch files of photographs, but without success. Karol Walshyk sat beside me, a cup of tea, long since grown cold, untouched in his hands.

'This is a horrible country,' he stated.

'Sometimes,' I agreed. 'Sometimes it's not so bad.'

'This story that Natalia told. You hear that often?'

'We do cruel things to each other,' I said. 'You must have seen similar in Poland.'

'It is so ...' he struggled to find the right word, 'thoughtless.'

I nodded, without looking at him.

'It must be hard not to become thoughtless too. To become used to it,' Karol continued, gesturing towards where Burke stood behind Natalia. 'Like him.'

I looked up at Burke, who was joking with the other members of his team. I missed Caroline Williams. I missed having someone I could rely on in a case. And I questioned why I was sitting in a draughty police station in Omagh in the early hours of a Friday morning, when I wasn't even supposed to be working.

Gilmore approached us. 'She doesn't recognize anyone,' he said. 'We'll keep an eye on this scarred fella you say works the markets, see if we can make a connection there. For now, we need to find her somewhere safe to stay. We've tried the Women's Centre but it's full. The duty social worker's not answering his fucking phone. We can get her placed tomorrow. Somewhere safe, until we can pick up this Pony Tail guy. All we need is for her to give us a positive ID on him.'

'She can stay with us for the night,' I said. 'My wife is at home.'

Behind Gilmore's shoulder Natalia sat at the desk alone, worrying the nail of her thumb with her small teeth.

*   *   *

175

I brought Natalia home with me and left her sitting in our kitchen while I went up to wake Debbie and explain the situation.

She was still groggy after I roused her and it took several attempts to explain why an eastern European woman was sitting in our kitchen.

'You brought a prostitute to our house?' she repeated for the third time.

'She has nowhere else to go,' I explained. 'She doesn't know anyone else.'

'What about Social Services?'

'They can't contact them.'

'So we're taking her instead?'

I smiled grimly, as if sharing in her exasperation.

'It's not funny, Ben. I don't want her in my house. Find somewhere else for her.'

'You can't throw her out on the street, Debs. She's nowhere else to go.'

'*I'm* not throwing her anywhere. You do it. What are you thinking, offering our home to prostitutes?'

'I had no choice.'

'How come no one else took her? Why did it have to be you? This is my home. We have children here, Ben, who don't need to share their home with a fucking prostitute.'

I tried to think of a reply, but Debbie got out of bed and brushed past me to get her dressing gown.

We went downstairs together. Debbie smiled stiffly at Natalia when she went into the kitchen.

'I'll make tea,' she said, twisting the tap so angrily the water sprayed out at force, on to both the kettle and the window behind the sink. Natalia smiled at me with embarrassment, then gestured around the room. She angled her head to catch Debbie's eye. 'S'nice,' she managed. 'Nice.'

Debbie thanked her, then finished making tea in silence. I brought the cups and milk and sugar to the table while Debbie carried over the teapot. She sat down opposite Natalia, smiling at her, attempting to engage her in conversation of some sort, though with little response.

Finally, glaring at me, she suggested that she take Natalia up to her room. I heard her explain to Natalia the whereabouts of the toilet and the fact that the children were sleeping in the next room. When she came back down, I was standing at the back door having a final smoke before going to bed.

'Thanks, Debs,' I said. 'She's a nice girl.'

'I still want her out of here in the morning,' she said, placing the dishes in the sink.

I continued smoking in silence, hoping to ride out her reaction.

Finally she asked, 'What happened to her?'

'She was raped.'

Debbie stopped what she was doing for a second and stared at me.

'And I think it was my fault,' I said, flicking the smouldering butt out on to the back path and closing the door.

Chapter Nineteen

Friday, 20 October

The temperature dropped overnight and our lawn was dusted with frost when I woke. Though past 7 a.m., it was still dark out and the house was silent. Something had disturbed me. Fearing that Natalia had absconded, I crept across the gallery and listened outside her bedroom door. From inside I could hear her gentle murmuring in her sleep.

I checked on the children, then returned to my bedroom. It was then that I noticed the light on my mobile phone, which was sitting on the dresser. I had missed a call from Jim Hendry.

'Wakey, wakey,' he said on answering his phone when I called him back.

'I'm meant to be off work, you know,' I said.

'Not so as anyone would notice,' he retorted.

'What's up?' I asked.

'Karl Moore is – since last night,' he said. 'He's ready to talk.'

'Any chance I can speak to him?' I asked.

'Not a hope,' Hendry said. 'Though we're all in Ward Two, Room C, in Altnagelvin, if you fancy dropping by for a wee visit.'

*   *   *

After the chill of the morning, the heat in the hospital was oppressive. The ward was loud with the clatter of plates and the activity of the nurses. In Karl Moore's room, two PSNI officers stood with a young female duty solicitor. I knocked on the door and Jim Hendry turned and beckoned me in. He introduced me to the others in the room and explained to the solicitor, Alex Kerlin, that I was present as part of a cross-border investigation into a crime in which we believed Moore was involved. One of the uniformed PSNI men went outside and took up position in front of the now closed door, to stop anyone from coming in and interrupting the interview.

Karl Moore lay back on his bed. His skin was the same green as his hospital gown and his dull eyes were sunken in their sockets.

Hendry had set up a tape recorder beside the bed and, having turned it on, introduced himself, the other officer in the room, Ms Kerlin and myself. He then advised Karl Moore of his rights. Moore waved his hand as a sign that he understood and accepted the advice given, a gesture that Hendry described.

'You understand why you are being questioned?' Hendry said.

Moore nodded his head.

'You are aware that your wife, Janet Moore, is dead?'

Again Moore nodded. He attempted to speak, but seemed to have difficulty in doing so and swallowed hard instead. Hendry added that Moore had nodded in response to the question.

'Were you responsible for your wife's death, Mr Moore?' Hendry asked.

The hospital ward seemed to have gone silent as Moore gathered his strength to speak.

He smacked his lips drily several times, then nodded. 'Yes,' he said, finally.

The noise began again and somewhere outside the room someone dropped a pan, the clatter echoing up the corridor.

'Can you repeat that, Mr Moore?' Hendry asked.

'My client has answered the question, Inspector,' Kerlin protested. 'Can we move on?'

'I just want to verify beyond all doubt that Mr Moore is accepting full responsibility for the killing of his wife.'

'My client isn't contesting that fact. Can we move on, please?' she insisted.

'Perhaps you can describe to us the events that led to your wife's death, Mr Moore. In your own words,' Hendry suggested.

What followed was one of the most painful things I have witnessed in my time as a Garda officer. Karl Moore did not attempt to hide his guilt, or transfer responsibility to anyone else. He struggled to speak and frequently whatever he was attempting to piece together seemed to die in his throat. His eyes glistened as he spoke. At points his hands gripped at the bedclothes, though without strength.

'I asked her if she was having an affair,' he said. 'She was. She told me she was. I couldn't . . . I couldn't stop. She was shouting at me about him. About Bradley.' He stopped and swallowed hard. Alex Kerlin handed him a plastic tumbler of water from his bedside cabinet and he sipped from it. In the close heat of the room, the foulness of his breath seemed to grow increasingly strong.

'I told her to stop. I . . . my hands were on her. I couldn't stop. I . . . I didn't stop. I didn't stop.' His eyes welled up and his mouth tightened as he attempted to hold back his tears.

'How did you know she was having an affair?' Hendry spoke softly. Karl Moore was admitting everything; there was no need for forcefulness.

'She mentioned "Leon" a lot. Kept getting calls from him. Then someone confirmed it.'

'Harry Patterson?' I asked, earning glances from those in the room to whom this information came as a surprise.

Moore nodded. 'He told me at the football . . . "Watch your wife," he said. "She's making a fool of you . . . Her and Leon Bradley." She'd got him a ticket for something, said it was for me.'

I nodded. Patterson's actions were inhuman and unprofessional at best, and quite possibly criminal. Whether he had foreseen the eventual outcome was irrelevant. Moore had, however, moved on to a topic in which I was even more interested.

'I asked her when I got home and she denied it . . . So I wanted to ask Bradley. I sent him a message from Janet's phone . . . the next day, asking to meet, so he'd think it was her . . . I hid her phone all day . . . so he wouldn't call her and find out it wasn't.'

'What happened when you met Leon Bradley?' Hendry asked, pre-empting a further interruption from me. I nodded my head to let him know I appreciated the question.

Moore's eyes rolled backwards and closed, and for a moment I thought he had passed out. Then he swallowed drily and exhaled noisily. 'He denied it. Said they were doing some story on pollution. I said I didn't believe him . . . Told him I knew he'd been at that goldmine with her when it opened. He said they'd thought, the mine was to blame, that's why they'd been there . . . Said they'd been wrong. They were working together, he said. That was all.'

He coughed, the sound rattling in his throat. Taking a sip of water, he continued, 'When Janet came back from Belfast I told her I'd seen him. She went mad . . . Then she admitted it. She said I was pathetic . . . I wasn't worth lying to. She was proud of it . . . She didn't even think I was worth a lie. Not even worth a lie.' He continued to mutter to himself, his face turned slightly from us, his gaze starting to lose focus. He was regressing to somewhere inside his own mind, reflecting on some unspoken thought or memory.

I couldn't let Leon drop. 'If he denied it, why did you kill him?' I asked.

He looked at me in bewilderment. He glanced at each of the people assembled in his room as if noticing their presence for the first time.

'I didn't kill him,' he stated, simply.

I found it hard not to believe him. Having already confessed to killing his wife, there was little to be gained by his denying killing Leon.

'He was found the day after you met him in the River Carrowcreel. Someone shot him,' I said.

Alex Kerlin stood up from her seat. 'This is the first I've heard of this.'

Hendry raised his hand in a placatory fashion. 'When I introduced Inspector Devlin I explained that he was investigating a cross-border element to this. Janet Moore's lover was also found dead last weekend. By his own admission, your client arranged a meeting with him. The last person to see someone alive is generally the person who killed them.'

'Trite, Inspector Hendry,' Kerlin retorted with more ire than I'd expected from her. 'But Mr Moore hasn't admitted to being the last person to see this Leon Bradley alive. He simply said he had met him.'

Moore himself looked from one to the other, attempting to follow the conversation, his mouth forming the words of each speaker like an echo.

'He was going somewhere after I met him,' he said to Kerlin, who indicated that he should address his comments to Hendry and myself. 'He was going somewhere else . . . He said he knew where the pollution was coming from. He was angry that I wasn't Janet. He said he'd broken the story himself.'

'Where was he going?' I asked.

Moore shook his head and swallowed. Kerlin held the tumbler of water to his lips and he drank again.

'You're shaking your head,' Hendry said for the tape. 'Does that mean you don't know where he was going?'

'He didn't say,' Moore said.

Hendry turned to me to see whether I had any further questions, but there seemed to be nothing further to ask. I was more frustrated than ever. Instead of getting a solution to Leon's killing, I had been led a step further, only to hit a brick wall. Then Moore seemed to remember something.

'His camera,' he suggested, timidly. 'His camera will show you where he went.'

'What camera?' I asked, my heart rate rising.

'He had a camera. He was going to take photographs of where the pollution was, he said.'

'You're sure of this?'

Moore nodded his head slightly. 'He showed me his camera, to prove he'd come to meet Janet for work.'

I tapped Hendry on the shoulder and let him know that I was going out on to the ward. I took out my mobile and was about to call Helen Gorman when one of the nurses stopped and, hands on hips, nodded towards a sign on the wall stating that the use of mobiles was not permitted. In the end, half gratefully, I went downstairs and, standing outside the main door, lit a smoke. After a few attempts I managed to get a call through to Gorman. She was more than a little reluctant to speak to me.

'I'm not looking for a favour,' I explained.

'They found pollution,' she said, perhaps assuming that that was the purpose of the call. 'You were right. They found pollution in the water in his lungs. High levels.'

'That's good to know,' I said. 'Thanks.'

'I had to tell the Super, sir. I'm sorry. It's my job,' she stated frankly.

I was disarmed by her honesty, though I knew Caroline Williams would have been more circumspect.

'I know. That's fine; I shouldn't have put you on the spot. I just want to know something. When Leon Bradley was found, was a camera recovered?'

She paused for a second, either trying to recollect the

184

details of the find, or trying to gauge whether my request was one that could land her in trouble. Finally she answered: 'No, I don't think so. Why?'

'Just wondering,' I said. I wasn't surprised. If Leon had gone into the water upriver, his camera would have sunk, possibly destroying any evidence it might contain.

There seemed little point in going out to the Carrowcreel myself at this time of day. The light would already be dimming, particularly under the tree canopy. The best thing to do would be to go to Patterson first thing the following morning and demand a search of the river. After what Moore had told us, he was in no position to refuse.

I called Gilmore while I was still outside to see whether he'd had any luck in picking up Pol Strandmann. I was not particularly surprised to learn that his house in Ballymagorry had been empty.

'We'll keep an eye out for him,' Gilmore said.

'He'll be doing the market on Sunday,' I said.

'So you told us. We're sending a team down. You're welcome to come along,' he added. 'After all, you know what he looks like.'

'What about Natalia?' I asked. 'Have you a place arranged for her?'

He paused and I guessed where this was going. 'I was hoping you could keep her for another day or two. The Women's Centre is looking for somewhere, but the language issue is causing problems. And we can't really put her in a hotel on her own. Some of the places we've tried are reluctant to take in a foreigner.'

'What about Social Services?'

'They're not being the most helpful. We're really stuck.'

'I'll need to check with my wife,' I said finally. 'She's the one looking after her today.'

'It's only for another day or two,' he said, as if I had already agreed. 'We'll speak before Sunday about going for Strandmann.'

I hung up and called Debbie to explain the situation. She reacted as I had feared, though I could tell that Shane and Penny must have been in earshot, for she moderated her language accordingly.

'I told you I wanted her out, Ben,' she hissed. 'Look, I feel sorry for her, but I don't want her here.'

'Fine,' I said, disingenuously. 'You tell her she can't stay.'

'Don't be such a hateful—' she said, cutting herself short before she said something that Shane would no doubt repeat in front of his grandparents for the next month.

'I'm sorry, Debs. Honestly. I feel responsible. I can't – I can't just abandon her. I can't let her down.'

'No,' Debbie said, the anger gone from her voice. 'But you don't think twice about letting me down instead.'

I knew, though, that she would allow Natalia to stay. I gave her Karol Walshyk's number in case she needed help in communicating with Natalia, and promised her I'd be home when I was finished with Moore.

Hendry and I sat in the café after the interview with Moore was completed. The other officers had remained outside Moore's room, for he was now under arrest for the murder of his wife. Alex Kerlin, meanwhile, had been called to attend a client in the local police station and had turned down Jim's offer of a cup of tea and a sandwich.

'Shame,' Hendry commented as he watched her leave the hospital.

'Bit of a soft spot for Ms Kerlin, Jim?'

'Nice girl,' he said in response. 'Not often you meet them in our line, eh?'

I reflected that, despite having worked with Hendry on and off for several years now, I didn't know much about his home life. I knew he had been married at one stage, though he never spoke of his wife.

'Are you on the look-out, then?' I asked.

'Always be on the look-out,' he retorted, playing with the tip of his moustache. 'Otherwise you'll know you've died.'

We drank our tea and I attempted to read the headlines of the newspaper sitting in front of a man at the table beside us.

'The missus is remarrying,' Hendry said, apropos of nothing. 'Next week. The kids told me. They're calling him Daddy, apparently.'

'I . . . I'm sorry, Jim. I didn't know.'

'No need to apologize; it's not you she's marrying.'

'I'm only—' I began to explain.

'I know what you meant,' he said, chuckling lightly.

'How many kids have you?' I asked.

'Two girls. We had a boy, but he didn't make it.'

I stopped myself from saying sorry a second time.

'You've one of each, isn't that right?' he continued.

I nodded. 'The gentleman's family.'

'I'd have liked a boy. What do they say? "Girls do your head in, boys do your house in." Is that it?'

'Something like that,' I replied.

'They live in Manchester now. I don't really see them much. Speak to the girls every night. It's not the same though, is it? You miss stuff.'

'Are you going over – for the wedding, I mean?' I asked.

'Are you fucking mad?' he asked, looking at me incredulously. 'I'm not allowed within two hundred yards of her since the restraining order.' He winked and smiled so I was unable tell if he was joking.

By the time I got home, Debbie and Natalia had made dinner. Natalia was dressed in some of Debbie's clothes. She looked younger than she had the night before. She had applied light cosmetics and had washed and styled her hair. She and Debbie moved wordlessly around one another in the kitchen, handling pots and pans, smiling politely when one got in the path of the other.

'Things seem to be going well,' I said, gesturing towards Natalia, who was laying the table.

'As if I have a choice,' Debbie replied, though I could tell from her tone that she had reached some sort of grudging acceptance for now.

Penny and Shane were sitting in the living room on the floor, playing with a teaset. Penny had laid cups and saucers for several of her dolls, while Shane was chewing on a plastic apple and banging the floor with a small plastic fork. They looked up and smiled when they saw me in the doorway, then went back to their play. I walked over and kissed both on the head, smelt the scent of their shampoo.

The doorbell rang and I was a little surprised to see Karol Walshyk standing outside, dressed in his neatest suit, a bottle of wine in his hand.

'I called him earlier today to tell him how Natalia was doing,' Debbie explained, as he and Natalia spoke in the kitchen. 'I suggested he come for dinner. I thought it might be nice for her to have someone to speak with.'

'You're the best, Debs,' I said.

We shared a meal of chicken and roast potatoes. Natalia and Karol spoke frequently in Chechen, which Karol would then translate for us. We avoided speaking of Natalia's husband, or her feelings about Ireland. Debbie asked if Natalia had any children, which Karol answered without asking her, presumably to avoid the topic of the miscarriage which had first brought her to his attention. Still, I suspected that she had understood the timbre of the question, for she became suddenly subdued and spoke little, even with Karol, for the remainder of the night.

'He likes her,' Debbie said, after Karol had left and Natalia had gone to bed. 'He feels guilty about it, but he likes her a lot.'

'Are you sure it isn't just the romantic in you, looking to match-make?' I said.

'No. He really likes her. He cares for her. You can tell in the way he speaks to her. The way he didn't translate that bloody stupid question I asked about children. He wants to protect her.'

'She's just lost her husband,' I pointed out.

'I didn't say he was going to do anything about it. Or her either. But I think it's mutual. They're a nice pair.'

'Would you?' I asked.

'Would I what?'

'Date again? Remarry? If something happened to me?'

'Now, who would I have to fight with then?' she said. Then after a pause she asked, 'What about you? Bearing in mind what I've put up with this week. Would you marry again?'

I thought again of Karl Moore. 'I don't think I could live if anything happened to you, Debs.'

'That's the right answer,' she said, her hand flat against my cheek, her smile reaching her eyes.

Chapter Twenty

Saturday, 21 October

It took several attempts before I got the car started the following morning, and even at that it was so cold my breath froze on the interior of the windscreen within seconds of my clearing it.

I sat at my desk, drinking a mug of coffee, still wearing my coat as I waited for the station's heating system to rattle itself into life. Patterson arrived just after eight, while the sky was still lightening. He looked surprised to see me.

'You're at least two days early,' he said, making his way into his office. I followed him, mug in hand.

'My suspension ends today, Harry,' I said. 'What have you got on Leon Bradley?'

'Are you stupid, Devlin?' he said. 'Get out of here.'

'Karl Moore woke yesterday,' I said, sitting down in front of his desk.

'Tell someone who gives a fuck,' Patterson blustered, though without his usual conviction.

'The press would have a field day with it, Harry. One of their own killed by a jealous husband, fired up by a cop protecting an American investor the reporter was investigating. It would make a great conspiracy theory.'

'That's all it is – a theory.'

'That's all it has to be. It won't matter.'

'What's your problem, Devlin?' he said, sitting heavily in his seat. 'Still pissed off that I got this job instead of you?'

'I just want to do *my* job without being blocked at every step. And today, I want a search party out at the Carrowcreel, looking for Leon Bradley's camera. He went out there chasing this pollution angle.'

'That nonsense again?'

'I know the autopsy showed up pollution in the water in Leon's lungs, Harry,' I said.

'Of course you do. Suspension has meant fuck-all to you; you may as well have been at work anyway,' he snorted.

'I know I've ballsed up on this, Harry. But it's starting to fall into place now. Bradley thought he knew where the pollution was coming from. And I doubt it was from Orcas.'

This piece of information had the effect I had hoped. Anything that vindicated Orcas and Weston would appeal to Patterson.

'Go on,' he said, leaning back in his chair.

'I think he saw or found something up there; something he shouldn't have. I believe he went up there to take photographs of the pollution's source. If we can find the camera, we might find out who's poisoning the river.'

'The camera might have nothing on it. What if he died before he took any shots?'

'Then at least we might know where he was killed.'

Patterson rubbed his jawline with his knuckles. Finally he picked up the receiver of the phone on his desk and dialled.

'Burgess? Patterson here. Get on the blower and round up as many as you can for a search of the Carrowcreel. They're to meet at the campsite within the hour ... Yes, overtime payable. Ben Devlin will be leading the search ... Well he's back now, if that's OK with you, *Sergeant*?'

He slammed the phone down and stared at me across the desk. 'Don't fuck it up this time.'

An hour later a group of us had gathered at the edge of the Carrowcreel. Ten Gardai had turned up. Most had been foresighted enough to wear waterproof boots. In addition, a dozen of the gold prospectors had agreed to help, among them Ted Coyle and a number of Leon's friends, including the older man, Peter.

We spread across the river, walking side by side upstream, each of us carrying a stick with which to test for unexpected dips in the riverbed. The Gaida officers led from the centre of the river; the prospectors stuck mainly to the edges. On the banks, the search was repeated; here the sticks were being used to poke into the longer grass and bushes.

As we moved slowly upstream from the point where Leon's body had been found, Ted Coyle approached me and took the spot to my left. He still bore the fading bruises from his attack.

'I thought you'd have had your fill,' I said.

He laughed hollowly. 'I'll stick it out.'

'I take it no one else has struck it lucky,' I said.

He shook his head. 'Nah. A couple of people thought they'd found stuff. Mostly fools' gold. Iron sulphide.'

'So you're still the only jackpot winner.'

He snorted. 'Yeah,' he replied, after a pause. 'Look at that.'

I followed the direction of his upraised finger towards a pool to the side of the river. Trapped between two rocks, a dead salmon floated, its scales shimmering green in the autumn sunlight.

'They're everywhere,' he said. 'Every day now, I see one or two dead fish floating downstream.'

'There's pollution in the water,' I said. 'You were right. It's being investigated.'

'That's how Leon and I met,' he said.

'I know. You told me at the funeral,' I reminded him.

He nodded absent-mindedly. 'That's right.'

We trudged upriver in silence. Some of the prospectors dipped their hands into the water at various points and lifted out stones or silt from the riverbed.

'Where did you find your nugget?' I asked, for want of anything else to say.

'Upriver,' Coyle replied quickly.

'Further up than this?'

He squinted into the middle distance, then turned and glanced behind us. 'I can't recall,' he said.

'It must have been quite a day,' I said.

'It *was*,' he replied.

The answer sounded unnecessarily forced. 'How did it feel,' I asked, 'striking gold?'

'Oh, it was incredible,' he replied. 'Proud as Punch.'

I noticed that he wore a wedding ring. 'Have you family? What do they think of it?'

'They ah . . . they're very pleased,' he said.

'I thought you'd have gone back to your wife after the attack.'

'No,' he replied slowly. 'No. I thought I'd wait it out.'

'What about your kids? Don't you miss them?'

'Of course,' he said earnestly. 'I'm here for them. If I can find gold, it'll justify everything.'

'You seem to have done pretty well already, haven't you?' I said.

He glanced at me sideways, then flicked his gaze at the others around us. Most were either engaged in conversation with their nearest neighbour, or staring intently at the water.

'I have,' he said. 'That's right.' He ran his hand through his hair.

I stopped walking and looked at him directly for the first time. He held my stare for a second at most, then glanced down at the river.

'Where does your family live?' I asked, moving forward again.

'Newry,' he said. 'Just outside of Newry.'

'What brought you this far north?'

'I heard about the mine. I just had a feeling I'd discover something if I came here. I always wanted to, you know. Be at one with nature. Make a fortune with my bare hands.'

'What did you do? Before you came here?'

'Should I call my lawyer?' Coyle said, laughing forcedly.

'Do you think you'll need one?'

'I was an accountant,' he said, pushing his glasses up his nose with a single pudgy finger.

'Does your boss not mind you taking so much time off work?'

'No, they . . . they were OK about it.'

I began to see where this was going: a middle-aged man, leaving his job and family to commune with nature.

'What happened? Did they lay you off?'

He looked at me and laughed again, nervously.

'Why would you think that?' he asked, his eyes shifting quickly away from me.

'I don't know. Maybe I'm wrong, but I don't think so,' I said. 'It doesn't matter to me. There's nothing illegal in it.'

We walked in silence for another few moments.

'Divorce first,' he said finally. '*Then* I packed the job in.'

'What happened?' I asked. I suspected he wanted to talk. Maybe I was just the first person to ask.

'We just seemed to drift. Neither of us noticed at the time. Then our youngest went to university and we were left in this big house by ourselves. We thought it would be great – get to know one another again. Instead we found that we'd both changed into people that the other one didn't really like.'

'I'm sorry to hear that,' I said.

Having started to speak, Coyle clearly wanted to continue.

'I gave her the house and I bought a camper van. You've a lot of time to think at night, when you're on your own. You know – I found out she was right. I had become some-one *I* didn't even like. I was disappointed in myself. I'd never had any great adventures. Then I heard about the goldmine here. Something told me I had to come here. To find my fortune.'

'And you did,' I said. 'You were vindicated.'

A redness crept up his neck into his face.

'Mr Coyle?' I said.

He looked across at the people to my right, then shook his head so slightly, I was not entirely sure I had seen the gesture.

'What? But I saw the picture?'

He nodded. 'I bought it online,' he said, without looking at me.

'Why?'

He raised his head. 'How much of a loser would you want to appear to your kids? I'm fifty years of age and I'm driving round Ireland in a fucking camper van. How the fuck are my kids meant to be proud of their father? *I'm* not even proud of me.'

'What made you do it?' I stopped walking, wanting to give Coyle my full attention. The other searchers beside us continued their slow movement upriver. Coyle stopped too, though while we spoke he scanned the trees behind me, as if afraid to look me in the eye.

'One of the papers wanted to interview me. "The nutcase camped out by the river looking for gold." I knew they'd take the piss, whether I agreed to an interview or not. So I figured, what if I told them I'd found something? They couldn't take the piss then, could they? So I got a nugget online.'

'How much?'

He muttered a figure in the hundreds of euros. The financial price was irrelevant anyway – the stunt had cost Coyle much more in terms of the dent to his self-esteem.

'How did your kids react?' I asked.

'They thought it was great,' he smiled. 'They thought I was a hero.'

'A father is always a hero to his kids,' I said.

'Your kids must be young,' he said, squinting at me through his glasses.

'That's right,' I agreed.

'You're a hero when they're young,' he said. 'As they get older, they'll start judging you. How long did you spend in work? Why did you put your job before us? Why did you teach us not to lie when you lie all the time?'

'They come through it though,' I reasoned.

'We make mistakes,' Coyle said.

'I'm sure your kids would be proud of you no matter what you did.'

He smiled at me sheepishly. 'Don't tell anyone, will you?'

I nodded. 'Not a word. Though perhaps someone should let the gold rushers down there know that they're on a high road to nowhere. What if there is no gold to find?'

'Then Mr Weston in there is going to be the only one to make any money out of this place,' Coyle said, nodding towards Orcas, which had now appeared to our left.

We had travelled two miles or so upstream and people were starting to get bored. I noticed several of the searchers on the bank swinging their sticks from side to side through the long grass without actually looking at the ground. It seemed like a good time to stop for a break and something to eat.

I sent one of the uniforms back downstream with orders to drive out to the nearest chip shop and stock up on burgers and fish suppers. The rest of us climbed up on to the bank and rested. Someone broke out cigarettes and lighters were passed around.

The river ran slowly, the water beer-brown where it poured over rocks. The trees around us were losing their foliage. The autumn sun was still fairly high in the sky, but its heat had weakened considerably. Still, its rays caught the smoke of our cigarettes, creating a blue haze above where we sat.

After we had eaten and gathered up our scraps, we began making our way upstream again. About a mile up from Orcas, when the afternoon sun was dropping fast and the sky was cloudless but for the ragged scar of an aircraft's vapour trail, we finally found what we were looking for.

About twenty yards from the river, on the left bank, discarded in the middle of a forsythia bush, lay a digital camera. The screen on the back had cracked, and when I tried to switch it on nothing happened. Still, I was hopeful that some of the technical staff in Letterkenny would be able to recover something from the camera's memory.

We asked the prospectors to take a break while the Gardai began a fingertip search of the immediate area. Thirty yards upstream we found traces of blood on the stones lying on the higher parts of the bank. We had, at least, discovered where Leon Bradley was shot and, as the camera was discarded thirty yards downstream, it was safe to assume that he had been chased from that direction.

It would be too late at this stage to get a forensics team out to examine the site before dusk settled. Two of the men headed back downstream to bring up a roll of tarpaulin and some crime-scene tape to shelter the area, in case rain should further damage a crime scene left undiscovered for the guts of a week.

First thing in the morning, the SOCO team would need to get up here. And, I remembered, I was also supposed to be accompanying Gilmore on the stakeout at the market outside Derry.

When I got back home I phoned Patterson. One of the uniforms who lived near Letterkenny had taken the camera to the technical specialist to see what, if anything, could be retrieved. Patterson agreed to dispatch a team to examine the site of Leon's murder first thing in the morning. I explained that I had a lead to follow over the border and asked him to assign someone to take responsibility for the integrity of the site.

I had a shower to warm myself up, and ate dinner with Debbie and the children. Karol Walshyk had taken Natalia out for a few hours to Derry, where a shop specializing in Polish and eastern European goods had opened.

As we ate I reflected on my conversation with Ted Coyle. Shane was balancing a lump of mashed potato on the spoon he held clamped in his fist. Penny held a fork in her left hand and lifted the food from her plate with her right hand. As Shane attempted to manoeuvre the spoon to his mouth, the food fell off and splattered on the table. He grinned with pleasure and rubbed his hands through the potato, while Penny giggled at the mess.

Afterwards we washed Frank, our basset hound. As I towelled the dome of his head dry, the wattles of skin at his throat shook, causing the long laces of saliva hanging from his mouth to fleck the window above the sink. 'Dirty Frank,' said Shane, pointing to the spatter marks.

They were the most normal few moments I had spent in the past weeks and, happy as I was to help Natalia, I was glad to have my home back to just my family and me for a while.

Chapter Twenty-one

Sunday, 22 October

Gilmore called me at 8.30 the following morning, just as I was making my way home from early Mass with Natalia. She had spoken little, though I had attempted to explain to her that I was going that morning to search for Pol Strandmann. I had pointed on my own scalp to where his scar ran. She had nodded and smiled gently.

Five giant metal sculptures of Irish dancers and musicians dominate the border crossing between Strabane and Lifford, and it was beneath these that I met Gilmore. Two carloads of officers were to make their way to the market. A number of them were Excise and Duty officers, looking for illegal cigarettes and pirate DVDs, the sale of which was common at such markets and car-boot sales. We were piggy-backing on their team, ostensibly providing support, but also keeping an eye out for Strandmann.

We arrived at the market shortly before eleven. A queue of cars waited to make its way on to the football pitches where the market was held. Several hundred cars were already parked there and we could see a large number of stalls set up, many pitched beside white transit vans. Already crowds of people were shuffling their way between the stalls. To the rear of the market we could see the tarmac strip of the local airport runway, along which a light aircraft was taxiing before rising unsteadily into the sky.

One of the lead Excise officers stopped at the small shed at the entrance to the market where each shopper had to pay an entrance fee. He asked to speak to the organizer and we waited for someone to fetch the man.

Owen Corrigan, a small, stout man with greying hair, arrived within a few minutes. Over his suit he wore a fluorescent vest.

He read through the warrant with which he was presented, before protesting that all the stalls in the market were completely above board, and that, for his part, he had done all he could to ensure that no illegal activity was taking place in the market. He pointed to a tattered notice pinned to the side of the hut, warning traders that the sale of counterfeit goods would be punished by expulsion from the market.

The lead officer, whose name Gilmore had told me but which I had quickly forgotten, gave us a nod, and we made our way through the gate into the market. A few hundred stalls were set up, and already a queue had formed at the first van to our left, which was selling burgers. The smell of frying onions so early in the morning made my stomach churn.

The next few stalls were selling clothes, some second-hand, some factory seconds by the looks of them. One stall had a pasting table piled high with pairs of jeans. A crowd of women pushed and jostled for position, tugging the jeans off the table, examining the sizes. I could discern amongst them several I took to be east Europeans.

We made our way down the first row. Near the bottom, two young fellas had set up a card table on which they had laid thirty or forty bundles of counterfeit DVDs. On the ground beside them was a travel bag, piled high with more. By the time they noticed us coming towards them, two Customs officers were already behind them, cordoning them in against their own table.

Gilmore nodded for me to keep moving on round the market, looking out for Strandmann. Some of the sellers seemed to peg us as policemen, for I noticed some of them busily removing things from their tables as we approached, then trying too hard to look casual.

It was at the final row of stalls that I finally spotted Strandmann. A large white van had been parked in the bottom corner, catching prospective buyers coming from either direction. Strandmann was standing inside the back of the van. Around him was piled roll after roll of toilet paper, yet I could see him handing people long packages wrapped in blue plastic bags.

'Is that him?' Gilmore asked. He had sidled up to me and was standing, hands in pockets, pretending to examine the porcelain dogs on the table in front of us.

I nodded my head.

'Selling shit-roll? Hardly a criminal mastermind.'

'I never said he was,' I retorted. 'And he's selling more than toilet paper.'

Gilmore squinted in his direction. 'Looks like fags,' he observed. 'At least it gives us another reason to lift him.'

He took out his mobile and phoned through to his colleagues, instructing them to approach Strandmann's van from the left, whilst we would approach head-on.

'He knows me,' I said. 'We'd be better coming from the side.'

Gilmore waved away my concern as he continued to speak into his phone. Then he began to make his way towards the van, and I had little choice but to follow.

As it transpired, Strandmann made the other two first. When we were about forty yards from him, I noticed him looking up to his left, looking away and then doing a quick double-take. It was clear that he knew they were cops.

Then he looked straight ahead and caught my eye. For a split second I thought he was going to smile, almost as if he couldn't quite place me. Then he dropped the parcel in his hand and dashed around the side of the van.

By this stage the other two cops were almost on him. Cursing to himself, Gilmore set off in pursuit. I ran after them as best I could. Strandmann's van was parked against a barbed-wire fence that separated the market from the airport. Strandmann had climbed on to the bonnet of his own van to clear the fence, and Gilmore was struggling over it by the time I reached him. Dropping over to the other side, he set off at a trot in the direction his colleagues and Strandmann had taken.

I started to climb on to the bonnet with the intention of scaling the fence but decided I was so far behind it would be a waste of time. Getting back down, I noticed a logo on the driver's door. The image was of a freight lorry, and underneath was the name: V M Haulage.

As I came around the back of the van, the man from the next stall was reaching into the back of Strandmann's van.

'What the fuck are you at?' I demanded.

The man jumped back, clutching five cartons of cigarettes to his chest.

'I . . . I thought youse had all gone, Officer. I was going to hold these for him – make sure no one stole them or anything.'

I held my hands out, but the man was reluctant to surrender his find. He licked his lips nervously as his eyes darted. I followed his gaze into the back of the van and saw another bundle of cartons stacked behind the toilet rolls. The man had clearly been planning on stocking up for a while, during Strandmann's forced absence.

'If you want him, there's only one place for him to go,' the man said, slyly, adjusting the cartons in his arms into a more comfortable position but not letting go of them.

'I'm all ears,' I said.

'Drive back out and head towards Deny. About half a mile up the road, you'll see a turning on your left; a wee gate thing. He'll have to come up there. All the rest's fenced off by the airport,' he said. Then he added, 'You'll need to be quick.'

'Leave at least one, if you don't want me coming after you,' I said. We would need some evidence that Strandmann was selling illegal cigarettes. But I doubted that either the cigarettes or the man to whom I was speaking would be there on my return.

I jogged back towards the entrance, passing one of the Excise officers.

'There's a guy in the corner with a shitload of illegal cigarettes,' I said. Then, remembering I hadn't brought my own car, I turned and went back to him. 'I need your keys,' I said. 'Pursuit of a rapist.'

The officer fumbled in his pocket for his keys then tossed them to me. Within a minute I was driving out of the market. I followed the cigarette man's instructions and, just as he'd said, about half a mile up the road I spotted the gateway. I pulled in and parked a little past the opening.

I sat in the car, adjusting the rear-view mirror so I could keep an eye on the gateway. Sure enough, within a few minutes a figure climbed over the gate and dropped heavily to the ground. His trouser-cuffs were caked with mud. He looked down the pathway along which he had just come, then began walking towards me.

Suddenly, he began to sprint. Looking beyond him, I saw one of Gilmore's men scrambling over the top of the gate. Just when I judged Strandmann to be level with the driver's seat, I flung open the door. He thudded into it, spun sideways and fell to the ground.

He bellowed something at me as I climbed out of the car. Half sitting on his torso, I managed to hold him while we waited for Gilmore and his men to arrive. My weight being probably twice his own, he soon stopped struggling.

As Gilmore's men cuffed him and hefted him to his feet he turned to look at me. One side of his face was pocked red where the gravel had bitten into him, and his skin was still flecked with grit. He glared at me, then spat.

Instinctively, I raised my fist, but one of the PSNI men pulled him roughly away from me while the other placed a warning hand on my arm.

He was taken to Limavady PSNI station and booked. While he was being processed, Gilmore and I returned to the market and searched his van. The cigarette man had left three cartons, as well as two boxes of loose tobacco, a pile of pirated pornographic DVDs and several bags of hash. Opportunistic grabbing of ciggies was one thing; getting caught with someone else's drugs was clearly a step too far for him.

I searched my own pockets for my cigarettes and realized that I must have dropped them along the roadway when I had been struggling to keep Strandmann down.

'What's wrong?' Gilmore asked, having heard me swear.

'I've lost my cigarettes,' I said, patting my pockets for the umpteenth time, with no success.

Gilmore, clearly elated with the success of the operation, tossed me one of the cartons from Strandmann's van.

'Consider it a bonus for a job well done,' he said.

'We haven't even questioned him yet,' I said. 'He could give you nothing.'

'He'll talk,' he replied. 'They always do. Fear of deportation. They have it cushy here and they know it. That fucker'll be singing by teatime.'

'V M Haulage,' I said out loud, as I tore open the cigarette carton. 'Jesus Christ.'

'What now? Lost your fucking lighter too?'

'No. I've just realized something,' I said.

Chapter Twenty-two

Sunday, 22 October

I phoned An Garda Research Unit and placed a request for details on V M Haulage. The woman who answered promised to get back to me as soon as possible. Then I called Letterkenny station to see if our techies had had any luck with Leon's camera. They were, I was told, off for the weekend and would be available on Monday morning, if I wished to call back.

Finally, Gilmore and I made our way to Limavady, where Strandmann was being held pending interview.

He was slouched in the chair when we came into the interview room, his legs stretched under the table at which he sat, his blue jeans tight against his thin calves.

On the table was a polystyrene cup of watery tea and he played with a packet of cigarettes as he waited, rotating the pack between his finger and thumb. Every so often he would lean back to look at the clock on the wall behind him, as if he were waiting for someone to come. If so, he was to be disappointed, for despite his making a phone call, no one arrived to represent him.

Finally the duty solicitor was called, a tall, uninterested-looking young fella, who spent most of the interview doodling on a page in front of him.

The Customs and Excise officers started the interview. They cautioned Strandmann, putting to him that he had been seen illegally selling cigarettes from the back of his lorry. In addition, counterfeit DVDs had been discovered. Could he explain their presence?

Strandmann looked at them, his legs crossed at the ankles. He sucked between his teeth and twisted his head until the bones cracked. But he did not talk.

Next Gilmore spoke to him. Drugs had been found amongst his possessions. Could he explain that?

Again, Strandmann said nothing. Even his solicitor looked at him askance and stifled a yawn with the back of his hand. 'Do you speak English?' the young man asked. Strandmann looked at him for a second, then returned his gaze to the cigarette box in front of him.

'You've been hung out to dry,' Gilmore said finally. 'I know you've been told to say nothing if you get lifted, but you've been landed in it, pal. You called your boss, I'm guessing. They didn't even send you legal representation – you're on your own, pal.'

Strandmann stared at him, one eyebrow slightly raised.

'Of course,' continued Gilmore, 'all this stuff today is minor in comparison with rape.'

Strandmann smiled, a tight feral twist of his mouth that extended no further than his lips.

'You think that's funny, pal? We have your victim. An illegal immigrant you helped bring into the country, whom you raped and then forced into prostitution. We have her, pal. Which means we have you, too.'

The duty solicitor had perked up at finding himself involved with a case more serious than a driving offence. Strandmann, for his part, still did not speak, but nor was he smiling any more.

'You're screwed, *pal*,' Gilmore said, gathering up the contents of the folder in front of him, as if to leave. It was a trick it seemed Strandmann's solicitor hadn't seen before, for he looked up at Gilmore open-mouthed, wondering why it was all over so quickly.

'*Pol*,' Strandmann corrected.

Gilmore slowly sat again and opened the folder.

'Pol,' he agreed.

Over the course of the next hour or so, Strandmann admitted to selling smuggled cigarettes and, after some denial, the counterfeit DVDs. He denied any knowledge of Natalia or the other Chechen illegals. He did not know, and had never heard of, anyone fitting the description of the pony-tailed man.

'We have a witness who can place you at the scene of various crimes,' Gilmore said. 'A woman who claims you raped her before forcing her into prostitution—'

'A hooker?' he interrupted. 'You'd trust a whore!'

'Don't get smart-arsed with me, son,' Gilmore said. 'All we need is her evidence and you're sunk. Are you going to carry the can for whoever's above you? You're a bottom-feeder, son – you didn't set up these girls. But you know who did. Time to be selfish, Pol.'

Strandmann simply smiled. If it was a show, it was good. I decided to follow a different tack.

'What is V M Haulage?' I asked. Gilmore turned and looked at me quizzically, clearly wondering where I had plucked the name from.

'Why?' Strandmann asked edgily.

'I noticed the logo on the side of your van,' I explained.

His shoulders relaxed, almost imperceptibly, but the change in body language was enough to let me know that the mention of V M Haulage had struck a chord of some sort.

'I work for them,' he said.

'Selling girls?'

'Selling toilet paper,' he retorted.

'Is that what they do? Sell toilet paper?'

He shrugged his shoulders. 'They do all kinds of stuff.'

'What exactly?' I persisted. 'You work for them – you must know what they do.'

'Stuff,' he repeated, as if it was in itself sufficient explanation. Which, in a way, it was.

'We'll need Natalia in to ID him,' Gilmore said as we stood outside the interview room. I looked into the room, where Strandmann reclined in his chair, his legs stretched under the table, while the duty solicitor seemed to be vainly attempting to engage him in conversation. 'Where did you get V M Haulage from, anyway?'

'Like I said, it was on the side of his van,' I explained. And, of course, the name had cropped up before. I suspected that Eligius had not been using V M Haulage to buy toilet paper.

Excusing myself, I went outside for a smoke and to call Karol Walshyk to tell him the PSNI would collect him and Natalia within the hour. Then I called the lady in the Research Unit with whom I had spoken earlier.

'It is Sunday, Inspector,' she replied a little irritably when I asked her had she found out anything for me about V M Haulage. 'In fact,' she continued, 'I shouldn't even be here today. I came in to catch up on stuff left over from the last week.'

I apologized and empathized with her about having to work Sundays, which seemed to mollify her.

'V M Haulage,' she said finally. 'Owned by Vincent Morrison. Started in 2005. Freight Company – specializes in cross-Europe transit of goods. Does a lot of charity deliveries. Permanent staff of five. Based in Derry.'

After she read out the address, I thanked her for her work.

'You could have Googled it,' she said. 'That's all I've done.'

Gilmore showed me to his desk, where I could access the Internet. I was able to access the information Research had given me off the home page of the VM website. Googling the name also brought up a number of articles from local papers about the aforementioned 'charity work'. Seemingly, a number of Northern Irish groups who had collected goods for under-developed eastern European countries, particularly in the wake of the Bosnian conflict, had found in V M Haulage a free method of transport for their donations. The owner, Vincent Morrison, explained that, as his drivers were often taking or collecting deliveries to or from Eastern Bloc countries, there was no reason why they couldn't do some good at the same time.

None of the articles had accompanying photos, so I did an image search to see if I recognized Morrison's face. Several images were brought up. The first few showed Morrison shaking hands with various charity representatives, or helping load boxes of goods into the back of one of his lorries. I recognized the man as Vinnie, Strandmann's companion at the market. One other photo in particular interested me. Morrison was standing with some of his team, who were preparing to drive to Chechnya on an aid-delivery mission, according to the banner on the side of the van behind them. Standing to Morrison's left, his hair tied back from his face, his weasel features accentuated by the image's lack of colour, was Pony Tail. Behind him, almost out of shot, I recognized a second face: Seamus Curran.

Gilmore was in the station canteen, sharing a story with some of his colleagues. I showed him the picture, which I had printed out.

'You're sure it's him?' Gilmore asked.

'Absolutely,' I said. 'We need to show it to Strandmann. He can't deny knowing him.'

'He's made another phone call,' Gilmore explained. 'He's trying to post bail. We need Natalia here before he gets out.'

'Has anyone gone for her?' I asked.

Gilmore nodded. 'We'll try him with this while we're waiting,' he said.

*   *   *

Strandmann looked at the picture once and tossed it back across the table at us. He pulled a face, sniffed, rolled his shoulders.

'You don't know him?' I asked.

He shook his head, refusing to speak.

'Answer the question. You don't know him?'

Strandmann shook his head again, then stopped himself. 'Never seen him.'

'That's very strange,' I said. 'You see, this man works for the same company as you. A full-time staff of five, apparently. I find it hard to believe that you don't even know his name. His name would mean nothing – nothing suspicious about knowing a colleague's name. *Not* knowing the name of someone you work with, now that *is* suspicious. That makes me think you're lying.'

'Ford,' he said. 'Barry Ford, his name is.'

'Why didn't you tell me that straight away?' I asked.

'I thought you'd use it to get him in trouble too. I know his name, is all.'

'What does he do?'

Strandmann stifled a smile. 'He's a handy-man. He does odd-jobs.'

'His address?' I asked.

'I've no idea. I work with him, that's all.'

At that, someone rapped sharply on the door. Gilmore left the room and spoke to someone, then asked me to join him outside. He led me into an adjoining room in which now stood Natalia and Karol.

Gilmore explained slowly that he wanted Natalia to look at the images of Strandmann being relayed from the room

215

next door onto a video monitor. Karol translated, pointing at the monitor as he explained what she was being asked to do.

Natalia leant close to the screen, squinting at the seated figure. Finally she said something to Karol.

'She can't make him out,' he said. 'He's too . . . indistinct. She needs to see him closer.'

'We need to set up an identity parade anyway,' Gilmore said. 'It makes no difference – we can still charge him with the ciggies and stuff, see if we can make the other charges stick later.'

Natalia seemed to follow the gist of what Gilmore had said, for she spoke forcefully to Walshyk.

'She said she only needs to see him for a second, to be sure,' he explained. 'Just for a second, she says.'

Gilmore looked at me and shrugged. He led Natalia out to the corridor and, standing at the door of the interview room, flicked up one of the slats of the blinds covering the window. We could all hear the breath catch in Natalia's throat. She turned and nodded slowly, then spoke quickly to Karol, who moved over and stood beside her, his hand on her arm.

'It's him,' he said.

Later that evening I found myself back in Seamus Curran's pub in Derry. He was standing behind the bar, listening to two musicians playing an Irish reel. I scanned the bar and noticed that many of those slapping their knees in time with the music were tourists. The locals sipped on their Guinness and waited for the noise to die down to resume their conversations.

'Mr Curran,' I called, raising my hand. 'A Coke, please.'

He brought a Coke and a glass over to me.

'The Guard. I remember your face, but not your name,' he said, clicking the top off the bottle and placing it in front of me.

'I never gave it,' I said. 'Benedict Devlin. I think we should talk.'

Curran smiled as he gestured around the crowded room. 'I'm a little busy,' he said. 'You'll have to come back.'

'You didn't tell me you were involved with V M Haulage.'

His smile faltered slightly and then was back in place.

'You never asked. So what if I am?'

'You called Hagan an arsehole the last time we spoke.'

'That opinion hasn't changed, Benedict. And you don't need to be a cop for me to confess to that.'

His use of my forename rankled.

'If you think he's such an arsehole, how come your company is doing business with his? Is it not a bit hypocritical, chanting anti-war statements from the window of a business partner's office?'

'Who told you we work with Eligius?'

'The documents Leon Bradley sent out. Funny, actually, you were the only one I discussed it with, the one who told me it would arrive the day after we spoke. Then the local postman gets robbed. Coincidence, eh?'

'And that's all it fucking is,' Curran snapped, his hair flicking into his face.

'So what's the deal with Hagan?' I asked again. 'How do you know him?'

'We met on a Peace and Reconciliation visit to Chechnya. We led a group on conflict resolution. He supports some of our charity work from time to time. A way to appease his conscience, perhaps.'

'But you have no problems with yours, I suppose.'

'None,' Curran said. 'I have to serve someone.'

He walked away from me and dealt with his customer. For the next half-hour he avoided my edge of the bar and did not look at me until I stood to leave. I placed £2 on the counter.

'For the drink,' I said.

As I drove home, I considered what he had said, if Hagan had made charity donations, V M wouldn't be invoicing the company; the work would have been done for free. But like all practised liars, Curran probably retained an element of truth in his story. I believed that he probably had met Hagan on a 'Reconciliation' tour in Chechnya. I had little doubt that V M Haulage, or someone working for them, was carrying something for Eligius to Chechnya, and on the return leg was bringing back illegal immigrants. A mercy-mission lorry would be the last place someone would check for illegals. Plus the lorry would already have any necessary paperwork to explain the cross-country journey.

Whatever they were carrying for Hagan, it was clearly illegal; otherwise, why the secrecy? Why the attack on the Strabane postman, unless the documents he was thought to be carrying were potentially damaging? All I had to do now was work out whom they were damaging to, and in what way. Then make sure that the damage was done.

Chapter Twenty-three

Monday, 23 October

That evening Natalia had seemed unusually jumpy, and even Penny and Shane managed to elicit only the briefest flicker of a smile from her as they danced wildly to a TV theme tune. I suspected that she knew she would have to give evidence against Strandmann, and that this in turn would lead to questions about her status and the work she had been engaged in before her arrest. If Strandmann could be charged with something significant – say, people-smuggling – then Natalia would be spared the trauma of having to give that evidence.

On Monday I went into the station legitimately, for the first time in a fortnight. Several officers approached me and welcomed me back. I was aware that some of the younger Guards didn't want to be seen to be too friendly, lest it affect their promotion chances. Even Helen Gorman was circumspect.

I phoned through to Letterkenny and asked to speak to the techie who had been given Leon's camera. I was forwarded to someone called Marty, a civilian IT specialist who, for the first few minutes of the conversation, explained to me the processes by which he had retrieved the photographs from the camera. I tried to sound suitably impressed.

Finally, I interrupted him: 'So, did you find any shots?'

'A load,' he said. 'He had a memory card, and images saved on the internal drive. He has over a hundred here. Which ones are you looking for?'

'Any of someone brandishing a shotgun?' I asked, half jokingly.

'None, but there's some right dirty stuff on this. Must be shots of his missus. Very artistic.'

'Were they the last shots he took?' I asked, assuming that the woman in question was Janet Moore. If the last shots he had taken had been of her, then he had not used his camera on the night of his death.

'No, the last photos are of some old bloke working in the woods.'

'What kind of work?'

'Shifting stuff,' he said quickly. 'Look, do you want me to send you these? You can look through them at your leisure.'

'Can you e-mail them to me?'

'There are too many,' he said. 'I'll save them to a Shared Documents file and you can download them from there.'

Sure enough, several minutes later, the techie sent me an e-mail with details of the file in which he had saved the images. I noticed that he signed off his message with a yellow smiley face.

I opened the file and began to scroll through the contents. Most of the pictures were of no interest. Leon and his friends. The old grey dog I'd seen out at Carrowcreel with the crusties. Images of trees, taken at artistic angles. Then I opened an image of Leon and Fearghal. They were standing side by side. Leon slouched slightly, though still a few inches taller than his brother. His arm rested across Fearghal's shoulders, his legs crossed at the ankles. He sported a half-smile. Fearghal stood erect, his hands behind his back, his body upright, though he had inclined his head just slightly so that it rested against his younger brother's.

I printed the picture off, then continued moving through the images. Janet Moore was photographed in various stages of undress, in a manner Leon had probably considered artistic: her breasts obscured by cushions, her face alive with mischief. Then there was one image of her standing naked, uncovered, her hands by her sides, her expression a little plaintive. I flicked on to the next image quickly.

It became clear that I was moving towards the most recent shots. Several images of the crusties out at the camp appeared. One of Peter, the older man, a joint hanging from his mouth. Ted Coyle, half bent over his prospecting pan, his hand raised in salute. Other campers whose faces I recognized, some posed, others caught unawares.

Finally, I saw an image that made me start. I almost missed the person in the shot, for the image was ostensibly of an area of woodland. In the background was an old barn-like structure, its corrugated-iron roofing riddled with rust-edged holes. Just emerging from the barn, though, was a man I recognized, his greying hair pulled back into a pony-tail. The next shot was a better image again. It was also the last. Pony Tail was facing the camera, his features clear, his expression one of bemusement. I suspected that he had seen Leon taking his picture.

I printed off that image too, then lifted both pictures from the printer tray.

Helen Gorman was completing an incident report on a traffic accident when I went across to her.

'I want you to gather up a team and go back out to the Carrowcreel and find that building,' I said, handing her the shot of Pony Tail.

'Why?' Gorman asked.

'Because this fucker was obviously up to something in it. Something bad enough to kill Leon Bradley to stop him revealing it. Now gather up a team, Helen.'

'Yes, sir,' she said, standing up quickly and moving off.

Vincent Morrison worked out of a unit on an industrial estate on the outskirts of Derry, near Campsie. When I arrived at his depot, two vans were parked in the garage bays. One had the engine exposed and a young man in a boiler suit was lying on the floor underneath. A girl sat at the reception desk doing a newspaper crossword.

'I'd like to see Vincent Morrison,' I said.

'Have you an appointment?' she asked, barely glancing up at me.

'No, I'm the police.'

'Not up here, you're not,' a male voice said. I looked up to see Vincent Morrison standing in the doorway of his office, leaning against the doorjamb with his arms folded. I recognized him from the photographs I had seen on the

Internet the day before. He was a slight man, small-framed and underfed. He wore a loose T-shirt which had the effect of making his arms look even more spindly than they actually were. His face was narrow, his mouth slightly pursed, his moustache thin on his upper lip. He wore glasses, behind which he blinked several times in quick succession.

'That's true, Mr Morrison,' I conceded.

'You're one of the ones that lifted my van yesterday,' he said, wagging a finger playfully in my direction.

'I was there, that's correct,' I agreed, stopping myself from asking how he knew. 'Your employee was selling all manner of things from the back of your van.'

'You give these people jobs and what happens?' he said, hands out, palms raised in a what-can-you-do? gesture.

'All the same, the man was selling illegal goods from your van, Mr Morrison. I'm sure the PSNI will want to discuss it with you at some stage. Meanwhile, I was wondering if you could help me.'

He tilted his head slightly to the side. 'If I can,' he said.

'I'm trying to locate one of your employees. Barry Ford?'

Morrison's mouth pursed a little tighter, and he shook his head.

I took out the photograph of Ford that I had printed out and handed it to Morrison. 'No one seems to remember this man,' I said. 'He works for you, apparently.'

Morrison looked at the picture, then folded it and handed it back to me.

'I know Barry. He used to work for me. Haven't seen him in a few days. What has he done?'

'I'm not sure where to start,' I said. 'I'd like his address if you have it.'

Morrison clicked his fingers in the direction of the girl still sitting behind her desk, chewing on the top of a biro as she struggled with her crossword. 'Get Barry's details, Sharon,' he said.

'Thank you,' I began, but Morrison interrupted me.

'Where was that picture taken?' he asked.

'We're looking into it now.'

Morrison nodded and moved out from his doorway. 'If that's everything? I had hoped you'd be bringing me back my van, but as you say, I need to discuss that with the PSNI.'

'There is something else,' I said. 'What business does your company have with Eligius Technology?'

'None of yours, actually,' he replied with a laugh.

'Your name came up in the investigation of a murder, sir. Invoices from you to Eligius. Your partner Seamus Curran already confirmed that you are carrying something for Senator Cathal Hagan. He tells me they met in Chechnya. Do you send lorries out there much?'

'We are a freight carrier,' he explained. 'We work with a lot of companies, some better known than others. And we go to a lot of countries.'

'What do you transport for them?' I asked.

'Whatever they pay us to transport. Now, this really *is* none of your business, Inspector. If you want to see our records, you can get a warrant and see what happens. Except, of course, your warrant will be meaningless up here.'

224

'A contract from a company the size of Eligius and you really expect me to believe that you don't know what you transport for them?'

'That's not what I said,' Morrison replied, smiling. I noticed that one of his two front teeth was slightly crooked and overlapped with its neighbour. 'I said it was none of your business. And I don't really give a shit whether you believe a word I say or not; you've no authority here. I'll give you that address, because I'm a good guy. Ask me any more questions and I'll kick your arse out of here.'

Morrison's aggressiveness only served to strengthen my determination to find out why his contract with Eligius was so important. I also had the sheet of productivity reports; they meant little to me, but I suspected that someone with a head for figures might be more successful in identifying their significance to Leon Bradley. I was reluctant to ask someone within my own station, in case word would get back to Patterson that I was investigating Hagan. There was someone else, though, who I knew would be delighted to dig for dirt on Orcas.

Ted Coyle had told me he used to be an accountant. As I drove out to the Carrowcreel, I phoned Gilmore and gave him the address Morrison had given me for Barry Ford. He lived in Derry, which was out of my jurisdiction. The PSNI, however, could legitimately go after him, armed if needs be.

I was about three miles from the turning to the Carrowcreel when I got a call from Helen Gorman. She and three other officers had trekked up the river again, she said. They had located the barn in the images we had retrieved from Bradley's camera. It was a five-minute walk to the east of where we had found the camera. It had looked deserted but as they had approached they noticed a car parked near by. Someone was inside.

I told her to wait for me and then drove back towards Orcas. It would take too long to drive to the campsite and make my way upriver. I recalled seeing the fence at Orcas near the spot where we had found Leon's camera.

I parked the car against the fence, where I estimated the spot closest to the river to be. Before locking up, I removed my gun from the floor locker between the two front seats, in case Pony Tail was armed. He'd already taken one shot at me with a sawn-ofF shotgun, and I knew a shotgun had also been used to kill Leon. Best to be sure, I told myself. I was able to haul myself up over the chain-link fence, dropped heavily on to the other side and stumbled down to the river's edge.

Within a minute or two I spotted the crime-scene tape and cut up on to the bank and headed east. At jogging pace, even with the smoker's cough that made me stop and gasp for breath every couple of hundred yards, I caught sight of the barn through the trees within a few minutes.

The building, which was constructed of corrugated metal, was located in a clearing in the middle of the forest. Nearer the edge of the treeline close to it, the forest floor was thick with undergrowth. As I approached I saw the four Gardai crouching behind a tangle of bramble bushes about fifty yards due west of the barn. Then I saw Helen Gorman rise, gun drawn, and step out through the bushes behind which she had been crouched. One of the other officers rose to his feet uncertainly, while his two colleagues held their positions.

Beyond them in the clearing, just past Gorman, I could see Barry Ford. He was dressed in a white protective suit, a paper mask covering his mouth. He was leaning into his car and I guessed that Helen had decided to stop him leaving. He looked up at her approaching and his eyes widened slightly. He leant back into the car again. Gorman shouted to him to get out of the vehicle, thinking he was trying to escape. Too late, I realized that that was not the case. From the passenger seat he pulled out a shotgun and twisted quickly towards Gorman, holding the stock firmly in two hands, at waist level. Gorman froze, her own gun held aloft. Then she lowered her arm as if readying for a shot. I shouted to her as I drew my own weapon. But it was too late.

The blast echoed through the trees, causing the birds above us to break into a cacophony of cries. None, though, matched the visceral scream Helen Gorman made as her body was flung backwards. She landed on the ground near where her colleagues were stumbling to their feet. I managed to discharge two shots in quick succession at Ford, but he ducked behind his car and began to stumble towards the treeline to the far side of the barn.

I dropped to my knees beside Gorman, gripping her hand. The blast had caught her on the chest, shredding her Garda shirt. Deep wounds were gouged from the flesh of her breast and shoulder and blood pumped through my fingers as I pressed my hand on the wounds.

'Call for help,' I shouted to the three who stood behind me, staring open-mouthed at their colleague. 'Call a fucking

227

ambulance!' I screamed. Finally one of them pulled out his phone, whilst the others knelt beside Helen. One pulled up his sweater and tore a strip from the hem of his shirt to use to plug the deepest of the wounds. I had a first-aid kit in my car, but it was too far away.

Gorman screamed as we pressed on her wounds. She gritted her teeth and gripped harder on my hand, twisting my fingers in her own as each spasm of pain hit her. Absurdly, I recalled my wife, holding my hand in the same manner as she gave birth to Penny.

'You're going to be OK, Helen,' I said, smoothing her hair back from her face. In doing so, I smeared her blood from my hand across her forehead, which was already cold and damp with sweat.

'Jesus, I'm freezing,' she said. 'I'm fucking freezing.'

I put my arm around her as her body shook with cold. Her teeth chattered uncontrollably and her muscles began sporadic contractions.

She screamed once more, a high-pitched yowl such as I had never heard before. Her back arched as she twisted around. She gripped my hand tighter, brought it to her mouth and bit down to relieve the agony she was experiencing.

'The ambulance will be here soon,' the officer behind me said.

Gorman attempted to smile, her mouth a tight grimace. Then she looked at me, our hands held together in front of her face. 'I can't feel your hand,' she said. 'I can't feel your hand.' Her voice rose as she started to panic. She began to weep, her words spluttering on her lips, and I realized that

228

tears were dripping from my face too, though I had not been aware that I was crying.

Finally, she gasped once, tightened her grip forcefully, then relaxed. Her eyes shifted their gaze past me to the canopy above and slowly lost their focus. Her jaw slackened and her mouth gaped open. One of the other Guards started CPR, leaning close to her mouth in the hope that she might start breathing, but it was obvious that she was gone.

I marked the sign of the cross in the smear of blood on her forehead, and silently mouthed an Act of Contrition. I pressed her hand to my lips, then placed it by her side. Then, barking orders at the others to remain with her until the ambulance arrived, I lifted my gun and set off after Barry Ford.

As I passed his car, I noticed blood smeared against one of the side panels. If I had hit him, it had been fairly low on his leg, judging by the height of the bloodstain. Still, it would be enough to slow him down.

I ducked in under the branches and entered the woodland proper. To my left I could hear the rush of the river. The forest canopy was eerily silent, the wildlife seemingly scattered by the commotion. Ford must have heard Gorman too. Perhaps he felt some grim satisfaction in her screams.

The lower branches of the pine trees were bare of leaves and needles, and I was able to see a fair distance ahead. Far to my left, heading upriver, I could make out the white-suited figure of Barry Ford. He had a head start on me, though not as much as I had feared.

He obviously caught sight of me at the same time, for he twisted and, steadying himself, raised his gun and fired off a shot.

He was still too far ahead for the shot to count for much and it splintered harmlessly against the trunk of a tree twenty feet ahead of me. The noise of the gun reverberated around us and in its wake the silence of the forest seemed to return with a whoosh.

To return fire would only have been a waste of ammunition at this range. I picked up my pace and kept my head down.

Up ahead I noticed that Ford had stopped and was leaning against a tree trunk. I could make out a patch of bright red on his white trousers. Reloading his gun, he turned and fired a second shot. This one splintered the tree to my immediate left, causing me to duck for cover. At least I knew I had gained on him sufficiently that he was now well within range.

I heard another clunk as he shunted his cartridge into place and a third blast ricocheted off the trees around me. This shot blew off the bark of the tree beside me, causing splinters of wood to rain down on me. My stomach muscles clenched and my legs seemed to lose power.

I glanced around the trunk of the tree I had taken cover behind. Ford was struggling to reload his weapon and I used the opportunity to take aim and fire. The shot hit the ground a foot away from him, scattering dirt and pine needles and causing him to scurry backwards. In his turn he took aim again and fired, though his shot was wide and the pellets lodged in a tree some ten feet away from me.

Figuring I had thirty seconds until his next shot, I broke cover and ran towards him, trying to keep cover between us. He fired again, the shot hitting the trees in front of me. This time, as he leant back against the tree he was using for cover, the white of his shoulder was still visible. I took aim, steadying one hand with the other, and squeezed off a shot.

The spurt of blood from his shoulder was enough to let me know I'd been successful. Ford twisted onto the forest floor, still attempting to aim his gun despite his diminishing strength. Finally, he seemed to give up and his arm flopped useless on the ground, the stock of his gun heavy in his hand.

I came out from my cover and approached him warily, my gun trained on his chest.

'Let go of the gun,' I shouted. 'Now!'

Ford half laughed a gasp. 'I can't. You've fucked my shoulder.'

'I will shoot you,' I said. 'Drop the fucking gun,' In the distance I could hear sirens, and I was aware that somewhere behind me someone was calling my name.

'I can't, you stupid prick,' he spat.

I trained my gun on him as I approached. He was on his side, his arm lying partially beneath him. His shoulder was soaked with blood, the tear at the front of the white suit he wore showing that the bullet had passed through his body.

'How's the girl?' he wheezed.

My gun twitched involuntarily. My mouth seemed suddenly dry. I tried to speak and had to clear my throat before I could form any words.

'You killed her,' I said.

'She startled me,' he said, frowningly.

I nodded, but did not trust myself to speak. My gun was suddenly heavy in my grip. I glanced over my shoulder, attempting to gauge how far behind me the other officers were. My mouth felt furred and I had to lick my lips several times.

Ford seemed to sense my thoughts, for he struggled to raise himself up on his weakened arm. 'I didn't mean to kill her, man—' he started to explain.

I raised my gun from his chest to his head and swallowed hard. It would be easy, I thought. No one could dispute my story. He still had his gun in his hand.

'Why did you kill Leon Bradley?' I asked, almost to prevent myself from acting rashly.

'Who?'

'Leon Bradley. You shot him in the back. Why?'

Ford raised his empty hand in a gesture of surrender.

'I don't know what . . . I can't . . .' His gaze moved beyond me, as he now attempted to see where the other Gardai were.

'Was it about Eligius? Something about Morrison?'

He shrugged.

'You mugged a fucking postman to try to retrieve letters that Bradley stole? Starting to remember yet?'

A laugh gurgled in his throat. 'I don't know what the fuck you're on. I never touched a post—'

'Tell me about Morrison,' I snapped.

He smiled again, then glanced past me. 'You don't know what you're messing with. Don't fucking get involved with him.'

'Why?' I asked.

'Just don't mess with him, man.'

'What's the connection with Eligius?'

Ford coughed roughly. 'I don't know, man. We take stuff into Chechnya for them.'

'What stuff?'

'I swear, I don't know. Something small. A few boxes just.'

'Who organized it? Morrison or Curran?'

'I don't know.'

'What about the people you bring back? Who organized that?'

Ford glanced past me again, his tongue darting onto his lips. He was losing blood and, I guessed, getting thirsty. His admission would mean nothing if I were the only person to hear it.

'Vinnie. The guys we delivered to in Chechnya made an arrangement. They had people who were looking to get out of the country, we had an empty lorry coming across Europe. No one got hurt.'

'Apart from the people you bring in. What about them?'

'I just drive the fucking van, man.'

'We're going back now. I'm going to remove your gun. If you even twitch at me, I'll shoot you.'

'No you won't,' Ford said. 'You need what I know.' He looked past me once more, and I knew that he had made his decision. I saw his jaw set, an instant before he attempted to raise his shotgun one last time, and seconds before I pulled the trigger of my gun. My bullet shattered Ford's cheekbone before lodging itself somewhere in his brain pan. His mouth gaped in a frozen O and his eyes rolled in his head as his body dropped again to the forest floor.

That's how I described the events during the investigation that followed into the shooting of Barry Ford, less than a hundred yards from the Carrowcreel.

Chapter Twenty-four

Monday, 23 October

Back-up arrived a few moments later in the form of one of the Gardai I had left with Helen Gorman. He stood beside me, his chest heaving as he attempted to catch his breath, and looked down on the lifeless form of Barry Ford.

He placed his hands on his upper thighs and leant over heavily, as if he were going to be sick. He spat a thick globule of bile on to the ground and stood erect again. Finally he managed to say, 'Fucker had it coming to him. Good work, sir.'

I wiped the sweat from my eyes. 'I got nothing from him. Nothing.'

My colleague, whose name I did not even know, placed his hand on my arm.

'You got *him*,' he said, and winked.

I could hear other voices approaching, the blue uniforms standing out against the dull hues of the forest. They ran past me as I made my way back to where Gorman's body lay, her face turned towards the sky, the light blue of her shirt almost entirely purpled by her blood.

The medical crew had torn her shirt open, revealing the extent of her wounds. One of them was comforting the man who had been giving her CPR when I left. Several of our colleagues stood near by, smoking and whispering in hushed tones as they glanced at Gorman's corpse.

'Cover her up,' I said to one of the crew as I made my way over to the barn.

Ford's protective suit suggested he had been up to something in there and my first thought ran to drugs. Then, as I approached, I caught the strong smell of fuel.

The barn itself was around three thousand square feet. The metal sheeting on the roof had started to rust in places and tiny shafts of light streamed through the gaping holes above us. Inside, there were ten home-brew vats, down the sides of which a corrosive sludge dripped. In the far corner were stacked almost a hundred metal drums. I went over and picked a stick from the ground to lift one of the lids. As I prized up the lid of the nearest vat, the air sharpened with the smell of diesel and another more acrid smell.

'Green diesel,' a uniform said, appearing next to me.

I turned and looked at him and either my expression, or the bloody state of my face and hands, made him shift his step.

'Johnny McGinley,' he said, holding out his hand then withdrawing it again, quickly. 'It's green diesel.'

'How the fuck do you know?' I asked.

'My da owns a farm. He uses green diesel for the machinery and that. That's what it's for. This guy was cleaning it, so it can be used in normal cars and that. Remove the dye so the customs men can't get you. Fucks up your car, though.'

'What's that sludge?'

'Something nasty,' he said. 'You use acid to clean the fuel – sulphuric acid usually. That's the remains of the acid and the dye and shit. There should be a shitload of that stuff about somewhere, though, judging by the state of those pods. He must have dumped it.'

'How much "it" are you talking? Where would he dump it?'

'Could be as many barrels again as those in the corner. Those pods have been used for a while. Where would you dump it? Look around, Inspector. The whole bleeding woodland would make a perfect dumping ground. Problem is, that stuff will just burn through the barrels or whatever he's been putting it in, run out onto the ground.'

And straight into the river, I thought.

I sat down by the Carrowcreel, waiting for Patterson. As I lit a smoke, my phone rang. I recognized the number as Gilmore's.

'No sign of Ford at that address. If he ever lived there, he's not been back in a while. Pile of post lying behind the door. We've asked the Community Branch to keep an eye on the house for him.'

'Don't bother. He's not coming back.'

'How do you know?'

'I've just shot him.'

'Is he dead?'

I dragged on my cigarette and grunted through the smoke. 'Result,' Gilmore said, cheerily. Why was everyone *not* involved in the killing so pleased about it?

'I lost one of my own colleagues,' I replied.

Gilmore was quiet for a moment, then I heard him snuff with embarrassment. 'Shit, I'm sorry. Who was he?'

'She,' I corrected. 'Helen Gorman.'

'I'm sorry to hear that. It's not easy to deal with. I lost a couple of mates to the Provos,' he began, but I wasn't in the mood for old war stories. And I couldn't shake the thought that I was the one who had sent her out here in the first place.

'Ford was laundering fuel,' I explained. 'He worked for Morrison's haulage company, and he was laundering green diesel. Morrison is involved in this.'

'Sounds promising,' Gilmore agreed. 'Fuel-smuggling is Customs and Excise. I'll phone up our friends from Sunday, get them to drop round on Mr Morrison, check his tanks.'

'That's a plan,' I agreed.

'Take it easy, Devlin. I'll let you know what happens.'

I closed my phone and put it away. My arm muscles were twitching now with delayed shock. I stubbed out my smoke and washed my hands in the cold water of the river.

Patterson arrived about half an hour later with a further cohort of officers. I ran through the episode with him. Then he spoke with each of the officers who had been with Gorman and they confirmed that she had told them they were to hold their position until I arrived. The man who had followed me into the woods also confirmed my description of how Barry Ford was shot.

'What about his confession?' I asked. 'Is any of it usable?'

'None,' Patterson said with disgust. 'Unless we can get someone to corroborate it. You had no witnesses, nothing recorded.'

'I had no *choice*,' I protested.

Patterson grunted and raised his hand to shield his eyes as he stared upriver. 'Lean on this prick Curran and see what he has to say. But stay away from Weston and Orcas for now, do you hear me?'

I nodded. 'We can get Morrison on something, though,' I said. 'Fuel-laundering.' I gestured towards the barn, where McGinley was standing with a number of other officers. Patterson looked at them, turned his head and spat onto the ground, then went over. I followed.

Patterson inspected the contents of the barn, then ordered several teams to head out in search of the missing drums of acidic waste which, we assumed, Ford had been dumping.

'He'd have to travel by car with them,' McGinley added. 'Follow car tracks.'

A number of the more senior men looked at him scornfully. Patterson turned and glanced at him appraisingly. For my part, I was impressed with how he handled himself.

And he was proved right. Half a mile due north, one of the teams discovered over two hundred oildrums piled under a tarpaulin stretched between a number of trees, the tarpaulin covered with leaves and pine needles. A number of the drums at the bottom of the pile had already been corroded through, the thick sludge running into a stream nearby, whence it had made its way into the Carrowcreel.

I stood with Patterson, surveying the dump. If the waste could do this to steel, I could only imagine what it had done to the river.

'No matter what you think about Weston, you can't blame him for this,' Patterson concluded, nodding towards the barrels, then rubbing vigorously at his nose with his index finger and thumb. 'Maybe you can lay the fuck off him now, eh?' he added, then turned and walked away.

'Maybe,' I said. Killing Ford had effectively killed that whole line of enquiry. The discovery of the fuel laundry explained the death of Leon Bradley, and the pollution in the river. And Karl Moore had confessed to the killing of his wife. But there still remained the issue of Natalia and the smuggling of illegal immigrants in which Ford and Strandmann were involved and in which Morrison had some hand. He had trucks going out to Chechnya on charity missions. Natalia had told us she had been smuggled into the country in the back of a truck.

And none of this explained the significance of the sheets that Leon had stolen from Eligius. Or why someone wanted them badly enough to attack the postman on the day they were to be delivered. Ford denied that attack, even as he admitted people-smuggling. Maybe he had been telling the truth.

Patterson had warned me to lay off Weston. Ted Coyle, on the other hand, had not been mentioned.

I found him downriver. He was one of the few stragglers left, panning the river. Most of the others had either left or were sitting outside their vans, watching the comings and goings of the Gardai. Overhead, a V-formation of wild geese traversed the cloudless sky.

I explained to him what I wanted him to do. Then he gave me a lift back to Orcas to collect my car. There I gave him the brown envelope containing the documents Hendry had given me and which I suspected he would soon realize I had yet to return. Coyle looked at them, then at me, blinking quickly behind his glasses.

'I'll take a look at them, see what they mean,' he said. 'Give me your mobile. I'll ring you later.'

'You never saw these,' I said. 'You know nothing about them, and I'll deny giving them to you, if anyone asks.'

He nodded and turned as if to leave. Then he came back towards me. 'You know, you should really ask Peter Daniels about this. He went into Eligius with Leon.'

'I would if I could find him,' I said. 'No known address for him, apparently.'

Coyle blinked behind his glasses, staring at me as if I was stupid. 'He's sitting downstream. Daniels is one of the guys Leon was camped with. They're packing up today.'

Chapter Twenty-five

Tuesday, 24 October

Peter Daniels was sitting on the step of one of the camper vans when I got back to the site. A rolled cigarette drooped from his mouth as he scratched the neck of the dog I had seen wandering around.

'You didn't tell me you were Peter Daniels,' I said.

'Should I have?' he asked, smiling mildly.

'You were at Eligius with Leon.'

'That's right,' he said, scratching his nose with his thumb.

'You didn't tell me,' I said.

'Why would I? It's irrelevant.'

'Irrelevant? What about the shipping lists he posted out?'

'Oh, *you* got them,' Daniels said.

It was then that it occurred to me that Ford was not the only man with a greying pony-tail.

'It was you who jumped the postman, wasn't it?'

'I have no idea what you're talking about,' he said.

'It was out of my jurisdiction,' I explained. 'I don't care. But it made me think the documents were more important than they are. I thought someone killed Leon over them.'

'Sorry about that,' he said. 'An unintended consequence.'

Which was as close to a confession as I was going to get, I thought.

'What was so important about the documents? What did you want information on V M Haulage for?'

'We didn't. We went in to protest against the war. Leon was a wiz with computers. When we actually made it in, he suggested we look for the names of any Irish companies working for Hagan. Stage protests at their offices, send them stuff in the post – hoax devices and that, you know.'

'Green Alliance?' The group Janet Moore had told me was behind the hoax threats against Hagan.

Daniels smiled broadly. 'It's nice to be known,' he said.

'So what happened?'

'Nothing. Leon found those shipping invoices. We realized they were a local company, thought we'd keep the details. Plan something a little further down the line. Always useful to have these places on the radar.'

'What's the other sheet? All the figures?'

Daniels shrugged. 'Something Leon found. He came across a protected file. Spent the evening trying to crack into it. That's all he found. He reckoned it must be important, the hassle they'd gone to to protect it. I didn't get a chance to study it. Maybe I could see it now,' he added slyly. 'I might be able to help you.'

'You've helped me enough already,' I said. 'I'm told you're leaving.'

He nodded through a haze of sweet-smelling smoke, then squinted at his wristwatch. 'We'll be on our way in an hour, I'd say. Heading to Derry. It's been a pleasure, Ben.'

He stood and extended his hand. We shook. When I got back to my car, I phoned Jim Hendry and told him that the man responsible for the attack on the Strabane postman would be crossing the border in an hour's time, if anyone wanted to pick him up.

I discussed events with Debbie over dinner, but her words of reassurance had little effect and I slept badly that night. In my dream I relived the shooting of Helen Gorman. I saw her moving in slow motion and tried to shout a warning, but my mouth couldn't form the words. I watched myself shoot Barry Ford, but in my dreams his hand remained motionless on the forest floor, his gun unmoving.

Waking at five in a cold sweat, I showered and went downstairs. As I passed Natalia's bedroom door, I could have sworn that I heard her crying softly. I thought of knocking and checking on her, but there was nothing I could say to her, no words of comfort that would mean anything, or express the sorrow and guilt I felt at what had befallen her. I recalled hearing of a Ukrainian woman in the North who, having lost her job over the Christmas period, was forced to sleep outdoors. Over several winter nights she suffered such extreme hypothermia that, when found, she had to have both legs amputated. It seemed vile that such things could happen in a country that had been enjoying an unparalleled period of prosperity.

At six-thirty, my mobile rang. It was Ted Coyle.

'You sound like shit,' I observed when he had introduced himself.

'Likewise,' he remarked. 'I've been up looking at your sheets. I can't see what's so important about them.'

244

I tried to keep the disappointment out of my voice. 'Don't worry about it. It was a stab in the dark. I'm not even sure the content *is* important. Maybe it was just the fact that it verified the link between Eligius and Vincent Morrison's outfit.'

'No ... no,' Coyle muttered. 'No. I thought that myself. But why would Leon have lifted the sheet about Orcas? There's something in those figures. Something important.'

'What are they anyway?' I asked. 'I guessed they were productivity things.'

'They are,' Coyle interrupted. 'It's a breakdown of how much rock was processed and what minerals came out of it. The headers, Au, Ag and that, are gold, silver; all the minerals they extracted.'

I couldn't see their relevance and said as much. 'It was a long shot, to be honest. Thanks for looking at them anyway,' I added, ready to cut the connection.

Coyle hadn't finished. 'The only thing about this that might be important is how little gold they actually extracted. According to this.'

'What do you mean?' I asked. 'It's been a profit year for Orcas.'

'Not on these figures, it hasn't,' Coyle said. 'Their gold extraction is negligible. Not enough to run a profit, anyway. Most of what they found is listed under Fe – iron sulphide, I guess; fool's gold.'

I felt my pulse begin to pound in my throat. 'That can't be right.'

'Take a look yourself,' he said. 'It's all down there.'

245

'You have the only—' I began, then recalled my first trip out to Orcas. Weston had handed me and Patterson leather-bound folders. 'Everything you could ever want to know about our company is in those packs,' he'd said.

'I'll call you back,' I said, snapping my phone closed.

I found the folder under a pile of junk in the study. Sure enough, it did contain productivity reports on the mine. According to my copy, though, the percentage per tonne of gold was significantly higher than any of the other minerals. Either Coyle's figures were from a different year, or one of us had the wrong set of figures.

One phone call confirmed that, like mine, Coyle's figures were dated in February of this year. One set was incorrect. And I suspected I knew which. If Coyle's figures were right – and they were the ones that had been password-protected in the computer system of Eligius – then Orcas was making nothing. Which raised the question, where had the record profits come from?

I copied Coyle's figures onto my own sheet and headed for the station.

Patterson groaned when I handed him the sheets. He laid them on the desk in front of him and looked up at me awkwardly.

'Will you sit down, for fuck's sake?' he snapped.

I sat, but could not control the continual pumping of my knee. I became aware of the thudding of my heart and a tightening across my scalp. Recognizing the early signs of a panic attack, I took a deep breath.

'So, what am I meant to see here?' he asked.

'One report states that the total grammes per tonne of gold extracted from 100 tonnes of rock was 58.75. Which is a remarkable amount.'

'Right,' Patterson said, flicking the sheet in front of him. 'So?'

'The other figures are from a sheet Leon Bradley posted out of Eligius the night he broke in.'

'And you have them how?' he asked.

'The PSNI forgot to get them back from me,' I explained. 'According to these figures, for the same period, the grammes per tonne were less than one gramme per hundred tonnes.'

'Which is bad?' Patterson asked, with a hint of sarcasm.

'Which is unprofitable. It wouldn't be worth their while operating if these figures are right.'

'So where did the profits come from?'

'That's what we need to find out. If he chose these two pieces of information, he must have guessed they were linked in some way. Ford told me that they were transporting stuff for Hagan to Chechnya.'

'This was before you shot him,' Patterson said, glancing up from the sheet.

'Orcas reports massive profits, then these figures surface which suggest the land contains negligible levels of gold. Leon Bradley must have been on to something.'

'The problem, Devlin – which you seem to be ignoring – is that you can't keep accusing John Weston without corroboration. You accused him of polluting the river and he wasn't.'

'Though the river was being polluted.'

247

'Not by him, though. You have a real chip on your shoulder about Weston. After him giving you that necklace.'

In a perverse way, it was *because* he had given me the necklace that I distrusted the man, though I couldn't tell that to Patterson. 'I think we need to get someone from the NBCI in to go through Orcas's books. And ask the PSNI to go through Eligius's. There's something not right about it all.'

'Get some evidence. Chase up Curran; he's the weak link. Let the PSNI pressure this Polish fella and Morrison.'

I went down to Derry that afternoon to question Seamus Curran once more. When I went into the bar, a man I didn't recognize was standing behind the counter.

'Help you?' he asked with an upward tilt of his chin.

'I'd like to speak with Seamus Curran,' I said.

'You and the rest of us, pal,' the man replied.

I looked at him quizzically, though I already had a leaden sensation in my gut.

'He didn't turn up to open at lunchtime,' the man explained. 'No one can raise him.'

'Would you have a number I could contact him on?' I asked.

'No point, pal,' the man said. 'I've just told you, no one can raise him. I went round his house and there's no sign.'

I left my card on the counter. 'Can you give him this if he turns up? Tell him I need to speak with him?'

The man took the card, glanced at it and tucked it against the side of the till. I suspected however that Seamus Curran, wherever he was, would be unlikely to receive it.

* * *

That evening, I drove to see Fearghal Bradley. He had called me to say he was in Letterkenny for the day to organize a headstone for Leon's grave. I wanted to see him one last time before he went back to Dublin. I also wanted to give him the photograph of himself and Leon that had been recovered from the camera.

We met at a bar, where Fearghal ordered food and drink for the two of us. Linda Campbell, he explained, was working in the museum and hadn't been able to get the time off to come up again. They were working hard to salvage something of Kate, he told me.

'What about you?' I asked.

He shook his head. 'Let go, Benny. Jesus, they couldn't keep me on, after what I did.'

'Would they not have shown a little understanding – after all that happened with Leon and that?'

'I'm sure they might have,' he replied. 'I didn't want them to. I'm not going to use Leon to excuse myself. I did what I did for a reason. I'd do it again today, if I had to.' He placed his pint glass firmly on the table, his fist gripping its circumference, his eyes bright.

'Why *did* you do it?' I asked.

'Was her being sacrificed once not enough?' he replied, wiping spilt drops of beer from his beard. 'We have to sacrifice her again for fucking gold. Fuck that, Benny. We shouldn't take that shit.'

I smiled mildly. I had had enough of having to justify myself. And I was tired of feeling that my job was making little difference to a world where even a human life was just one more commodity.

'How's Linda?' I asked, if only to change the topic.

'Working, like I told you,' he retorted.

'I think I put my foot in it with her. I thought you two were an item, you know. She said you aren't.'

He lifted his beer and took a mouthful, his eyes mournful and wet beneath the pub's lamplight. 'Linda had a tough time. She's not ... she's not the marrying kind. Maybe someday.'

'Something happened to her at college, she said.'

'She was assaulted. One of my fellow lecturers attacked her.'

'Jesus.'

'He runs the department now. And I was shifted to the museum for taking her side. The Guards did fuck-all. That's the difference you lot make. Fuck-all.' He spat the words at me.

'I'm sorry you feel that way, Fearghal,' I said.

He stared at me as if willing me to argue back. 'What happened to us, Benny, eh?'

We sat in silence for a few minutes. Finally I rose to leave. 'I brought you this,' I said. 'I thought you might want it.'

Fearghal took the picture from me and looked at it. His eyes brightened with tears, and he ran his hand down his cheek.

'He was the only one of us,' he said, turning the picture around to me. 'He was the only one that didn't sell out.'

'I'll see you around, Fearghal,' I said, lifting my coat.

He looked up at me and smiled briefly. 'No you won't, Benny.'

'It was good to see you, Fearghal,' I said. 'Despite the circumstances.'

He nodded slowly.

'You too, Inspector,' he said.

Chapter Twenty-six

Wednesday, 25 October

'They've found a body out at the mine.'

It took me a few seconds to realize that Patterson was talking to me. I looked up from my desk.

'What?'

'They've dug up a body out at the mine. We're going out,' he repeated irritably. 'Out to Orcas. It's a dead body,' he explained, turning to leave as he did so.

'They gen—' I began.

'Fuck up,' he retorted. 'It looks like it's Seamus Curran. Let's go.'

Curran lay in the same pit from which Kate had been recovered a few weeks earlier. Like her, he had been strangled, the rope burns vivid around his neck. He had also been bound, his arms behind his back, the wire binding his wrists biting deep into his skin. His body lay face-down, his mouth pressed in a final desperate kiss against the clay at the bottom of the pit.

'It's him all right,' I said to Patterson.

'Everyone you speak to seems to wind up dead,' he observed, looking down at the corpse.

'It's a fairly clear message,' I said. 'And not for me. Morrison's telling Weston something.'

'How do you know it was Morrison?'

'He knew that I'd spoken with Curran. Maybe he figured that with Ford dead and the Polish fella in custody, Curran would be the one we'd go after. There's nobody else left.'

'Best get in touch with the PSNI, get Morrison in for questioning.'

'Was he not lifted the other day, over the fuel-smuggling?'

'How the fuck should I know? Call them and find out.'

I called Gilmore myself and explained the situation. He wasn't hopeful about getting much out of Morrison.

'We had him in the other day for questioning over that fuel dump youse came across. He's one cool bastard, I'll tell you. He just sat listening to all we had to say, didn't answer back, didn't let a thing slip. Didn't even bring a fucking lawyer.'

'He's the obvious candidate for killing Curran.'

'Maybe he is,' Gilmore said, 'but don't be holding your breath waiting for him to break down and confess. No doubt he'll have an alibi tighter than a gnat's chuff. The best we'll get him on is duty evasion on that fuel. Every one of his trucks we tested was using green diesel.'

'Enough to hold him?'

'We didn't even oppose bail,' Gilmore stated. 'No point.'

'Fair enough,' I began.

'We did oppose bail for that other guy, Strandmann, but they let him out.'

I couldn't believe what he had said. 'What? He raped a woman. And he's an immigrant.'

'He still gets treated the same as everyone else. We couldn't hold him on anything. He opened up after you killed Ford. Everything was Ford's fault. He forced him to help him, against his wishes. The Chechen girl is lying to stay in the country.'

'So that's it?'

'He had a clean record, good lawyer,' he explained. 'He had to surrender his passport and has to report to his local station every evening at six.'

'Who posted his bail?'

'Vincent Morrison, obviously.'

I knocked on the door of Patterson's office and opened it without waiting for his response. He was on the phone when I entered. 'I'll come myself, sir. We'll be with you in a half-hour.' Then he laid down the receiver. 'I didn't hear your knock,' he snapped.

He listened while I told him about Strandmann's release. 'He's the North's problem now anyway.'

'What about Weston?' I asked.

'That was the NBCI,' he said. 'They're sending up a team tomorrow morning. They've requested the Fraud Squad in the North do likewise with Eligius. We're to go in today and seize all documentation, shut the place down. We better hope things are the way they look. Or we're both fucked.'

'Weston's dirty,' I said.

'Why? Because he's rich?'

I started to deny the accusation, then thought of something. 'I'll *come* myself,' he had said. Not '*go* myself'. He had told the person on the other end of the phone that we'd be with them in half an hour.

'You told Weston we're coming?' I asked incredulously.

'It's common fucking courtesy, Devlin. Like knocking on a fucking door. What's the man going to do in half an hour?'

I could think of several things, but held my tongue.

Patterson stood. 'You can take that fucking look off your face too,' he added, pulling on his cap. 'Weston brought a fortune into this county with that place.'

'He brought nothing; the place isn't producing enough for a fucking ear stud.'

'We'll soon find out. Let's go.'

The drive out to Orcas seemed to drag. I watched the clock: Patterson had given Weston plenty of time to destroy any evidence and prepare his story. I couldn't help but wonder what hold Weston had on Patterson. Was he just being political in keeping on Weston's good side? Or had Harry been bought off? I recalled again the necklace Weston had given me, and Patterson's response. Had Weston already paid him off by the time we had first gone out to Orcas?

We pulled up in front of the main building just as dusk started to settle across a sky thick with grey cloud. The landscape beyond us was unnaturally scarred, the troughs in the ground's rugged features darkening slowly.

The girl we had met on our first visit, Jackie, was already coming from behind the counter when we entered.

'This is outrageous,' she said, then blushed deeply at her own words. 'Mr Weston's a great man.'

'We'd like to speak with Mr Weston, please,' Patterson said. I moved past them to the foot of the steps which led up to his office.

'We know where he is,' I said, taking the steps two at a time. 'He knows we're coming.'

The girl called after me about warrants and trespassing. I was more concerned that Weston hadn't come down himself. I imagined him in his office, shredding as much documentation as he could while Patterson wasted time in the foyer.

Several people were standing in the corridor at the top of the stairs. Their heads were turned towards the closed door of Weston's office, their voices a quiet murmur.

'Excuse me,' I said, pushing through. I could hear Patterson behind me, calling me to stop.

I approached Weston's door and rapped sharply once, then twisted the door handle. It moved only a few millimetres, but wouldn't shift. 'Open up, Mr Weston,' I shouted, leaning my weight against the door.

By now Patterson was behind me. He grabbed my arm and attempted to pull me back from the door. 'Step back, Inspector,' he snapped.

I pulled my arm from his grip and shoved my weight against the door with as much force as I could. I had to repeat the action several times before I felt the door give as the wood around the lock cracked and splintered.

As I stumbled into the room through the open doorway, I scanned the office but Weston was nowhere to be seen.

Then I noticed the window lying ajar, the canopy of the forest beyond visible in the distance. Patterson and I ran towards the window though I knew we were already too late.

John Weston's body lay on the pavement below, haloed by his own blood.

Chapter Twenty-seven

Wednesday, 25 October

It was almost nine o'clock by the time I got home. The NBCI team were dispatched from Dublin as soon as Patterson contacted Garda headquarters to let them know what had happened.

I waited at the site until the Dublin team arrived. There were twelve officers in all and within twenty minutes of their arrival they had begun to unearth all kinds of documentation that they told us they considered 'significant'.

As it became increasingly apparent, even to Patterson, that Weston had been involved in something he shouldn't have been, the mood began to become more workmanlike. Still, none of us could ignore the glare of the arc lights that had been set up in the car park below. Eventually, Patterson told me I could go home. Neither of us mentioned the fact that the call he had made to Weston before our arrival had given him time to consider his options. Ultimately, he had decided on the most extreme.

By the time I got home, the kids were already in bed. Debbie was curled up on the sofa, watching some American comedy series featuring impossibly attractive young people whose worst problem seemed to be where to get a cup of coffee. I had watched too many people dying over the past few days to be in the mood for sharing the entertainment. Instead I went and stood under the shower, until the water ran cold and I could bear the chill no longer. But it made no difference, and as I stood with my face turned against the force of the water, I could still see Weston in his last moment, and Helen Gorman as she shuddered her last breath, and Barry Ford slumping to the ground. I climbed out of the shower and vomited into the toilet bowl.

As I lay on the floor by the toilet, I gradually became aware again of the noises of my home: the sound of a television; footsteps on the stairs; Penny reading softly to herself in bed. I lay on the floor for ten or fifteen minutes, until I began to shiver with the cold. Then I got up and dressed.

As I came out of the bathroom, Natalia passed me on the way into her room. She smiled lightly and I noticed that she was wearing a little make-up, her face slightly rouged.

'Where's Natalia going?' I asked Debbie when I came downstairs.

'Karol is taking her to a dinner.'

'On a date?' I asked.

Debbie shushed me and, glancing up at the ceiling, lowered her voice. 'Not quite, though I think he's hopeful it'll be the start of something. I told you he was very fond of her.'

'Where are they going?'

'Apparently a group of immigrants meet once a month for dinner and a few drinks. He invited her along.'

I looked at my watch. 'It's very late to be going out for dinner,' I said.

Debbie threw a cushion at me. 'She is an adult, you know.'

'I'm just saying. It's very late.'

Debbie tutted. 'God love Penny when she grows up,' she said, turning her attention back to the television.

As I heard Natalia's soft footfalls on the stairs, the headlights of Karol Walshyk's car swept across the blinds of our front window. Natalia came into the living room and stood before Debbie, waiting to be inspected.

'You look lovely,' Debbie said.

Natalia glanced at me and I felt Debbie's foot strike my calf.

'Sorry. You look very well,' I said.

Natalia blushed and straightened her hair with her hands, presumably to hide both her embarrassment and her pleasure.

The doorbell rang and Natalia waved at us with her fingers and went out to the door.

'Aren't you going to tell her not to be late?' Debbie said teasingly. In response, I leant towards the doorway as if to call out to Natalia.

The words died in my mouth, though, when I looked out. Pol Strandmann was there in my hall, Natalia held in front of him, a knife pressed against her throat, as he tried to shove her towards the front door.

'Don't move,' he snarled, bearing feral teeth. 'I'll cut the bitch's throat.' He pressed the knife's edge against her skin, the pressure leaving a long white line on her neck.

'Let her go, Pol,' I said. 'You've nowhere to go.'

He glanced behind him to his left and right, as if to ascertain whether he had an escape route. 'They've nothing,' he spat. 'Nothing without this bitch. They can't get me for anything.'

'And what then?' I asked. 'You think you'll get away with it? I've seen you here. You think I won't come after you? Don't be stupid. Put the knife down. We can talk. Give me Morrison and I'll see you're treated lightly.'

'Bullshit! Do you think Morrison'd let that happen?'

'Where are you going to go? Eh?' I edged closer towards him and he moved back towards the open doorway. I couldn't let him get out with Natalia. 'Where are you going to go, Pol? Walk out that door and I'll have half the fucking force on you in ten minutes. Morrison'll be the last of your worries.'

'I'll disappear,' he said, his voice rising hysterically. 'How the fuck do you think we bring them in? You think I can't disappear? Make a new name and vanish?' He giggled a little manically. Under the light of our hall, I could make out his eyes, his pupils pinpoints, the irises ringed with red.

I moved towards our fireplace, where the hearth-set contained a poker.

'Not another fucking step,' he said. 'I'll saw off her fucking head.' He laughed again, a queer, high-pitched giggle that he seemed to have some difficulty in controlling.

'You can get help,' I said. 'Morrison is the one we want. You could give him to us. It'll make things easy for you.'

'Easy? Morrison? He'll skin me alive.'

'You'll be protected,' I reasoned. 'It's the only way.'

He stared at me as if weighing up my proposition. He shook his head violently and in doing so applied more pressure to the blade he had pressed against Natalia's throat. She cried out.

At that moment Karol Walshyk stepped through the open door, holding aloft a piece of rock he had lifted from our garden. He brought it down with force on the back of Strandmann's skull before the man had even had a chance to register his presence.

Strandmann dropped heavily to the ground and his knife clattered across the wooden floor. Natalia fell forwards and clawed her way into the living room, where Debbie rushed to her.

Karol was kneeling over Strandmann's motionless body, the rock raised above his head. Again he brought it down hard on Strandmann's skull, the thud sickening, the force causing blood to splatter against him and onto the wall to his left. He raised his hand a third time, his face contorted in rage.

'Karol, don't!' I shouted, approaching him, my hand held out for the rock.

'He deserves it,' Karol barked, his words a tumble in the thickness of his accent. 'He deserves it for what he did.'

'He does,' I said. 'But not like this. He can give us the man who brought Natalia in. He can help us get the person responsible.'

Karol stared at me, his body heaving with the effort of his exertions. He looked down at the prone figure lying beneath him, then looked at his own hand, thick with gouts of blood.

Finally he stood erect and, stepping away from the body, let the rock fall from his hand. It lay on the ground while around it Strandmann's blood was pooling. Upstairs I could hear my children getting out of bed, wondering what the commotion below was. Debbie rushed to get to them, to prevent them coming onto the landing and looking down.

Karol stepped past me and went into the living room, where he wrapped his arms around Natalia, who hugged into him, her body shuddering with tears, her face pressed against his blood-stained shirt. He held her tight and looked at me, willing me to ensure that her tears were not in vain. I had convinced him that keeping Strandmann alive would serve justice. I had only now to convince myself.

Epilogue

Friday, 24 November

In the week following those events, the NBCI and the PSNI worked closely in piecing together the relationship between Orcas and Eligius. Eventually, the evidence and documentation they found prompted them to reach the following conclusion.

Orcas had opened after initial exploration suggested they had found a sizeable gold deposit. The early vein they found had been used to produce the jewellery I had seen on my first trip out to the mine. However, after setting up the mine, Weston and the funders must have quickly realized that the vein had run dry sooner than expected and the mine was going to incur huge, potentially embarrassing losses for the Irish-American businesses behind it.

Meanwhile, Cathal Hagan, or someone acting on his behalf, agreed to the sale of military software to Chechen rebels. Seamus Curran, a friend of Hagan's, was engaged to use the freight firm in which he was a partner to take the goods into the country, as part of a delivery of charity goods. Someone, presumably Morrison himself, had then reached an agreement with the rebels to bring back illegal immigrants. Increasing profits further, Morrison, through Barry Ford, had not only continued to extort money from the immigrants after their arrival in the country, but had also begun laundering fuel for use in the transit of goods across Europe.

Hagan turned Orcas's misfortunes to his advantage by using the company, in which he was an investor, as a means to launder the money he had made through the illegal sale of software. Weston had participated in the deception, falsifying the productivity reports to make it seem as if the mine was as successful as its profits suggested. It all came to light when Leon Bradley, initially attracted to the area on the promise of a new gold rush, began to investigate the pollution in the river caused by Morrison's fuel dump.

All of this was reported back to me by Patterson after the NBCI had completed their search of Orcas.

'What about Morrison?' I asked him when he had finished relating the findings of the NBCI team. 'What can he be held accountable for?'

'Nothing apart from the fuel thing. There's no evidence that he knew what was being taken to Chechnya was illegal,' Patterson said.

'What about Hagan? What's going to happen there?'

Again Patterson shrugged. 'It's not our concern. I suppose it'll be embarrassing for him, with his War on Terror thing. Looks bad for people to find out you've been selling parts to terrorists yourself. The NBCI will pass on what they have to the Yanks, I imagine. It'll be up to them, really, but Hagan's well connected.'

'So, who answers for what happened?' I asked, attempting to control my frustration.

'Weston takes the blame for everything. You were so desperate to get something on him. *Well done!*' he added.

Before I could respond he continued, 'Of course, you were out of order in so many ways this time too, Devlin. And yet you still manage to come out of it smelling like roses.'

'I don't think anything that happened here turned out the way I wanted, Harry.'

'Whatever. I've put in a request for a transfer,' Patterson said suddenly.

'I'm not going anywhere,' I said. 'My family are settled here.'

'Not for you. Costello set up the Super's office here when his wife was sick. I've decided to move it back to Letterkenny. That leaves you responsible for this station.'

I was more than a little taken aback. 'Why? I mean, thank you. But – why?' The move was in a way a promotion, though I would remain under Patterson's command as Superintendent.

'You were right,' he said.

'Truthfully?'

'Truthfully. It'll keep you out of my hair for a while and I'll not have you barging into my office every time you feel like it.'

And, I reflected, it reduced the risk of my revealing his involvement in the murder of Janet Moore (for which her husband was awaiting sentencing), or his tipping off Weston about the impending Garda searches of his premises.

Suddenly I felt as uneasy as I had when Weston had gifted me the gold necklace.

'I'm moving next week,' Patterson added. 'I'd love to say I'll be sorry to leave you here, but it wouldn't be true.'

Despite my assurance to Karol Walshyk, Pol Strandmann ultimately could play no part in bringing Vincent Morrison to justice. He never recovered consciousness following Karol's attack on him in my home and remained in a vegetative state at the time Morrison finally came to trial.

In the absence of any living witness to corroborate our knowledge of Morrison's activities, the Public Prosecution Service in the North decided that the only charges that could be successfully prosecuted related to the use of illegal fuel in his fleet.

I attended the court on the day of Morrison's case. About fifteen minutes before he was due to appear, I stepped out to the side of the building to have a smoke. Several barristers stood, in gowns and wigs, cigarettes clamped in their mouths as they conducted business over their mobiles.

To my far left a family stood, the man obscured by his wife and children. The youngest child, a girl, was sobbing uncontrollably. Her father squatted down to her level and I could hear him speaking to her in a placatory manner.

Even when I saw his face, it took me a few seconds to register that the man was in fact Vincent Morrison.

'Thought it was you,' he said, winking conspiratorially.

Initially I tried to ignore him, dragging deeply on my cigarette to finish it faster.

He said something to his wife and broke away from his family to approach me. His daughter hugged his leg, but he disentangled himself from her and walked over.

'Here to gloat?' he asked, lighting a smoke.

'Here to see you get what you deserve,' I said. I was aware of his wife watching me with open hostility. The elder child, a boy, scraped the toe of his shoe along the edge of the kerb, his hands in his pockets.

Morrison tilted his head from side to side, as if weighing up my words. 'What I deserve? Aye, maybe that's true. But then, as you know, it could have been much worse.'

'It should have been,' I retorted. 'It'll catch up with you.'

'No it won't,' he replied with a sharpness at odds with the friendly nature of his opening banter.

'Aren't you ashamed of yourself? Curran's kids are left without their father. For what?'

'You're the only one can answer that.'

'Do *they* know what you do? Your son? Does he know his father's a killer?'

'Does yours? Barry Ford's shooter. Do you go home and tell your kids about all the fuck-ups?' he snorted. 'Thought not. I'm just providing for my family – same as you.'

'You destroy people's lives. You deserve everything you get.'

He ground out his cigarette and came close to me, close enough for me to smell the tobacco off his breath.

'Don't be so fucking naïve. You know what I'll get? Six months, a year max. You've done me a favour. The Assets Recovery Agency took my vans. I've been bankrupted to pay back duty on fucking fuel. I'll do six months. But that's it. That's the best you've been able to do. I'll have earned twice what they took from me a year after I get out, and neither you nor anybody else will be able to do a sweet fucking thing about it.'

I met his glare and tried to appear defiant, but what he had said was true. For all that Morrison had done, the worst that would happen to him was a six-month sentence. He had cleaned up behind himself so carefully, had taken out every witness who could possibly incriminate him, that no one could prove anything. And what he said frightened me. Most criminals are stupid; that's how they get caught. Morrison was growing sharper all the time.

'Six months,' he repeated. 'I'll be sure to look you up when I get out. We'll catch up.'

'You do that,' I said. 'I'll be waiting for you.'

'I don't doubt it,' he said, smiling broadly, then winked at me, clicking his tongue as he did so. He put his hands in his pockets and turned back to his family.

Fifteen minutes later I watched as he hugged his wife, son and daughter, and then was led away to start a fourteen-month sentence for fuel-smuggling and evasion of duty. With good behaviour, he would be out in half that time.

As they left the courtroom, his son turned and stared at me angrily. And then he started to cry for his father.

Early last week, Natalia and Karol called on us. Following the hospitalization of Strandmann and the collapse of the immigrant-smuggling case, Natalia had been told her evidence was no longer required. Four days later she received a letter telling her that, as an illegal immigrant, she would be deported back to Chechnya by the end of the month.

The day they called was chilled, the air sharp with the scent of decay. The boughs of the apple tree at the front of our house bent heavy with the rotting fruit of the autumn. Natalia stood outside our house, Karol at her side, as in her best broken English she thanked Debbie and me for our hospitality and kindness.

Debbie listened while she spoke, her eyes moist with tears, her fingers playing with the necklace that Weston had given to me just a few weeks ago. When Natalia had finished speaking, they embraced tightly, as old friends might.

'You take care,' Debbie said, holding her hand.

'I'm sorry for everything,' I said. Karol began to translate but Natalia held up a hand to silence both of us. She spoke quickly in Chechen, then turned and looked at Karol.

'Don't apologize,' he translated. 'You opened your home to me. You made me welcome.'

Her words were not enough though to assuage the guilt I felt at all that had befallen her.

'I tried my best,' I said, my own eyes filling. 'I'm so sorry.'

'No sorry,' Natalia said. 'Family. Thank you.'

'I—' I started to speak, but could think of no expression as eloquent as the one she had just made. 'Thank you,' I said, finally.

Karol spoke himself then, without prompting. 'I'm going to go with her.'

'Are you coming back?' I asked, though I already knew the response.

He shook his head. 'I don't think so. I'll stay with Natalia until she finds her feet. Then we'll see what happens. Who knows?'

'Are you two—?' I began, but Debbie thumped my arm and rolled her eyes.

Natalia laughed.

'Friends,' Natalia said, smiling warmly at Karol in a manner that left her answer open to question. Then she leant down and kissed first Penny and then Shane on their foreheads.

Karol approached them too and, stooping, offered his hand to shake. Penny pulled her hand away from him and stepped back a little.

'Penny,' Debbie said sharply.

Karol smiled gently at her. 'I must say sorry, Miss Devlin. I said bad things to your daddy when we met in the shop. I was wrong. He's a fine man.'

Penny looked up at me, then back at Karol. Finally she put out her hand and shook his.

'He's a fine man,' he repeated to her, and she rewarded him with the gift of her smile.

When we had said goodbye, Karol and Natalia climbed into his car and he started the ignition. Debbie, who had been standing beside me, gripping my hand, suddenly let go and ran down to the car. She bent down at the passenger-side window and tapped on the glass.

Natalia rolled down the window and smiled uncertainly. Then Debbie reached up to the clasp of the necklace she wore and, having unhooked it, passed it in through the window to Natalia.

'For you,' she said. 'God bless you both.'

With that, she patted the roof of the car and came back up the driveway to me. She stood beside me, her hand in mine, and in that single gesture made me feel that I could, perhaps, begin to forgive myself too.

One morning, after stopping in at the station, I drove out to the Carrowcreel. As I pulled to a halt under the cover of the fir plantation, several cars passed me.

I walked upstream with a bunch of flowers to leave at the spot where Helen Gorman died. I stood by the river and said prayers for the happy repose of her soul. And, in the silence of the woodland, as the river passed with hushed whispers, I like to think that my prayers were heard.

On my way back downriver, towards the car, I spotted Ted Coyle. He was wading upstream, a sieve in his hand. He dipped and lifted a handful of silt from the riverbed and dropped it into the sieve. He then held it just at the water surface and let it wash away the dirt. He inspected the remnants, then upturned the sieve and spilt the contents back into the river. When he saw me he waded back downstream.

'You're not leaving then?' I asked, nodding towards the now almost deserted car park – only my car and his van remained.

'No,' he said, drawing the word out. 'First here, last to go.'

'Have you anywhere to go?'

He looked at the river, then turned his face towards the sky. 'Sure where else would you go? Where could be nicer than this?'

I took out a cigarette and lit it. 'You can't stay here for ever, Mr Coyle. Go home. There's nothing left to find here. Your kids must miss you.'

He squinted at me from behind the lenses of his glasses. 'I suppose so. I'm just . . . I thought it might be nice to wait until I make a find – a real find. Let me leave with my head held high, you know?'

'You could be waiting for some time. Orcas had no gold in the end,' I said. 'Apart from that first vein. There was nothing else.'

'One vein is all you need, Inspector,' he said. 'That's all it takes.'

I regarded the man and his attempts to retain some sense of pride. His own gaze shifted from me to the river and back again, and I could sense that he was waiting for me to leave.

I held out my hand. 'Good luck to you then, Mr Coyle.'

'And you too, Inspector Devlin,' he replied, shaking my hand in his.

Then he pushed his glasses up his nose, turned and stepped back down into the river.

Just this morning I saw Ted Coyle one more time. He was smiling from the front page of the local newspaper, holding in the palm of his hand a twisted nugget of gold. He had discovered it a few days before, while panning the river. He could not believe his luck, he said.

The last of the prospectors, and ultimately the only man to profit from the gold vein in Donegal, was finally leaving the Carrowcreel. The paper speculated that the

273

nugget was worth up to €15,000. I suspected that its true value was much greater; it was all that the man might need to return to his family, to face his children with a sense of dignity.

That is, perhaps, the best for which any of us may aim.

Acknowledgements

Thanks to all who helped in bringing *Bleed a River Deep* to fruition, not least Ed Harcourt for permission to use the name of a great song for the title.

Thanks to my friends and colleagues in St Columb's who have been incredibly supportive of the Devlin novels, especially Sean McGinty, Nuala McGonagle, Tom Costigan, Eoghan Barr and the members of the English Department. Special thanks to Bob McKimm.

I received valuable advice on various aspects of this book from Moe Lavigne of Galantas Mining, and Paddy McDaid and Carmel McGilloway, who offered advice and help with legal procedures. Any inaccuracies are entirely my own.

Thanks to the various bookshops and libraries that have been so supportive of these books, especially to Dave Torrans in No Alibis and Dave and Daniel in Goldsboro.

Thanks to Peter Straus and Jenny Hewson of RGW, and Will Peterson and Emily Hickman of The Agency, who have been terrific in supporting and developing my writing. Also Pete Wolverton and Liz Byrne at Thomas Dunne Books, Eva Marie Von Hippel and AJ at Dumont, and all involved with Pan Macmillan: Maria Rejt, Caitriona Row, Ellen Wood, Cormac Kinsella, David Adamson, Sophie Portas and especially my UK editor, Will Atkins, to whom this book is dedicated and without whom the Devlin series could not have come this far.

Thanks to Michael, Susan, Lynda, Catherine, Ciara, Ellen, Anna, Elena, Karl, Paul, Rosaleen, Jessica, Zenita, Phelim and Alex.

Special thanks to my parents, Laurence and Katrina, for everything that they have done and continue to do, and likewise to my sister and brothers, Carrael, Joe and Dermot.

Finally, as always, this book is for my wife, Tanya, and our children, Ben, Tom and David, with all my love.

A new Brian McGilloway mystery for 2021 …

THE NEW BEN DEVLIN THRILLER

BRIAN
McGILLOWAY

BLOOD
TIES

How can a dead woman avenge herself
on her killer twelve years after her murder?

How can a dead woman avenge herself on her killer twelve years after her murder?

This is the puzzle facing Ben Devlin in his latest case. He is called to the scene of a murder - a man has been stabbed to death in his rented room and when his identity is discovered Devlin feels a ghost walk over his grave as he knows the name Brooklyn Harris well. As a teenager, Harris beat his then-girlfriend Hannah Row to death, and then spent twelve years in prison for the murder.

As Devlin investigates the dead man's movements since his release it becomes apparent Harris has been grooming teenage girls online and then arranging to meet them. But his activities have been discovered by others, notably a vigilante, who goes straight to the top of Devlin's list of suspects ... until he uncovers that Harris was killed on the anniversary of Hannah's death - just too big a coincidence in Devlin's books. So Hannah's family join the ever-growing list of suspects being interviewed by his team. And then forensics contact Devlin with the astounding news that blood found on Harris's body is a perfect match to that of Hannah Row's. Yet how can this be; the girl was murdered many years ago - and Devlin doesn't believe in ghosts.

CRIME AND THRILLER FAN?

CHECK OUT **THECRIMEVAULT.COM**

The online home of exceptional crime fiction

KEEP YOURSELF IN SUSPENSE

Sign up to our newsletter for regular recommendations,
competitions and exclusives at **www.thecrimevault.com/connect**

Follow us

@TheCrimeVault

/TheCrimeVault

for all the latest news